FATED HEARTS

A SHADOW BOUND NOVEL

GARRETT LEIGH

Cover Art: Garrett Leigh @ Black Jazz Design

Editing: Posy Roberts @ Boho Press

Proofing: Jennifer Griffin @ Marked and Read. Annabelle Jacobs.

FOREWORD

It's 2020 and the wolf packs of western Europe have been waging a war for a hundred years. Pushed back to the north, Alpha Varian's pack stands alone against the huge numbers of allied southern packs. Only their greater skill on the battlefield and their alliance with Shadow Clan, the mismatched family of the most powerful shifters the world has ever seen, keeps them from total destruction.

For years, the Shadow Clan has stayed out of the war, for fear of plunging the world into a greater conflict of all supernatural creatures, but when Varian calls on his oldest friends for help, their restraint is stretched to the limit.

Note: in this supernatural world, the wolves are shapeshifters, not werewolves. They are not influenced by the moon or killed by silver bullets.

Shadow Clan are something more, ultra shapeshifters, if you like. They are venomous and have enhanced powers, gifts, and strengths. When they are changed, they may choose the form their animal side takes. More on Shadow Clan can be found in Shadow Bound, which tells the story of how Dash and Luca found each other. It is a free story and the link to it is in my newsletter, which you can find at the end of the book.

CHAPTER ONE

Bomber leaned against the tree. "You should be down there with the rest of them. She was your best friend."

Zio didn't answer. Crouched in the branches, fists clenched, he watched through hooded eyes as Emma was brought forward to be scattered in the forest clearing where so many wolves had been scattered before her. He didn't believe in the afterlife, but she had. *I hope she wasn't disappointed.*

Varian, alpha of the northern pack, stepped up to perform the sacred cutting ritual that would finally set Emma free. The ancient rope was uncoiled from the urn carrying her ashes and severed with a dagger older than every supernatural being gathered in the clearing. A breeze whispered through the forest. Leaves rustled. Birds took flight.

It began to rain. Light drizzle turned to fat drops that sent mourners hurrying for shelter until only wolves—only pack—remained.

Varian gathered them close. "Emma was our healer and our sister. The imprint she left on our lives will never fade, but we must go on. Our time for grief is short. War is with us, and it will be until we can find peace with the southern packs." His gaze drifted skyward, letting Zio and Bomber know he sensed their presence. "Peace was something Emma craved. She dedicated her life to it. From this day forward, our quest for it will mean more than ever."

The words washed over Zio as the rain battered him, soaking through his clothes, running down his face in place of the tears he'd never shed. *Peace.* He curled his fists tighter, letting his claws slide out and bite into flesh, grounding himself in the scent of his own blood, fighting the urge to bend the earth to the tune of his rage. Peace was a joke. Too many lives had been lost. All that was left was revenge, and Zio meant to take it.

He would take it, whether the war continued or not. Tired of life and hungry for death, he was the perfect killing machine, the perfect soldier for Varian's combat squad.

And until Emma's killers were burnt to dust, that was all he'd ever be.

CHAPTER TWO

Devan entered the old church Shadow Clan favoured for important meetings. Years ago, a summons like the one he'd received from the elders would've terrified him, but he wasn't a freshly changed teenage boy anymore. Shifter life was the only life he truly remembered, and Bratislava was home.

The church was quiet and still, but Devan sensed the presence of those who had summoned him, and in the crypt, he found Dash and Luca waiting for him.

Dash greeted him with a warm embrace, Luca the cool nod that was typical of him. The mated elders were fire and ice. Light and dark. The warm sun and frigid sea, though Devan knew Luca to be far friendlier than his reticence belied. *And he used to be a vampire, remember? He's died twice to be here—human, vampire, shifter.*

Even in the supernatural world, it was a tall tale to accept, but Dash's healing powers were legendary. He'd found his mate in a dying vampire and saved him, bonding them forever.

Devan envied their love. Craved it. Not being able to hunt for his own mate was his only regret at choosing the safe life in Slovakia Dash had offered him.

One day.

"Take a seat," Dash offered when the pleasantries were done. "This shouldn't take long, but you'll need to focus."

Ah, focus—the one trait Devan had retained from his human self, or rather, an inability to do it unless he was strict with his thoughts.

He took a seat, settling against the engraved wood. "What do you need?"

"We have a task for you," Dash said.

"A mission," Luca interjected.

Dash rolled his eyes, the gesture allowing his boyish features to belie his great age. "Yes, all right. Call it a mission if you like, but the particulars of that are semantics. Devan isn't a soldier."

Truth. Devan could fight—he'd proven so many times—but that wasn't why he'd been changed. Why his human life had been upgraded to the supernatural. Do no harm. Life, not death. Though he lacked Dash's centuries of experience, he was and would always be a healer. "What's my mission?"

"We need you to travel to England," Luca said. "Join up with the Northern Wolf Pack."

Wolves. Devan struggled to keep the shock from his face. "You mean, the *only* northern pack left. Why?"

"Their medic was killed in action a few weeks back," Dash said. "There are no wolf healers left in northern territory now, and with the pack wars still raging, their need is greater than ours."

"What do we care about that?"

"We always care," Dash said. "But this pack is . . . special. I think the world would be darker without them."

"You want me to join them as their resident healer to keep them alive."

It wasn't a question, more a collection of words Devan had to speak aloud to legitimately believe, but Dash nodded, and Luca folded his strong, corded arms across his chest.

"We know it's a big ask," Luca said. "But within the alliance, Alpha Varian is a long-time ally of ours, a friend, a brother. And his pack is young. They need help and guidance, even if they're not yet willing to accept it."

And there was the other thing. Devan didn't share the vitriolic hatred of wolves that many of his kind did. After all, they were kin now—brothers and sisters—had been for more than a century since the Shadow Clan, Dash's family of misfit shifters, had forged a treaty with the ancient wolf packs. But old rivalries and differences were hard to ignore, and there was every chance the young wolves in the northern pack would resent his presence too much for him to be of any use. "How intense is the fighting right now?"

"There's a lull at the moment," Luca said. "The healer was killed in a skirmish in London, and the northern pack lost a lot of ground. They retreated to regroup, and the southern packs let them. They won't cross the border. . . at least, not yet."

Luca's ominous tone made Devan shiver, though it had been decades since he'd last felt cold. "If the southern packs take the whole of England, it's only a matter of time before their aggression spreads to the rest of Europe."

"It is," Luca agreed. "We've stayed out of the war so far, as agreed when we forged the alliance so long ago, but if the southern packs claim that much territory, there's no telling how much more they'll want."

Devan nodded slowly. The southern wolf packs were known for their power-hungry alphas: men and women who ruled their communities with terror and oppression. It was only fear of Luca's military might and lack of support from the wolves in the north that had kept them in check this long. "How long will I need to be there for?"

"There's no way of knowing that," Dash said. "Which is why we're giving you the opportunity to refuse."

"You are?"

"Of course. Bratislava and the healer's commune is the only home you've known as a shifter. Asking you to join a potentially hostile wolf pack is a momentous task, and I told Varian we'd only be able to help if I found a healer willing to accept the role."

5

"Why did you ask me?"

"Because you're unmated and young and known for your lack of aggression," Luca said.

"Are you calling me a coward?"

"Far from it." Luca shook his head. "The opposite, actually. It's far easier to fight first and ask questions later, and it takes more courage to stand in the face of a challenge and ask why."

Dash's gaze flickered between Devan and his mate. "It's true, though I wasn't expecting Luca to explain it so succinctly. There were other candidates, but you're a shifter who thinks before he acts. Dropped in the middle of a war-hardened pack, you're going to need that quality."

"What about actual fighting? What if the war advances north and the southern packs threaten Alpha Varian's remaining territories?"

"We'll cross that bridge when we come to it," Luca said.

But Dash frowned. "I think we should cross it now. Extraction will be difficult if the war spreads into previously safe territory, and also, Devan's healing instincts, even among wolves, may prevent him from even wanting to leave."

"So he fights?" Luca said.

"I hope not." Dash turned bright blue eyes on Devan. "Because that would start a much bigger war, but whatever happens, we'll support you. Just as if you want to come home, we'll make it happen."

"You literally just said extraction would be difficult."

"It will be, but above all else, you're clan, and we'll protect you no matter what." Dash spoke with the alpha timbre that let Devan know there would be no further discussion, and warmth flowed between them, a familial bond that was absolute.

Devan reached out to touch him. Their hands clasped, and Dash leaned over and nuzzled his neck.

"I'll go," Devan whispered. "When do I leave?"

CHAPTER THREE

Devan flew to Norway from Bratislava, then caught another plane to Greenland, passing through the shifter sections of the human airports and abiding by the rules the human governments enforced to keep shifters in check. Before joining the wolf pack, Dash wanted him to visit the last surviving wolf elders, who lived far north of where the military units were based in England.

Jonathon met him at the airport and took him home to meet Madhi, his mate. In human years, they outnumbered Dash and Luca combined, but they'd stopped shifting a decade ago and were finally growing old.

Their cabin in the woods was small and rustic. They'd made Devan a bed by the fire.

"It's okay," he said. "I don't need much sleep, and I'm eager to join the pack in England."

"We're sorry you have to," Madhi said. "Many years ago, we had hundreds of healers, more so than even your clan, but so many have been lost to the wars."

"Shadow Clan has fought wars too," Devan said. "It's only Dash and Luca's leadership that has kept us at peace for so long."

Madhi conceded his point with a nod. "This is true, but Luca demands the respect of all supernatural beings, and there is much love for Dash. It has been a long time since a wolf commanded such affection. We are no longer great leaders."

"You are still greatly respected," Devan said. "It's why Dash sent me to you. He says you know more about the northern pack as it is now than anyone, that I need your counsel before I can join them. I'm truly grateful for any guidance you can give me."

"Sit down, young blood. We'll tell you everything we can."

A few hours later, Devan left the cabin armed with as much information about Alpha Varian's pack as he could cram into his mind. On the way to the airport, he listed the names he'd learned from the elite combat squad he'd be embedded with: two betas—Gale and Zio—and eight soldiers. They were young, as Dash and Luca had said, but gifted too. Two pack members could influence the elements, another was a shield. The information went some way to explaining how such a small command unit had resisted the southern threat for so long.

But their healer is dead. Pain lanced Devan's heart, grief for a shifter he'd never known. Madhi and Jonathon had spoken nothing but kindness for the healer Varian's pack had lost. *"She was a good woman and a fine wolf. The world will be darker without her."*

Devan would never know if that was true, but one thing was certain, he had big shoes to fill.

Nerves carried him all the way to England, and he deplaned in Manchester with an unmistakable itch under his skin. But away from the safety of his home in Slovakia, for the first time in years, the urge to shift had to be ignored. Dash had warned him that the human population in this strange country tolerated shifters only if they stuck to their own lands when they took their animal forms or stayed out of sight. For the wolves based in Cumbria's Lake District, that meant a military compound hidden within the sprawling five-mile township under their protection, and the surrounding countryside. And even then, Devan would need Varian's permission to shift at will—no wolf pack would want an outsider roaming their territory unchecked.

He passed through shifter security and left the terminal. Outside, he scented the air. The earthy musk of wolves hit his sensitive nose like a punch to the chest, and the beast within him bristled, but Devan battled the fight-or-flight instincts that roared to life. He'd arrived a day or so earlier than he was expected, but he *was* expected. Any wolf who caught his scent would hopefully know it.

Still, alone on potentially hostile ground, Devan didn't fancy getting cornered. The sensible thing would be to take a cab north to the township and make his presence known. *But . . .*

In Devan's experience, the urge to shift could only truly be dulled by something else . . . something he was unlikely to find once he was embedded with the wolves. Besides, in war-torn territory, he'd be a fool not to scout the area while he had the chance. Before his every movement was beholden to the will of an alpha he'd never met.

Screw it. He slung his bag onto his back and headed into the city.

Zio sucked in a breath that burnt his lungs and pressed himself against the sticky wall. The club was dark and smoky and the only establishment outside of London that served booze strong enough to keep him drunk for longer than ten minutes.

And fuck was he drunk. Had been ever since Varian had gifted him some "time to process" but in the week that had passed since he'd fled the township, nothing had changed. He missed his life in London, the friends he'd lost. And he missed Emma, forever and always.

I need another drink.

"No, you don't," her soft voice counselled. *"All that happens when you're drunk is bad decisions and regret. You're not built for a reckless life."*

But she was wrong about that. War was as reckless as

anything in the world, and Zio had been born in a pool of someone else's blood.

Reborn.

Whatever.

He pushed off the wall and found the bar. The air was thick with human emotion and arousal, and much of it was directed at him. Most humans wouldn't have known he was a shifter, but their bodies did and instinctively called to him. Men, women, and everything in between.

Zio couldn't deny that excited him. It was why he'd come to the club in the first place, to find something—*someone*—to help him forget, even if it was just for one night. A single moment, even. Maybe then he could go home, make ready for war, and face the rest of his life without his best friend.

More booze passed his lips. Vodka, mainly. Ukrainian. It was fifty proof—just enough to resist his superhuman metabolism. Rough and strong, its fierce heat seared his throat and dulled his senses, all the while bringing parts of him to life that he'd long forgotten about. Parts of him he could forget about all over again if he was lucky enough for the vodka to send him to sleep.

He stumbled away from the bar and found a quiet corner. Most of the humans—though his presence made them horny— gave him a wide berth, and he dropped onto a soft armchair with the space to stretch his legs and survey his surroundings through bleary eyes. Arousal was still heavy in the air, draped over the room like a cloak, but as he sat there, head spinning enough to soften the sharp spikes of grief, something else hit his consciousness—something hotter and brighter than the roiling mess of human emotions around him.

It started in his gut and bloomed into his chest, drawing him to his feet as his veins began a slow buzz, and it reverberated in every cell of his body. Deep, primal desire pulled him forward, and he followed the trail, hands already reaching for the fly of his grubby jeans as the drive to connect with whoever was tugging the invisible cord took over.

Down some steps and through a door. Another door. A blackened corridor, so dark even Zio's wolf eyes couldn't see. But gods, he could smell. And *feel* the addictive warmth heating his blood until a fire was lit within him, and an ache in his chest drove him to his knees. The scent that had drawn him to this dark place swirled around him and he drank it down, bracing himself on the cool tiled floor, gasping. *I need —*

Strong hands hauled him to his feet. His back hit the wall before he could blink, and his jeans dropped to his ankles.

Zio's cock sprang free and he gasped again, fumbling for whoever had come upon him, desperate to feel flesh against flesh. His hands hit warm skin, and blood as hot as his thrummed beneath his fingertips. A rough jaw. The hard planes of a man's torso. Slim hips and a thick, heavy cock that made Zio's mouth water. "I want to fuck you," he slurred, voice so distant it seemed to belong to someone else.

A man chuckled. "I don't think we'll make it that far."

Zio was too blinded by booze and desire to dissect the statement. He fought the man for dominance and lost. The corridor was narrow. Zio leaned on the wall behind him and braced a hand on the one in front. His other hand found the man's cock and another wave of beautiful scent slammed into him.

His wolf rumbled with want. His teeth tingled, but he fought the urge to let them slide free and search out the man's neck. Biting humans without their consent was strictly forbidden, and there was no time for conversation. Zio needed the man to come so he could smear his scent into his skin and return the favour. *I'll claim him later.*

Hot hands grappled with slippery flesh. Zio thrust into the man's hand, all the while jerking his cock. A coil of pleasure-pain built in his belly, ensnaring every nerve. He pushed off the wall and against the man until they were pressed together everywhere except where he needed it most. *Want — Need —*

But he couldn't think clearly enough to construct either sentence, and suddenly, any coherent thought he had left was gone. Orgasm roared through him, starting from the tips of his curled toes and sluicing through his entire body. His companion let out a guttural groan, but it was drowned out by Zio's own crazed yell.

Hot release coated his hand. He brought their cocks together and smeared their seed until he couldn't tell whose scent was whose, and his wolf howled with pleasure. *Mine—*

Fuck! As quickly as his senses had abandoned him, the strength of his wolf's desire brought them screeching back. Still panting from the sheer force of his climax, Zio reeled back in horror. *That scent. It's not—*

The other man gasped. "Shit, you're a wolf."

CHAPTER FOUR

For the thousandth time since he'd arrived in England, Devan scented the unfamiliar air, catching both human and wolf as he searched for that one magic scent he'd spent the last twenty-four hours frantically scrubbing from his skin. *Idiot. You've been on the mission a couple of days, and you've already messed up.*

And damn, had he messed up. Hitting the club was supposed to have been a last gasp of freedom before pack life took over. Instead, it had turned into the most surreal experience of his supernatural life.

Inexplicable and unforgettable.

Satisfied he was safe—for now—Devan found a bench outside the train station where he'd been instructed to wait for his wolf hosts. He should've been preparing himself to meet his new alpha. Instead his mind was stuck on the young wolf he'd stumbled across in the shadowed corridor of the smoky nightclub.

It had been no accident.

The young man swayed on his feet, drunk and disorientated. "I want to fuck you."

Devan couldn't remember what he'd said in response— which was worrying all by itself—but gods, he remembered the wolf's scent. How it had called to him, embedded itself in his every sense, drawing him back into the club when he'd been on his way out. Hands. Skin. Ragged groans and sweet release. Devan had never been so consumed by desire. So out of his fucking mind with want and need.

But the crazed attraction hadn't lasted beyond the final throes of orgasm, and the disgust in the young wolf's face as realisation had hit him would haunt Devan forever.

The fact that it had mirrored his own horror was irrelevant.

Or was it?

He'd yet to decide.

And he had bigger worries than his bruised ego. Because it wasn't enough that he'd hooked up with a wolf. No. He'd hooked up with a wolf in territory where the only shifters likely to be in the area were probably connected to the pack he was joining. Unless his fuck up had gone nuclear, and he'd shared his seed with a recon soldier from the enemy. *Yeah, cos you're that lucky right now, aren't you?*

Devan's only comfort was that since the wolf had fled the club, he hadn't caught his scent once.

At least not in the air. He fought the urge to sniff his skin, to chase remnants of the heady fragrance that should've sent him running in the opposite direction the moment he'd picked it up. *Again, you're an idiot.*

Devan was inclined to agree, but he'd run out of time to worry about it. A vehicle slowed to a stop in front of him. Blacked-out windows slid down, revealing the sharp shifter eyes of three men.

"Are you the healer?" one said.

Devan nodded, and the back door of the SUV opened.

"Get in."

Zio skulked into the gathering hall. He was late, but the meeting didn't seem to have started, and Varian's scent was too weak for him to be in the building yet. *Thank gods.* Anxiety clawed at Zio's chest. He rubbed it, torn between craving the comfort of his alpha and real fear that Varian would take one look at him and instantly know what a terrible mistake he'd made. That they'd all know—his brothers, his *family*.

He scented the air again, and then himself, but found nothing to draw him back to the club two nights ago. His heart twisted again. Relief warred with a gutting sensation he couldn't explain. And then disgust roared to life. *He wasn't a wolf. And he shouldn't have even been there. You should've killed him, not whacked your cock out for him. Rubbed yourself in his—*

"Zio."

"Wha—" Zio jumped, hackles raised, claws out. Somehow he'd missed his brothers coming up on him.

"Whoa." Bomber backed off and threw an arm out, forcing Danielo and Michael to do the same. "What's the matter with you?"

Zio blinked, and his claws retracted. "Nothing. Sorry. Half asleep."

"Right."

Bomber looked far from convinced but let it go. Danielo stepped around him and pressed his forehead to Zio's.

"What's up, brother? We've missed you."

"I missed you too. Sorry I was gone so long."

"It's been a week. We've coped. What about you? Where've you been?"

Zio shrugged. "Around. I ran for a bit. Spent some time in the city."

"Manchester?" Danielo's eyebrows shot up. "Did you find someone?"

"No."

"Ah. So that's why you're in a shit mood."

"I'm not in a shit mood."

"Liar."

It was true—Zio *was* a liar. Of all his brothers, Danielo knew better than anyone that the only reason he ever ventured into the human cities was to get laid. And that he was a grumpy bastard when it hadn't happened for a while. It wasn't unheard of for Zio to fall into Danielo's bed from time to time, and with Emma gone, he was Zio's closest pack brother. If Zio was to tell anyone about the unknown shifter in the club, it would be him, but—

I can't tell him. I can't tell anyone.

"Why are we here?" Zio changed the subject, all the while absorbing Danielo's closeness as though he could be a balm to his aching soul. "Varian hasn't called a township meeting in months."

Danielo's frown deepened. "You've missed a lot, but I don't want you to hear it like this."

Varian appeared from nowhere and called for silence. Danielo clamped his mouth shut, but worry seeped from him and into Zio, adding to the turmoil he'd brought home with him.

Zio glanced around. The hall was packed with wolves and humans, all residents of the pack township. Zio sought out his unit. Danielo and Michael were already close by. Bomber had wandered off. Sensing Zio's unspoken call to him, he came back and flanked Zio, their shoulders touching.

The familiar scent of Zio's unit soothed him, but tension was pouring from his brothers in ominous waves, and as Varian took a breath to speak, dread bloomed in Zio's gut.

This is going to hurt.

"Thank you all for coming," Varian said. "I was hoping to speak to some of you privately before this meeting, but time has escaped us."

His gaze darted to Zio before it settled on the crowd again. "As you all know, our resident healer and doctor of human medicine was killed in action a month ago. While we have managed to recruit a GP from outside the township to join us, Emma was the last wolf healer in northern Europe. Filling her position has proved . . . difficult."

Zio took a slow, shuddering breath. He'd known this was coming. All shifter packs needed a healer to survive, especially in times of war. Being without one for as long as they had been was already a huge risk. If the southern packs had pressed their advantage instead of holding their newly won positions in London and the southeast . . . gods.

Varian was still speaking. Zio shook himself and tried to focus.

"The alliance has acted faster than we could've hoped for. Shadow Clan has sent a healer from their own ranks to join us, and he will remain with us at least until the war is over."

An uneasy murmur spread through the crowd, more pronounced in the wolves. Zio found Danielo's arm and gripped it hard. "Is he serious? He's recruited a healer from a non-wolf pack?"

"From that weirdo hippie commune Shadow Clan has in Slovakia," Danielo said. "Sorry, Z. I wanted to warn you before Varian told the whole world. We all did, but we couldn't reach you."

Zio's phone was in a canal somewhere near Leeds. After two solid days of replaying the last voicemail Emma had left him, he'd hurled it into the cut. When he'd finally begun to crawl his way home, he'd sensed Varian reaching out to him, his unit brothers too, and Gale, but he'd ignored them all, too caught up in—

Oh fuck.

Realisation hit Zio in slow, taunting waves. He dug his claws into Danielo's arm. "When's he coming? Is he here already?"

"I don't know. Last time we spoke with Varian, we didn't know for sure that the clan would help us."

"We can't have a healer who's not a wolf."

"Technically, we can." Danielo removed Zio's hand from his arm and pulled him into a half hug. "Look, I know it's tough to see Emma replaced, but we've got to think of the pack. We can't defend ourselves without means to recover from battle wounds. How many times did Emma save each and every one of us? Without her, the southern packs would be halfway across Europe by now, which is probably why the clan has stepped up."

"True that," Bomber said. "As long as we're fit to fight, the southern packs are our problem."

17

"I think it's more than that." Michael spoke for the first time. "Shadow Clan of old could destroy the southern packs in one battle. Perhaps they're not as powerful as we think they are anymore."

"It doesn't matter how powerful they are," Danielo said. "If they attack the southern packs, their peace with every pack, coven, and clan around the world will crumble. You want to go back to fighting werewolves *and* vampires? Cos that's what will happen."

Most of them were too young to remember a time when the entire supernatural world had been at war with each other. The alliance between Shadow Clan and the wolf packs of northern Europe had formed to bring peace and to hold it as long as certain conditions were upheld. Danielo was right: military assistance from a non-wolf clan was never going to happen, which meant . . . there was only one explanation for the unknown shifter he'd encountered in the club.

Encountered. That's what you're calling it?

Zio bit his lip hard enough to draw blood. It didn't matter what he called it, the fact remained that the man he'd been drawn to so intensely, that he'd shared come with, all the while so blinded by his scent that he'd been seconds from sinking his teeth in, from claiming him, was almost certainly the incoming healer.

Fuck my life.

CHAPTER FIVE

Varian welcomed Zio into his home, a house set deep within the military compound, and directed him to wait in the office. The scent of his mate, Tomos, was close by, and Gale was there too. His unit hadn't been at the meeting. In Zio's latest act as the worst pack beta in the history of pack betas, he'd neglected to wonder why.

Gale drew him into a hug.

Zio returned his embrace, but as Gale's scent hit him, he stiffened. "You've been with the healer."

Gale pulled back. "Sharp as ever. Yeah. I picked him up earlier. Smells weird, huh?"

Zio couldn't speak. The healer's scent on Gale's skin was faint, barely detectable, but it permeated every facet of Zio's being. Varian's office disappeared, and the darkness of the club consumed him.

"I want to fuck you."

The man chuckled. "I don't think we'll make it that far."

"Zio." Gale shook Zio gently. "It's okay, honestly."

"How can it be okay? He's not a wolf."

Gale sighed. "The others were freaked out too, but what are we supposed to do? Fight on with no way of putting ourselves back together? Why do you think Emma was targeted in the first place? Every wolf alive knew she was the only—"

Zio's hackles rose. His teeth sharpened and his claws broke free, drawing blood. "Shut the fuck up."

"Why? We can't avoid facts."

Zio had made a point of avoiding facts from the moment Emma had died in his arms, but he couldn't deny what Gale was saying. The bomb had been planted in the area Emma had set up as a makeshift field hospital, *after* the skirmish had died down and the wounded had been evacuated. Killing her had been the only tactical advantage to destroying it.

He wiped his hands on his jeans, forcing his wolf down. "I know all that. But how can we trust an outsider?"

You trusted him enough to get your dick out for him.

Valid.

Zio knocked his fist on the side of his head.

Gale caught it and pushed Zio's hand away. "Look, I get it. But we have to face the reality that we can't fight a war without a healer in our ranks. We'd be dead in days, and then what? I'll bloody tell you what, the southern packs will overwhelm the north and kill anyone who gets in their way. You think Emma would be able to live with that? You think she wouldn't have welcomed a thousand Shadow Clan into our midst if it would save a thousand northern wolves and their families?"

Varian entered the room before Zio could respond. He glanced between them, eyebrows raised, though he'd have heard every word as he'd approached, his alpha senses stronger than the soundproofed walls of his office. "Have a seat," he said. "Everything okay?"

After a beat, Gale stepped back, removing himself from Zio's personal space and obeying his alpha. "Yeah. Everything's fine."

Varian nodded and turned his gaze to Zio, waiting.

With a heavy sigh, Zio fell into the closest chair, facing off Varian to the front and Gale to the right, as agitation rolled through him. Chances were, unless the healer's lingering scent had given him a boner, they probably thought he was reacting to Emma being replaced, but letting them think something that wasn't entirely true unsettled his wolf. The effect the healer was still having on him was disconcerting too. *It was a drunken hookup, for gods' sakes. And he's probably a grizzly bear or a ginormous cat or some shit. Why can't I forget him?*

"Zio? Are you with us?"

Zio startled. Varian had moved to stand directly in front of his chair. He was staring right at him, his gaze as gentle as his tone. Zio swallowed. "I'm here."

"Good. Listen, I'm sorry you had to find out about Devan joining us in the meeting like that. I wanted to speak with you privately, but you weren't here, and like I said, the clan acted faster than I expected them to."

"It's fine. The pack needs a healer. How I feel about it is irrelevant."

"How you feel is never irrelevant. Not to me. To your pack. You and Emma were very close for a long time. Replacing her was never going to be easy."

"Emma can't be replaced," Zio snapped.

"I know. Bad word choice, but it's been a long few days."

Guilt overrode even the lingering disquiet in Zio's heart. "Shit." He leaned forward and ran a hand down his face. "I'm sorry. I should've been here."

"No, you shouldn't have. I gave you some time because you needed it. What's happened in your absence is beyond your control."

"But—"

"No buts. Pack is about the individual as much as the whole, or who would we truly be?"

Zio was too frazzled to answer that question. His mind raced and his heart thumped.

Varian stood over him and placed his palm on Zio's neck, silent and still until Zio met his gaze. *"Pack."*

Zio nodded. "Pack."

Varian nodded and stepped away to sit in the chair on the other side of the desk he rarely used. "There's something else I need to ask you about."

Beside Zio, Gale shifted in his seat, crossing and uncrossing his legs, fingers tightening on the armrests.

Zio braced himself. "What?"

"I don't know how long Devan's going to be with us, but he's going to need somewhere to stay. Your quarters are closest to the clinic, so I was hoping he could move into Emma's old room."

"At the bungalow?"

"Yes."

Zio closed his eyes, picturing Emma's room exactly how she'd left it a year ago when they'd been called back to defend—and ultimately lose—London. Her scent was everywhere, but it'd be fading by now, and the scent of another would soon erase her entirely. *No.*

But even as he thought it, her voice haunted his protests. *"Zio, I have pages and pages of notes on every wolf that's ever walked this land. If a healer from another world is to be of any use to this pack, they'll need everything you make fun of me for hoarding under my bed."*

Zio opened his eyes. "It's fine."

"Are you sure?" Varian's gaze pinned Zio in place. "We could always—"

"It's *fine.*"

"Okay."

"Okay." Zio sucked in a breath and broke Varian's stare, turning his gaze to the window. It was shut, but as the wind rustled the bushes, Zio imagined it carried Emma's scent and then one that now had a name—*Devan*—chasing it away.

It was a long moment before he remembered that Devan's scent was as seared on his soul as Emma's, but for entirely different reasons.

His pulse quickened again.

Varian cleared his throat. "Zio, do you need to go? Maybe you should shift for a while—"

22

Zio stood with a screech of his chair on the wooden floor, out of the room before Varian could complete the sentence. He shot through the house and burst out of the front door. Sweet pain shimmered through him and he shifted, muscle and bone solidifying into his true form in the blink of an eye.

His paws hit wet grass. Scents and sounds intensified, and his vision sharpened.

The forest called to him, and he made for the break in the trees that surrounded Varian's house, dropping his clothes as he ran. Shifting was everything—to run and leap. Weave and dodge. Grief and turmoil faded to a dull roar, overtaken by wind and rain. Animals scattered as they detected his presence. Precious moments, for when Zio was a wolf, he was free.

———

Devan paced the cramped back office where the wolf beta—Gale—had told him to wait. Impatience clawed at him. Claustrophobia too. He hadn't been forbidden from leaving . . . yet, but he'd got the impression that it'd be better if he didn't.

Better for who?

Like it mattered. Devan was in wolf country now and part of a pack. What he wanted as an individual was no longer important.

"That's not entirely true."

Devan whirled around. A broad-shouldered black man stood in the doorway, alpha strength tied into every bone and muscle. *Varian.* "They didn't tell me you were a mind reader."

Varian shrugged. "It's not a consistent gift. Sometimes important things jump out at me; others can pass me by. There's no rhyme or reason to it."

"Interesting."

"It has its moments. Welcome to England and to our home. How was your journey?"

It was on the tip of Devan's tongue to repeat himself, but he caught it just in time. The journey had been interesting for many reasons, but he didn't trust himself to discuss it without giving himself—and the young wolf he'd yet to scent on the military compound—away. Who the hell knew what Varian had seen pass through his mind already? "It was fine. I took a detour to meet with your elders."

"Are they well? It has been some time since we last spoke with them. Their home is a guarded secret I trusted your alpha with for the good of my pack."

"It's safe with me."

"I know. Dash is an old friend of mine. If he trusts you, so do I."

"Is that why he chose me to come? I was under the impression it was because I have no mate."

"A little of both, I'd imagine. Can I get you a drink? Something to eat?"

"I'm fine."

"Tired, though, yes? You have not slept in a few days."

Devan had come across mind readers before, but he'd never get used to how exposed he felt when someone voiced his thoughts before he could. "I don't need much sleep."

"But you do need some. We all do, unless we are vampires."

Devan shuddered. "I thought there were no covens left in your country."

"There aren't, but that could change if we lose this war."

"That's why I'm here."

"Indeed." Varian moved to a filing cabinet by the window and opened it. He retrieved a set of keys and offered them to Devan. "I have secured you accommodation within the compound. It's close to the human clinic should you be called to assist there, and it was the quarters of our previous healer. You should find anything you need in her rooms, though we have removed her personal belongings."

"What was her name?"

"Emma." Varian's eyes tightened. It was infinitesimal, but Devan saw it. "We loved her very much, and you may find

24

some . . . resistance among our wolves at first, especially from those closest to her."

"I'm prepared for hostility."

"Well, hopefully it won't come to that, but I'm not an alpha who orders my pack to feel the way I want them to. If you encounter any problems, we'll address them individually."

"I can see why Dash likes you."

"He taught me well."

"He did?"

"Long story, dear friend. Perhaps when we're not so pressed for time, I will tell it to you."

"I'd like that."

"I thought you might. Dash told me you're a thinker. We could do with some of that around here."

"Your wolves are young?"

Varian sighed. "They are, and they can be . . . difficult to guide without methods I choose not to employ, but they have good hearts. In times of war, that matters."

"And in peace, I'd imagine."

"It's been a long time since I knew peace, brother."

"How long have you been their alpha?"

"Some of them a few years, others a few decades. We are comprised of decimated packs and fractured families, all of us survivors of some kind."

Devan filed the information away. Varian's warm welcome had relaxed him somewhat, but his mind was still haphazard, as though his thoughts hadn't quite caught up. Or maybe they had. Maybe they were miles ahead, and it was he who wasn't up to speed.

He fought the urge to sniff the air, to seek out the addictive scent that had kept him awake every moment since he'd first caught it in Manchester. Somewhere outside, a wolf called to the night sky.

Devan's blood rushed. His skin tingled, and he found himself drawn towards the window. He'd never heard a wolf running free before—there were no wolves in Shadow Clan, none had chosen the form.

The wolf howled again, drawn-out and plaintive. It was haunting and beautiful, and Devan wanted to hear it again and again. To commit it to memory so he'd hear it even after he left this strange place.

Varian joined him at the window. He turned his gaze to the horizon. "Zio. You'll meet him very soon, I'd imagine. He shares your bungalow, though he doesn't settle much."

"Restless?"

"Always. I'm hoping we'll tame him one day, though. He's special to me. To all of us."

"Was he close to Emma?"

"Extremely."

"They were mated?"

"No, but I did wonder many times if there was a potential bond there. If it would be triggered by the dangers they both faced. It would've complicated pack life considerably, but I don't doubt it could've been the making of Zio."

Curiosity burnt brightly against the myriad of other emotions rampaging through Devan, but he pushed it aside. He'd meet his wild roommate soon enough. For now, all he wanted was a shower, some food, and despite what he'd told Varian, a bed to faceplant on.

Perhaps reading his mind, or perhaps not, Varian pressed the keys into Devan's hand. "Gale is outside. He'll take you to the bungalow, but I'd like to meet again tomorrow, if that's okay."

"That's up to you, isn't it?" Devan said absently. "I'm here with you as my alpha."

"But you are still free. I will call on you only when necessary. Outside of those moments, your time is your own."

"Can I leave the township?"

"Of course. You can go wherever you choose, but I'd advise talking with your wolf brothers first. We like to know when one of us is leaving so we can be found quickly if something happens."

Wolf brothers. It wasn't a phrase Devan had ever imagined would be relevant in his life, supernatural or otherwise, but it wasn't as offensive as he might've assumed.

Dressed in Varian's rich voice, he liked it.

CHAPTER SIX

Zio lurked behind Emma's favourite apple tree. It had a broad trunk and was the only tree in her small orchard that reliably bore fruit. Not that there was much fruit around at this time of year. Winter was cold, grey, and wet, and it suited Zio's mood. Shifting had calmed his frantic thoughts, but the fact remained that even if the Shadow Clan healer wasn't the unknown shifter he'd dropped his pants for in the club, he still had to share his home—and Emma's space—with a stranger.

A stranger he was waiting for behind a tree despite the fact that any approaching supernatural being would catch his scent on the wind.

Loser.

But in this strange new world, Zio needed a few more moments out of sight.

The wind picked up. He sniffed the air, and his blood began to burn as the fragrance haunting his dreams reached him, faint but unmistakable. Sweet and perfect. Zio braced himself for impact, to run if the draw he'd felt in the club overwhelmed him again, but as footsteps trod the path leading to the bungalow, he didn't flee. Couldn't. *I have to see him.*

He saw Gale first, stone-faced and earnest as ever. He was

senior beta in the pack, and fuck, if he didn't take it seriously. *You wouldn't catch him losing his shit in a club.*

Of course you wouldn't. Gale was selfless and a good man. The best. Zio was . . . something else.

Gale's companion stepped out of the shadows. His white-blond hair caught the light of the streetlamp, and even from a distance, Zio's sharp wolf gaze picked up his ocean-blue eyes, so typical of Shadow Clan, or so he'd been told—that their eyes morphed with the change. He'd never seen one to test the rumour. Only heard tall tales of their famous alphas—the supreme healer and his vampire-turned-shifter mate.

Those eyes, though. Overcome, Zio fell to his knees. He hadn't seen the healer's face in the club. Hadn't catalogued his lithe frame and glorious cheekbones. He was smaller than Zio had imagined him, but he was glorious in every way . . . except his damn-fucking genes. *If he was a wolf—*

But he wasn't a wolf. He was Shadow Clan, and he was here to take Emma's place. To sleep in her bed and erase her scent from Zio's home once and for all.

Zio staggered to his feet, testing the gravitating pull in his gut. It was still there, had been ever since he'd first encountered the healer—*Devan. His name is Devan*—but muted by grief and unenhanced by booze, it simmered at a level Zio could handle. He took a deep breath, absorbing Devan's scent as he drew nearer to Zio's hiding place. A shiver ran through Zio, but he steeled himself against it, blocking out whatever sensation it had meant to leave behind.

A growl rumbled out of his chest. *Fuck you, healer. You won't get me like that again.*

"I knew it was you."

Zio blinked.

Devan was somehow in front of him, arms folded across his chest, Gale nowhere in sight.

"How did you do that?"

"Do what?"

"Sneak up on me. You were twenty feet away a split second ago."

"No, I wasn't. You spaced out, and I took advantage of your distraction. Do you want to fight me, Zio?"

"What?"

Devan tilted his head sideways. "You were growling. Your brother says you're like that with everyone, but I wondered if it was personal, considering we've met before."

"That didn't happen."

Devan nodded. "Suits me."

He turned on his heel and walked away, his booted feet leaving no imprint on the orchard ground.

Zio watched him go, astonishment warring with a crippling disappointment he couldn't decipher. It felt like an anti-climax. A painful one, and it shouldn't have done, because he'd already established that his reaction to Devan the first time around had nothing to do with Devan himself and everything to do with Zio.

Right?

With no answer forthcoming and lacking any better ideas, Zio left the safety of Emma's tree and tracked Devan to the bungalow. The front door was open, as though Devan had expected Zio to follow him. Zio stepped inside, shut the door, and leaned against it. Devan's scent ambushed him from every direction, and he closed his eyes, fighting the heat that rose through his resolve, searing the sides of it. Melting it. *How the fuck did this happen?* Even for shifters, this shit was unreal, and he couldn't help wondering if he was stuck in a nightmare. If his subconscious was playing him with the cruellest trick.

Devan was in the living room, sitting on the couch, his back to Zio. He didn't look up as Zio entered the room. "Are you okay?"

It was the dozenth time Zio had been asked that question since he'd returned from his city adventures but coming from the soul who'd upended his mental equilibrium so entirely was more than Zio could handle.

He turned on his heel and stalked to the kitchen. The fridge

30

contained nothing but beer and the cans of sickly sweet pop Emma drank. He grabbed a beer and twisted off the bottle cap, then he gathered the cans and dumped them in the rubbish bin.

In the living room, Devan shifted on the couch, leather creaking beneath his light frame. Zio pressed his head against the fridge, then forced himself to re-join him. "Where are you from?"

Devan kept his gaze on the pile of papers that smelt of Emma.

He's been in her room.

Zio didn't know why it mattered so much. For the foreseeable future, it was Devan's room. But it did matter. It mattered a lot.

"I live in Slovakia," Devan said. "At the healer's commune in Bratislava. Emma was there once. I never saw her, but I recognise her scent. And her handwriting from the research papers she contributed to while she was there."

"It's like a monastery there, Z. No computers or phones. Every resource they have is handwritten."

"It was ten years ago."

Devan hummed. "Before my time then."

"You weren't a healer ten years ago? I thought you were born into it?"

"I wasn't born a shifter, but I was a healer ten years ago, just not in the commune. I was still in Finland, which is perhaps what I should've said when you asked where I was from."

Devan finally looked up. Up close, his eyes were even bluer than they'd appeared outside, and they bore an intensity Zio had never seen in a wolf. The blue of his irises were ringed with a fiery glow and made him terrifyingly beautiful, if his attractiveness hadn't terrified Zio already. "When were you changed?"

"When I was eighteen. Dash intercepted me outside medical college. He offered me a new life and gave me a few years to think about it, but it didn't take that long. I found him a few weeks later and asked him to change me."

"The only humans I know who've ever asked to be changed have been mated to whoever changed them."

"Well, that wasn't the case for me or other Shadow Clan I've come across. Perhaps wolves are more sexually compelling."

"Sex and mating aren't always connected."

"Indeed." Devan held Zio's gaze for a long moment, then cleared his throat. "Just as changing isn't necessarily connected to sex or mating. It certainly wasn't for me."

"I was changed when I was a baby."

"I know."

"How?"

Devan held up a folder with Zio's name scrawled on it. "Emma told me."

Zio bolted from the room. The front door of the bungalow slammed, and Devan winced as the impact rattled through the old bungalow, shaking the windows. Wolves weren't known for their subtlety, but until that moment, Zio had been impossible to read. Dark, gorgeous, and brimming with anger and grief, he was everything Devan had feared he would be.

Beautiful.

Troubled.

A mournful howl pierced the air. *Zio's howl.* Devan pictured him as a wolf, roaming the forest that surrounded the compound and township, and itched to join him, even though Zio had shifted to escape him and had likely never run with a shifter of a different kind. *He's probably never seen one.* But Emma had, and speaking her name had driven Zio away.

Devan blanked out his twitchy feet and tingling skin and refocussed on the paperwork he'd retrieved from her room. He'd already made up his mind to make it the first and last time he entered her space, but the raw grief in Zio's liquid gaze had poured concrete on that decision. As long as he was here,

Emma's room would remain hers. He'd sleep on the damn couch.

And sleep was something he could no longer ignore. Days of fatigue caught up with him. He sent Dash a message to let him know he was safely ensconced with the wolf pack, then set Emma's diligently kept paperwork aside for the morning.

He kicked his boots off and stretched out on the couch. Emma's scent was everywhere, but light, barely detectable, as though it had been sprinkled through the house like fairy dust a long time ago. Zio's scent was more potent, and confusing. The addictive musk Devan had chased through the club was still there, but there were extra layers now, as though the earthy wolf scent had absorbed Zio's disgust at discovering Devan wasn't one of them and used it as a shield.

He doesn't like me.

It was the last thought to cross Devan's mind before he fell asleep.

CHAPTER SEVEN

Devan woke to darkness and a distinct absence of fresh scent—it was early, pre-dawn, and Zio had yet to return.

It felt wrong to be in Zio's home without him, and the idea that he'd driven him out was unsettling. Once again, the beast within Devan called to him to shift, to break free and run with the sun as it rose, but aside from not wanting to invade Zio's space any more than he already had, he hadn't discussed shifting with Varian.

Maybe today.

Stretching, Devan stood from the couch and surveyed his surroundings with more interest than he had the night before, when his focus had been solely on the young wolf he was destined to share a home with for who-the-gods-knew how long. Zio's presence had disturbed every instinct Devan possessed, and he could hardly fathom that he'd managed to sleep in a place he'd yet to pace out and assess.

No wonder you're no soldier.

But Zio *was* a soldier, and that frightened Devan. The young wolf was volatile and teeming with emotions that had no place on the battlefield. He was a ticking time bomb unless he found a way to let loose some of that rage.

Devan could think of many ways he could facilitate that, but none of them fell under the remit of a healer, and he could've done without the hot flash rioting through him as his imagination bolted the stable. *Focus.* His gaze fell on the paperwork stacked on the coffee table, but that could wait. First, he needed to take stock of his new home.

He left Emma's room alone and inspected the bathroom. It was clean and tidy but smelt of bleach rather than Zio. Same with the kitchen. The fridge and cupboards were pretty much bare, and wolf scents were faint.

The living room had the three-seater couch Devan had slept on, a TV, and a Bluetooth speaker. Photo albums were stacked beneath the coffee table, but Devan left them alone. Shifter families didn't always follow human customs, but logic told him he had no business nosing around in things like that.

Zio's bedroom was at the back of the bungalow. The door was closed. Devan hovered outside, curiosity and the still bright craving for *that scent* making his hands twitch. He wanted to slip inside and get a glimpse of the man who'd affected him so deeply, but at the same time, the reality that Zio would know Devan had been in his room the moment he came home kept Devan rooted to the spot.

He breathed in and out, filling his lungs with Zio's scent, testing his reaction to it. Heat simmered in his veins. His heart skipped a beat, and the pull to shift and track Zio down was strong, but for what? For sex? Something else? Were his healing instincts connecting with his new pack already? After all, Zio was unhappy. Grieving for his best friend. It made sense that Devan would want to help him.

Devan retreated from Zio's bedroom door and drifted to the kitchen, mulling over the theory that gave him a get-out clause for his current obsession with his surly housemate. It was . . . plausible, but it didn't explain what had happened in the club. How Zio's scent had overwhelmed him, robbing him of any coherent thought but *want want want*. But perhaps the two weren't connected. Perhaps Devan's shifter instincts had reached out to the only other shifter present, drawing them together to protect them at a time when they'd both craved the same thing, leaving the fact that Devan was still drawn to Zio now irrelevant.

The hypothesis was about as farfetched as most humans believed supernatural science to be, but it suited Devan. Gave him a reason to throw caution to the wind and give in to the craving deep in his bones. He took a step towards the back door, but a knock sounded from the front of the house, pulling him back to the present.

Cursing, he darted through the bungalow to open the front door. Gale's scent reached him long before he got there, and Devan found himself disappointed, though for what reason, he had no idea. It wasn't as though Zio would knock before he entered his own home.

"Morning," Gale said. "Varian sent me to invite you for breakfast at his house. He always cooks on a Saturday."

"That's quite domestic considering you're at war."

Gale shrugged. "We like to welcome visitors when we have them. Makes life easier for everyone. Besides, this is our home. Our families are here."

Devan didn't have a family to speak of outside of the healer commune, where shifters kept to themselves. Dash often invited him for meals when Luca was away, but those instances had grown rarer in recent years. Keeping the peace kept Devan's alphas busy, and it had been a while since he hadn't eaten alone. "Sounds good to me."

He stepped out of the bungalow and locked the door behind him. Gale had retreated to the end of the path. Devan joined him, and they fell into step together as they walked towards Varian's house. "Seeing as I've interacted more with you than anyone else, can I take it that you're my pack contact?"

"I guess so."

"Wouldn't it make more sense for it to be Zio? Considering he's a beta too and I live with him?"

Gale's lips twitched, as though he wanted to grin but had thought better of it at the last second. "You'd think, but Zio's . . .

distracted at the moment. Maybe when you've been here a while and you know each other better."

"He didn't come home last night." Devan regretted the words as soon as they were out of his mouth.

But if Gale thought the statement was out of place, it didn't show. "He rarely stays still for long," he said. "He's nicer than he'd ever let you see, though."

Devan believed that. He couldn't recall much about the Zio he'd stumbled across in the club, at least, not visually. But despite the scent-fuelled urgency that captivated them both so entirely, in the fleeting moments before perspective had come crashing down, there had been a softness to his touch. A gentleness that haunted Devan perhaps more than anything. Devan's instincts were having a riot right now, and Zio was a mess. But of one thing Devan was inexplicably certain: Zio was worth everything. He was worth *this*.

The realisation jarred Devan, but they were upon Varian's house before his reaction could manifest. The smell of bacon and sausages reached him, and his stomach growled, reminding him that he hadn't eaten in days.

Gale laughed. "My wife said you looked hungry."

"Your wife?"

"Yes. She has a gift that allows her to see me even when I'm not with her. Her visions aren't always clear, but she caught a glimpse of you when we picked you up yesterday."

Devan had been around enough gifted shifters not to be particularly alarmed by the notion of being watched without his knowledge. "Is your wife a soldier?"

"Yes. Intelligence, though. Not combat. Varian tries to keep mated pairs apart in the field."

"Makes sense. I can't imagine what it must be like for her, being able to see you in danger and not being able to help you."

"You'll know one day, when you find your mate."

"*If* I find my mate. My kind aren't as drawn to others as you wolves. Many of us exist alone for as long as we choose to live."

"That's sad."

"Is it? Or is it just different?"

Gale stopped walking. "You talk like her."

"Like who?"

"Emma. She said things like that all the time."

"Did you listen?"

"Of course. Everyone listened to Emma."

Devan reached out without thought and closed his hand around Gale's arm. He was the first wolf he'd ever touched that wasn't Zio, and he steeled himself in case that had been the true cause of everything that had happened in the club, that he reacted that way to *all* wolves. But all he felt was a faint warmth that signalled a potential pack bond Gale was almost certainly not aware of yet. *You care about these people already.*

He couldn't deny it, even to himself. "I'm sorry you lost her."

Gale nodded. "So am I."

They resumed their slow amble towards Varian's front door. Gale let them in, and a dozen wolf scents bombarded Devan as they made their way through the house. He dissected them all, searching for Zio, but he knew before they reached the dining room that he wasn't there.

Gale directed him to a seat in the middle of the battered table. "Guys, this is Devan. He's gonna be with us for the foreseeable future as our healer. Make him welcome."

Gale's voice carried a hint of beta authority. Eight wolves met his gaze and communicated their ascent before they turned to look at Devan.

Devan met their curiosity head-on. Four of the wolves he'd met already when Gale had picked him up—Track, Xan, Kate, and Ishmail. He presumed them to be Gale's unit. The other four wolves eyed him with open suspicion. *Yeah. Definitely Zio's crew.*

Varian entered the room as Devan's thought completed. He caught Devan's eye and nodded. "You are correct."

"Thought so."

"Thought what?" The wolf nearest him asked. "We don't do secretive shit here."

"It's not secretive to keep your own thoughts to yourself,"

38

Varian said. "Devan didn't ask me to invade his mind and answer a question he had not asked aloud."

Devan leaned forward and put his elbows on the table. "I've got nothing to hide, though. Varian caught me speculating if the four of you scowling at me belonged to Zio's unit. His reaction to me was much the same."

A murmur went around the room, half-amused, half-defensive. Varian's expression was inscrutable, but Devan was used to that from alphas. And he'd given up worrying if Varian knew about his club encounter with Zio. The less he thought about it, the better.

The conversation—such as it was—moved on.

Varian's mate, Tomos, brought breakfast to the table and chided Zio's unit to help him cut bread and slice fruit. He was, apparently, a quiet man, but Devan could tell his relationships with the pack were strong.

He added extra bacon to the plate of the only woman in the room—Kate, from Gale's unit, and glanced around the room. "No Zio again? He'll waste away if he doesn't come home to eat."

"He'll hunt if he needs to," Varian said. "The boy can't be tamed, you know that."

"I know that he's been running those woods every night since he came back from the city. Is he doing okay?"

Tomos directed his question around the table.

Devan kept his head down, devouring the first meal he'd had in days, but he couldn't help listening, hanging on every word spoken and straining his senses to catch those that weren't. Zio's crew were reticent at first. But Tomos pressed, and the wolf beside Devan—*Bomber*—eventually cracked.

"He's tired," he said. "But he won't rest, and I don't think that's gonna change until he gets used to having another, uh, healer in the pack."

"And in his place," another member of Zio's unit added. "No offence, mate."

Devan glanced up. "None taken. It's an adjustment for me to live among wolves too. I'm sure we'll get there in time."

Gale's half of the room nodded, tentative smiles warming their faces.

Zio's unit remained aloof, but Devan could live with that. Knowing they had their beta's back was worth every scowl.

CHAPTER EIGHT

Zio could avoid many things, but squad meetings weren't one of them. Three days after Devan arrived, Varian tracked him down in the woods.

"It's time to come home, Zio. We need you now."

It was a request Zio couldn't deny, even if he'd wanted to.

He shifted back to his human form and glanced down at his filthy skin. Cuts and grazes from his latest rampage through the trees were already healing, and the spectacle of his skin knitting together put Devan on his mind. *Some good your great escape has done you, eh?*

Zio found the clothes he'd stashed a few days ago and padded through the undergrowth until he came to the clearing behind the bungalow. Devan's scent increased in potency with every step, and resentment simmered in Zio's veins. *Of all the healers in the entire world, the freaky cat king had to send this one. Gods' sakes, I'd rather screw a southern wolf than a fucking Shadow Clan.*

The thought left a bitter taste in Zio's mouth. Southern wolves were his sworn enemy. Shadow Clan were allies, even if he'd never met one before Devan. Even if he knew nothing about them other than the fact that Devan had cast a spell on him he couldn't shake. *I—*

Stop it. It was the booze, remember?

Zio remembered.

He let himself into the bungalow. Devan wasn't home, but there were traces of him everywhere—his bag by the couch, spare clothes folded by the coffee table. Scent tracks on every surface, in every room except Zio's.

There was food in the fridge.

Bemused, Zio gazed at the groceries stacked away, and his mouth watered. He hadn't hunted in the forest. Hadn't been hungry enough to bother. But he was famished now, and somehow the fridge was stocked with every single thing he felt like eating. Devan had forgotten nothing, even though he'd had no way of knowing in the first place that Zio had a childish penchant for fruit yoghurt desserts and cheese slices. That mass-produced ham and mushroom pizzas from the township store were his favourite thing to eat in the entire world.

Zio claimed a strawberry yoghurt and a spoon. He ate it in two bites, dropped the pot and the spoon in the sink, and trudged to the bathroom. A hot shower rinsed mud and grass stains from his skin, but it didn't seem to matter how many times he soaped his body, he didn't feel clean. His brain itched, and his wolf grumbled, eager to ditch the real world again and run free. But Zio wasn't free. He was a soldier, and his pack was at war. *Get it together.*

Half an hour later, he made the pack meeting with a minute to spare. Varian's dining table was devoid of the tea and snacks Tomos supplied them with for regular business, and maps of southern England covered every available surface. *Yes.* Adrenaline surged in Zio's blood. This was what he needed—a return to the reason he continued to exist. To put an end to the southern packs, once and for all.

Varian's hand was warm on his shoulder and then on his neck. He pressed his forehead to Zio's, his silent question clear. *All right?*

Zio nodded, pulse jumping. *I'm good.*

"Sure about that? We've got a lot to get through today."

42

"I'm *good*."

After a fleeting pause, Varian inclined his head to the left. "Take a seat then."

Zio stepped out of his grasp and moved to sit at the table. A lungful of Devan's scent stopped him in his tracks. Devan was at the table, sitting with Gale and Xan, heads bent as they talked, apparently oblivious to Zio's presence.

Resentment unfurled in Zio's gut, at Gale and Xan for welcoming a stranger so easily, at Devan for existing at all, but with Varian's gaze drilling holes in the back of his head and his eagerness to pick up where they'd left off in the south, he swallowed it down. Claimed his seat between Bomber and Devan and resolved to breathe through his mouth.

Devan ignored him, his body angled so he didn't even have to look at Zio by accident.

Zio clenched his fists.

Gale laughed at something Zio had been too caught up to catch, and Zio wanted to rip his goddamn throat out.

Figuratively.

Or maybe literally, the mood he was in.

Varian called the meeting to order. "We've had a tough time," he said. "And we've taken advantage of the lull in aggressions to recover and regroup, but that time has come to an end. Drone footage from our intelligence unit has shown enemy activity as far north as Leicester. We need to act now to protect our border."

"How fluid is the division?" Devan asked. "It's not a hard border, right?"

Varian shook his head. "It wasn't until we lost London. Now we have gone back to ancient lines that existed long before this war, and so far the enemy have honoured them, though I'm not confident that they will for long."

"By now they'll know I'm here," Devan said. "Dash had to inform them to hold clan treaties and also promise to send healers to them if they should find themselves in need."

"So you're on both sides?" Zio spat as a collective growl rumbled through his unit.

Devan spared him a glance. "I'm committed to this pack for as long as I'm needed, but that couldn't happen without Dash giving the southern packs assurance that the clan wasn't invested in their enemy."

Bomber snorted. "How can you be committed to our pack and still have loyalty to your own?"

"Easily. Before I came here, I didn't have a pack. I'm loyal to my clan. It's different."

"Your alpha could still pull you out at any moment," Zio said. "Send you to the south. How can we trust you?"

Devan shrugged. "That's up to you, but if you're truly worried the southern packs might claim me, the simple solution would be to not kill their healers. That way Dash's agreement with them will hold."

Zio swallowed a growl. It was wrong. All of it. Devan didn't feel like a liar, but he wasn't pack. Whatever he said and everything about the exchange made Zio's skin crawl. *See? Definitely the booze.*

The meeting moved on. Surveillance footage was reviewed, and plans were drawn up to flank the enemy's recon crew and take them out.

"We move tonight," Varian said. "Zio's unit will lead; Gale's will back them up."

"Where do you want me?" Devan asked.

"Somewhere behind," Varian said. "I don't think they'll target you, but I can't risk losing another healer with my entire elite squad deployed."

Devan nodded his ascent. "Works for me, but before then, I need to scout your countryside. Gather some supplies."

Varian's gaze flickered to Zio and back again. "Did you not find what you need in Emma's room and her clinic?"

"Powers are individual to each healer," Devan said. "Emma used many tinctures and fruits of her native forests, but I have no connection to many of them, so they won't work for me."

"Sounds wacky," Bomber muttered.

Devan laughed. "Forest magic can be that way if you don't understand it."

"Where do you need to go?" Varian asked.

"Everywhere." Devan drew a map towards him and traced his finger along the wooded areas that surrounded the township and beyond. "I need herbs and ferns. Tree sap and heathers."

Varian leaned forward. "How long will it take you?"

"A few hours if I know where to look, less if I can shift to cover more ground."

"I can't allow that."

"You said I was free to roam."

"You are, but in your human form . . . for now. There's much tension in the air, at the moment, among wolves and humans, and I haven't had enough time to warn all folk of your presence."

It made sense, but Zio couldn't imagine his wolf ever living with such restriction. He waited for Devan to argue his case, to fight for whatever beast lurked within the man, but it didn't happen.

Devan sat back in his seat. "As you wish. Perhaps a wolf could accompany me then?"

"Of course. Zio knows the land the best. He'll take you."

Zio sighed. *Super.*

Zio brought Varian's car round to the front of the house and tapped his fingers on the steering wheel, waiting for Devan to emerge. In another life, he might've found it funny that he'd somehow become a taxi driver for a Shadow Clan healer, but there was nothing funny about the prospect of spending the rest of the day cooped up with a scent that drove him insane. Or with a man who hadn't met Zio's gaze the entire time they'd sat next to each other.

Fuck. It's gonna be a long day.

And an even longer night, if the plans they'd drawn up in the meeting came together. Zio ran through them over and over, calculating risks, weighing them against the advantage they could gain by destroying the southern pack's recon unit. The enemy would find replacements soon enough, but maybe it would buy enough time to retake some much-needed territory.

The passenger door opened. Despite the supercharged energy running through Zio, he jumped a mile and glared at Devan. "Don't fucking sneak up on me."

Devan raised an eyebrow. "I didn't. Perhaps you're not as alert as you think you are."

He spoke mildly, and Zio wanted to punch him. But a wave of scent hit him before he could clench his fist, and fighting quickly became the last thing on his mind.

Zio swallowed hard. "Whatever. Get in."

Devan slid into the passenger seat and shut the door behind him. The potency of his scent increased tenfold, and any hope that Zio may've harboured that he could handle being alone with Devan like this evaporated as though it had never been there at all.

He shivered.

Devan finally looked at him. "Everything okay?"

Not trusting himself to speak, Zio nodded and started the car. He pulled onto the road that would take them out of the military compound and through the township—a place Devan must've explored already if the stocked fridge was anything to go by.

Case in point, they passed the supermarket that sold Zio's favourite pizzas. Despite every nerve being tensed to breaking point, his stomach betrayed him and growled like a malfunctioning tractor.

Devan chuckled quietly. "Why don't you just eat? Or are you some kind of masochist?"

It was an accusation that had been thrown at him before, and he couldn't deny that he was starving. Besides, stopping for food would give him a break from Devan's scent— *Seriously? You've been in the car five minutes.*

Zio pulled over anyway. "Do you want anything?"

46

"Nope."

"Fine." Zio got out of the car and slammed the door loud enough for a human family to turn and stare at him. He stared back until they uncomfortably looked away, then jogged into the shop.

The supermarket sold hot pizzas from a counter by the checkouts. Zio bought a whole large pizza and ate three slices on his way back to the car.

He offered the box to Devan. "Sure you don't want some?"

"No thanks. I don't eat mushrooms."

"What?"

Devan shrugged. "I killed someone with them once. It's a thing."

"Did you kill them on purpose?"

"No."

"Wasn't your fault then." Zio dropped the box on the back-seat. "Don't be a weirdo about shit you can't change."

"That a life lesson, Zio?"

"Who the fuck knows."

Certainly not Zio. He restarted the car and resumed their journey as the food worked its way into his system, soothing the scratchy sensation in his gut. His muscles relaxed, and his grip on the steering wheel loosened. He forgot himself and took a deep breath, but far from agitating him, Devan's scent calmed him even further, and for the first time in weeks, he felt as though he could finally sleep.

Shame he was driving.

"Feel better?" Devan's voice was soft, barely a murmur.

Zio wanted to be irritated, but it wouldn't come. He nodded and took the turning that would lead them away from suburbia and into the countryside. "Yeah."

Devan didn't answer, and a silence settled over them as Varian's powerful car ate up the miles. Zio leaned back in his seat and tried to keep his eyes to himself. Failed, naturally, but much like the squad meeting, Devan seemed oblivious to his attention.

47

It was as though he'd drawn a line in the sand, and Zio couldn't reach him until he crossed it.

The desire for something Zio couldn't decipher hit him in slow, rolling waves, strong enough to shake the peace he'd found just moments ago but gentle enough to keep him upright. He bit his lip, drawing blood, as always.

Devan sighed and laid a hand on Zio's thigh. "Don't think so hard."

His touch was electric. Warmth spread through Zio like a smouldering wildfire and the cut on his lip closed over, the blood he'd tasted on his tongue gone. "The fuck? Did you just . . . heal me?"

"Not on purpose." Devan kept his gaze on the increasingly green landscape. "Sometimes my gift escapes me before I can catch it, not that I'd imagine I did much your body wouldn't have done for itself. Wolves have unique healing powers, the fastest and most comprehensive of all supernatural beings."

"Even vampires?"

"Vampires are harder to hurt in the first place."

"I don't like vampires."

Devan grinned, and in the soft sunlight, his face seemed to glow. "They probably don't like you much either."

Zio laughed. Couldn't help it. "Nah, probably not. Oh hey, we're almost there. See that railway bridge at the top of the hill?"

"Yeah?"

"There's a nature park on the other side. It's protected, so humans don't go there with their kids and dogs, churning up all the plants. We run there as a pack sometimes. At least, we used to when there were more of us."

"You've lost many?"

Zio pulled into a lay-by and turned the engine off. "Too many to count."

"I'm sorry."

"Why? You didn't kill them."

"No, but I can feel how much it hurts you that someone else did. You feel responsible."

"Fucking mind reader, are you? Like Varian?"

Devan shook his head. "It's not like that. If I've healed someone, I'm often connected to them for a while after. It's a kind of empathy, I guess."

"Yeah, well, knock it off. I don't want you all up in my feelings."

Another chuckle softened the air between them. Devan opened the car door and his hand—the one Zio had forgotten about—slid from Zio's thigh, taking with it the zen-like bliss that had allowed Zio to think clearly. "Suit yourself, brother."

CHAPTER NINE

Devan swung through the trees, gathering leaves and twigs he could grind into powder. On the ground below, he sensed Zio's gaze on him, but replenishing his supplies of healing aids took precedence over the strange energy between them. Claiming resources from the earth was a sacred ritual, especially if they one day helped Devan protect Zio from more pain.

Hands full, he dropped to the ground and deposited his bounty in the small bag Zio held. "I need to find some Plymouth pear trees."

"Not round here. They only grow in the south—in Plymouth, funnily enough, and a few places near Cornwall."

"Okay then . . . what about whitebeam?"

"In the wild? I've only seen them in human gardens."

Devan glanced around. "I can do without both if you can find me a really old yew tree."

"Yew trees are poisonous."

"I can make them safe."

Zio took Devan at his word and scaled a nearby oak tree to look out over the land. "There's some a few miles away, but we're running out of time. I can get there and back if I shift."

Envy warred with Devan's desire to have everything he needed safely in his possession as quickly as possible. *I need to run*. But he couldn't. He'd been forbidden by his wolf alpha. Letting Zio go in his place was his only option. "I only need a handful of foliage. Don't carry it in your mouth, though. It's not safe until I've mixed it with other things. Here, take the bag."

Devan emptied the bag onto the forest floor as Zio ripped his T-shirt over his head and unbuttoned his jeans. The unmistakable scent of bare skin bombarded Devan, taking him back, unbidden, to the club. His pulse quickened, and heat pooled in his groin. He counted seedpods and leaves. Recounted them. But it was no good. There was nothing on earth that could overcome the effect Zio's scent seemed to have on him.

"What's up with you?" Zio's jeans hit the ground. "You look like a human having a stroke."

Devan closed his eyes and held out the bag. "Go. Please."

Zio took the bag, and energy shimmered around them as he morphed into his wolf form. His pleasure-pain at shifting was so palpable, Devan could taste it, and he didn't open his eyes until he was sure Zio had gone.

Alone in the forest, Devan gathered Zio's clothes and folded them into a neat pile, noting, as he had in the club, that Zio didn't care for underwear. In an effort to dissuade himself from pressing his sensitive nose to the soft cotton of Zio's T-shirt or, worse, his jeans, Devan abandoned the clothes and paced the woodland Zio had brought him to. It smelt deeply of the northern pack, especially Zio's unit. Their scent was everywhere, while Gale's unit appeared to stick to the paths.

Devan pondered the significance. There was no denying the differences between the two units and their betas. Zio's crew were as closed off and suspicious as him. Gale's unit had taken Varian's orders to make him feel welcome to heart. *How does that work on the battlefield?* Devan imagined it was complicated, and he didn't envy Varian's job. Not least because Dash had been right when he'd said Varian's pack was special. That their existence meant something to the world. How could anyone manage that when their main occupation right now was war?

That's why you're here. To keep them alive.

Devan's gaze fell on the pile of twigs, roots, and leaves, and though he knew the magic they possessed, they suddenly didn't seem anywhere near enough. He delved deep into his healer's soul and searched for his own power, the strength that he'd given Zio an unintentional taste of earlier. For many years, Devan had walked the earth confident in his ability to heal any wound he truly wanted to, but what if he couldn't? What if after everything, *he* was the weak link?

A wolf rushed into the clearing before he found an answer, Devan's fabric bag hanging around its neck. The beast was dark and rangy, like Zio in his human form, and its black coat shone like silk. Devan reached out to touch it, to feel the inky fur against his own skin, but the wolf blurred in the late winter sunshine, and before he could blink, Zio stood before him, bag in hand and completely and utterly naked.

Zio's bones shortened and clicked back into place. He stretched his neck and dangled the bag of yew foliage in front of Devan. "Do you want this or not?"

Devan closed his fingers around the bag but made no move to take it. His gaze burnt through Zio's skin, sizzling his nerves, and Zio's breath caught in his throat.

"Stop looking at me like that."

Devan licked his lips. "Like what?"

"Like you want to eat me."

Devan blinked, and a rough chuckle escaped him. "You're ridiculous."

"Not on purpose."

"Uh-huh." Devan took the bag and stepped back.

Zio stepped forward before he could catch himself. Devan raised a wry brow, but Zio couldn't bring himself to care. His base instincts outran his brain, and the need to touch Devan was abruptly overwhelming. He took another step, closing the distance between them until they were an inch apart.

Devan was shorter than him, slimmer, but his body, frustratingly hidden by clothes, was lithe and powerful. Zio pondered what his shifter form could be. Agile and beautiful, he'd moved through the trees with a grace that told Zio he was no wolf, but he'd known that already. When the time came for them to choose, Shadow Clan rarely took the form of a wolf. Most of them were big cats, like their leaders, but that hardly narrowed it down.

"You wanna stop looking at *me* like that?"

Devan's voice was low, barely a whisper, and laced with enough of a growl to snap Zio out of his daze. Zio clenched his fists to keep his hands at his sides. "I'm not looking at you like anything."

"Yes, you are, and it's not fair if you're going to rip my head off every time I glance your way."

"Last time I checked, your head was on your shoulders."

Glorious fucking shoulders. Zio still couldn't believe Devan was smaller than him. In the club, he'd seemed huge, his presence so imposing Zio had submitted to him the moment they'd found each other, lured by his scent and powerless to resist the desire to devour every part of Devan he'd been coordinated enough to touch. Warm skin, strong jaw, hard chest. Zio's head swam, and frustration erupted, spilling out of him with a furious growl. "Fuck! How does this not affect you? I'm losing my mind."

He whirled away, intent on shifting and making a run for it until he was far enough away to regain his composure, but Devan caught him. His grip on Zio's wrist was firm, but the hold on a deeper part of Zio was absolute. "Wait."

Zio closed his eyes, impatience, panic, and utter bewilderment battling for dominance in his fucked-up soul. "Why?"

Devan didn't answer with words. He put his hands on Zio's shoulders and turned him around, pinning him in place. "*Trust* me, this is affecting me. More than you'll ever know."

"I want to know."

"No, you don't. You don't want me here at all."

"That's—" But the argument died on Zio's lips. Devan was right—he didn't want him here. He wished he'd never come, that they'd never met, so he could go back to the long days and nights when grief and revenge were the only things on his mind. Emotions he understood. Pain he could take a hundred times more than the bone-deep ache in his chest. "I don't know what to do."

A breeze shook the forest. Zio harnessed himself to the earth and felt the ground shake as desperation ripped through him. A nearby tree splintered.

Devan sucked in a breath. "The gods was that?"

"It's you driving me crazy." Zio snapped his eyes open. "What are you doing to me? Why do you have this . . . thing over me?"

Devan growled again. "What makes you think it's so one-sided? That this is what I want?"

The ache in Zio's chest increased tenfold. "If you don't want me, let me go."

"I can't."

"Why not?"

"For the same reason you can't push me away."

Zio had been lost for weeks, adrift on a tide he couldn't contain, but the impact of Devan's words was so great he swayed on his feet, kept upright only by Devan's unwavering grip on his shoulders. "I don't understand."

"You don't need to. We just need to ignore it until it goes away."

Zio frowned. "Until what goes away?"

"You really don't know?"

Zio shook his head, and a helplessness crept into Devan's intense gaze. He opened his mouth. Shut it again.

Then he sighed. "This would be a hell of a lot easier if you weren't naked."

Zio glanced down at himself, unsurprised to see he was hard. On the rare occasions shifting wasn't accompanied by violence or a desperate need to escape the world, it always left him horny. And Devan had already proved the effect he had on Zio's cock.

He shuddered as another gust of wind rattled through the clearing. His skin burnt where Devan touched him, but it was nothing compared with the need thrumming in his groin. The heat. The desire. The pure power that flowed between them. *Gods, I want him.*

The certainty of the thought should've shocked Zio. Repulsed him. But as need took over his every thought, he felt nothing but overwhelming desperation to feel Devan's skin against his.

He backed Devan against a nearby tree. "You should be naked too."

Devan hummed. "That right?"

"Yes."

"I don't want you to regret this like you did last time."

"You regretted that too."

"How do you know that?"

"I could tell."

"How did that make you feel?"

"I didn't feel anything."

Devan moved like a snake and spun them around, shoving Zio into the tree trunk with enough force to make it bend. "Don't lie to me."

"I'm not."

"Yes, you are. Just because you don't understand something doesn't make it less real."

"I don't know what the fuck you're talking about."

Devan caged Zio with his arms, and disquiet threatened the coil of heat simmering in Zio's gut. "You need to understand."

"Why?"

"Because—" Devan shook his head. "Gods, I don't know. Maybe we should do it your way. Follow our instincts and leave the words unsaid."

Zio palmed his cock and tugged at Devan's clothes. "No one can know."

"Then you'd better keep your hands to yourself and leave this to me."

Devan dropped to his knees before Zio could respond, freeing himself from Zio's clumsy, grasping hands. "My venom may feel a little strange at first, but it won't hurt you, I promise."

Venom? "Wha—"

"Don't worry. I'm only deadly to humans."

Devan's mouth closed around Zio's cock, cutting dead his power of speech, of coherent thought, of anything save the sensation of Devan's tongue sliding along his length.

Zio's head fell back against the tree. Rough bark dug into his skull and breath tore from his lungs in a ragged moan. He thrust his hips, chasing more, but Devan's hands held him firm, his unspoken assertion so distinct that he may as well have shouted it in Zio's face. *My terms, wolf.*

Fear that Devan would pull back overrode any desire to fight him. Zio drove his hands into Devan's platinum hair and tangled his fingers in the awaiting silk. Devan's scent was all around him, trapping him in a vortex of pleasure as it melded with Zio's, gathering his arousal in a storm cloud of fearsome heat.

Zio let out another groan. "How have you done this to me again?"

Devan's only answer was to draw sharp teeth over Zio's cock. A warning, or a gesture of affection? As Zio's thighs began to shake, he couldn't tell. He gripped Devan's hair tighter, tugging hard enough to hurt. Devan dug shaking fingers into Zio's tender flesh. Claws drew blood, but Zio was too far gone to make sense of what it meant. To catch sight of the beast within the man who held Zio's every nerve in the thraldom of his mouth.

Madness hit Zio, a punch to the gut that doubled him over, his hands still buried in Devan's hair. His wolf howled, undone by the pleasure-pain so akin to the wild thrill of shifting. Zio yelled, his gift unleashing before he could catch it, shaking the earth and finishing off the fractured tree he'd assaulted earlier.

Branches fell and the ground rumbled. Ecstasy rocketed through him, white-hot, unstoppable, scorching everything in its path as he spilled his seed into Devan's waiting mouth.

His roar echoed in the clearing. He slid down the trunk of the tree, but Devan caught him before he hit the ground.

Zio glanced at the darkening sky as his faculties returned to him. War had caught up with them, and they'd run out of time. "We need to go," he whispered.

Devan shook his head and pulled Zio's face against his heaving chest. "Not yet."

CHAPTER TEN

Varian scanned the horizon, tension seeping off him, merging with the worry tainting Devan's every thought. "Zio and Danielo have similar abilities. Danielo can influence water . . . the sea, the tides. Zio can move the earth."

Don't I know it. Devan recalled the moment Zio had shot down his throat with perfect clarity, from the hypnotic scent of his release, his quivering thighs, and the minor earthquake that rocked the earth. He couldn't imagine how effective Zio's gift could be in battle.

Or maybe he could.

Fuck, I want him. But he couldn't have him. Dash and Luca had sent him to protect Varian's most valuable military assets, not trigger instincts that would prove dangerous for everyone.

The train of thought brought him back to the present and the reason he was able to push his second ill-advised encounter with Zio aside. Shortly after they'd arrived back from the woods, they'd hit the road again with the rest of the combat squad. Devan had travelled with Gale's unit, but he'd sensed Zio's presence in the vehicle behind them the whole way to Leicester, the ride no less unpleasant than the one they'd shared an hour earlier when they'd driven home from the woods in silence. A silence that for once had been Devan's choosing and not Zio's dark moods cloaking the air. Much like the night they'd met, soon after release, Devan's senses had returned to him, and he'd withdrawn, though not as violently as the first time, and it had taken longer. He'd held Zio close for as long as they could both tolerate it before reality had driven them apart.

Zio rubbed his chest and his mouth, as though a bitter taste was dancing on his tongue. "We have to go."

This time, reading Zio's hostile body language, Devan hadn't argued. How could he when it was so painfully obvious that the young wolf had no idea what was happening to him? To both of them?

"Devan?"

Dammit. Focus.

Devan snapped to attention. Varian was staring at him. At any other time, the alpha's gaze might've been curious, but not now. Not while the closest thing he had to children were out in the field, risking their lives for the survival of their pack. More than that. For the survival of shifters everywhere who craved an existence where they didn't have to worry that their loved ones would be killed before their lives had truly got started. "What is it?"

"It's midnight," Varian said. "They should've reached their targets by now, but they haven't checked in."

"Might not have a signal if the enemy have disrupted communication lines."

"Maybe, but they won't have destroyed the masts—too much risk that the humans will retaliate—and besides, even if they've created a fault, the humans will fix it fast. You know how they are with such things."

Devan did. The human preoccupation with remote conversation was forever a mystery to him. How did they live without looking people in the eye? With emojis and text in place of touch and affection?

Not that Devan had experienced much affection recently. "They might've found the enemy base more guarded than they expected. Perhaps they're lying low for a while before they move out."

Varian made a noise deep in his throat, and his agitation was infectious. Devan jumped from the disused motorway bridge they were parked on, landing on the grass below. He sniffed the air. Even from a few miles away, perhaps further, Zio's scent was easy to pick out, but there were others too—Gale, Track, and Shannon. Bomber and Danielo. Devan hardly knew them, but something about the combined scent—the scent of the *pack*— called to him, and he understood how Varian felt more than he wanted to.

"I'm going to scout forwards," he called up to Varian. "Just to the next hill. I'll come back if I see anything."

"Come back anyway, brother."

It wasn't an order, but it didn't have to be.

Devan left his alpha behind and followed the scents of the wolves who'd moved out a few hours ago. He didn't have far to go, but the terrain was rough—the abandoned industrial site made it hard to move around undetected. At least it was for Devan. The combat squad, as Devan had learned, were protected by Gale's shield.

"It's not a reliable gift," Varian said. "Because that would be too easy for us."

Devan snorted. "Can't have that."

"Apparently not. Gale's ability seems to vary as much as the weather. Sometimes he can protect the pack mind from telepathic gifts such as mine, others he can keep us invisible to technology as we move through enemy territory."

"How do you know which it is on any given day?"

"We don't, and he can't control it. Luckily we have night vision and scanners of our own. If I can't find my pack, no one can."

"But you can smell them?"

"Of course, and so can any supernatural being downwind of them, but there are ways around that."

Devan had missed the part where Varian had attempted an electronic search for his team, and as he skirted around a derelict factory, there was no denying that he was downwind of them. Zio's scent was everywhere. Gale, predictably, had moved in a straight line.

Ignoring the pull to track Zio, Devan followed the combined scent until he came to an abandoned power plant, where it was clear the two units had, as planned, split up—Gale's crew flanking Zio's as they moved in to set explosives around the enemy camp.

Devan was still far enough away that he'd yet to pick up the scent of the southern packs, but he sensed their presence, and his hackles rose. He'd never been around wolves in such numbers, but somehow his shifter soul was already distinguishing between friend and foe. Between pack and the enemy.

Caught at a crossroads, Devan climbed a set of crumbling stairs to look out over the site. A flash of light caught his attention, gone so fast he thought he'd imagined it. Then an explosion rocked the earth, tearing through the quiet of the night, shaking the already fractured landscape.

A silence took hold, fleeting and deadly, and then screams. The injured and dying called to Devan in ways he couldn't explain, his healer instincts so strong he moved to leap through the glassless window, to advance on the explosion site and do all he could for any soul who needed him.

But as he leaned out into the night, another burst of pain hit him, stronger than any other, claws that hooked into him, yanking him back from the window.

Devan whirled around and sprinted out of the building. He ran towards the ever-growing scent of wolf blood, reaching out with his mind, filtering out the influx of distress to find the only one who truly mattered. He already knew it wasn't Zio who was hurt, but it was someone he cared about. It was *pack*.

Bonds solidified as supernatural power shimmered through Devan. The urge to shift was stronger than ever, but even in his human form, he was fast. It seemed as though no time at all had passed when he came across Bomber on his knees by a contaminated canal, his arm mangled, bones sticking out in every direction as blood poured from gaping wounds.

Devan dropped beside him. "What happened?"

"Grenade went off in my hand," Bomber ground out. "It'll heal, right?"

His vulnerability hurt Devan's heart. He examined the injury. "It's already knitting together, but not fast enough for you to not pass out from blood loss. I can help if you'll let me?"

Bomber hesitated, and Devan understood. Zio aside, of all the young wolves, Bomber had been among the most suspicious of his presence. The most hostile to an outsider in their midst. Allowing Devan to heal him would give Devan access to his emotions, more so than he had already as his links to the pack strengthened. A frightening prospect when you weren't sure of a stranger's intentions.

"Put it this way," Devan said. "This place is gonna be swarming with humans any minute now. You want them to find you unconscious and pick you up?"

"You'd leave me here alone?"

"Not if I can help it, but someone else might need me."

Bomber shuddered, face tight with pain. "Do it. Heal me, but don't be doing no voodoo shit with my brain after, you feel me?"

His vernacular gave away his age, in human terms, at least. Devan laid his hands on Bomber and pondered his backstory. Bowing to Zio's unit's aloofness, he hadn't done much more than skim the notes Emma had left behind. As his power flowed through his fingers and into Bomber, he wished he'd read them more thoroughly. There was nothing worse than not understanding the soul he wished to fix.

"Whoa." Bomber's low whistle broke into Devan's healing daze. "That shit is fast."

Devan's vision cleared, and he studied Bomber's injured arm. Bones had knit together, blood had clotted, and his skin was starting to close over the wounds. "How's your pain?"

"It's gone."

Bomber gazed at him, apparently awestruck, but they didn't

have time for conversation. Sirens were already sounding in the distance, and they needed to move out.

Devan hauled Bomber to his feet. "Can you run?"

"Yes."

"On two legs? The humans are going to have helicopters up. You don't want to be caught in your wolf form."

Bomber snorted but didn't argue. "Varian still on the bridge?"

"Yes."

"Are you coming with me?"

It was Devan's turn to hesitate. In the time it had taken him to tend to Bomber, no further distress calls had reached him, but the notion of leaving Zio—of leaving *pack*—was inconceivable. "I'll be right behind you."

"Is Zio okay?"

"What? Why are you asking that? Is he hurt?"

Bomber frowned. "He wasn't when I last saw him, but I can smell him all over you, so I figured you'd seen him since."

Devan fought hard to let his healer instincts overcome all else. To keep the worry and desire away and be the selfless pack healer Bomber needed him to be. "He was fine when I last saw him too. Keep going to Varian. I'll find the others."

Bomber nodded, his trust in Devan now solid, and vanished into the night. Devan watched him go, then turned back to the direction he'd come from to escape the explosion site. By now, the air was permeated with the scent of so many wolves—those he knew, and many he didn't—that it was hard to distinguish between them. To know whose spilled blood he could taste on his tongue. With his head still fuzzy from healing Bomber, even Zio's scent was too faint to track.

Devan closed his eyes and reached out with the instincts he'd tried so hard to ignore. Followed the trail of vengeful rage until he got a lead. *What the fuck are they doing that far west?*

He set off in the direction Zio's anger was coming from, weaving in and out of buildings and leaping rusted vehicles. Violence loomed around every corner, increasing in intensity until the harsh soundtrack of a fierce fight grew loud enough to stop Devan in his tracks.

Heart pounding, he crouched behind a wall, the caged beast within him prowling, eager to join the fray. But he resisted the battle call as the human shouts and wolf cries peaked. Man or beast, do no harm—an oath that was far easier to keep when your clan, family, or pack were living in peace.

The fighting faded. Victorious shouts and howls rang out, and Devan's heart lifted as Zio's wolf voice reached him. They'd won. But it wasn't much comfort as he waited for his newfound pack to emerge from the shadows. Blood was still the strongest scent, and the healer in Devan ached for every soul that had been hurt. *I'm not built for war.*

Minutes passed, each one longer than the last. Devan paced his hiding place, scenting the air every thirty seconds. His phone buzzed in his pocket, apparently finding a signal from somewhere.

Varian: *where are they?*

Devan didn't reply.

Didn't have to, because in the split second he'd torn his gaze from the scene beyond the wall, a troop of wolves had emerged from the shadows: Gale, Xan, Kate, Ishmail, with Shannon and Danielo bringing up the rear. Six of them when there should've been seven.

Tension coiled so tight in Devan's nerves he was sure they'd snap. *Where is he?* He stepped forward, power shimmering through him as he prepared to shift and find Zio, whatever it took, no matter the consequences, but as his claws slid out and his bones prepared to lengthen and crack, a final bloodied wolf limped free of the darkness of battle.

CHAPTER ELEVEN

Zio slumped over Varian's kitchen counter, tired. He rubbed his arm, kneading the sore muscles. The bones had been broken for a snatched few minutes before his wolf healing had repaired them, but the dull ache remained.

"You should've let Devan fix you," Bomber murmured as the others kept their collective attention glued to the human news reports on the explosions and carnage they'd caused. "I was good as new in ten minutes, no aches or fatigue. It was wild."

A low growl rumbled through Zio, and his gaze drifted unbidden to where Devan sat on the floor with Shannon, close to the TV and about as far from Zio as it was possible to be without leaving the room. "I didn't need him to heal me."

"So? Why not let him anyway if it causes you less pain?"

"I'm not in pain."

"Liar. I don't get your problem with him."

"That's because you let him into your brain. What if he really was the enemy, huh? If Shadow Clan sent him to infiltrate us? Didn't take him long to flip you, did it?"

Bomber opened his mouth to respond, but Zio pushed off the counter before he could speak and stomped out of the kitchen. He'd seen the news reports already. Watched them on the internet hours ago. He didn't get why Varian had insisted they study them together.

"Because it helps to regroup and collectively assess a mission. You know this, Zio, we've done it a hundred times."

Zio sighed as Varian came up behind him, alpha hands firm on his shoulders, and steered him into the living room. "I know all that. I just don't get why it had to be right now. I need to sleep."

"So sleep," Varian said. "Do you not feel safe enough with your family to rest your head?"

Safe. Zio turned the notion over in his head and discarded it. Pack was the only family he'd ever known, and Varian had always been his greatest comfort—his alpha—but, no. He didn't feel safe. Never had. "I don't want to sleep here. I want to go home."

Varian sighed and wrapped his arms around Zio, caging him in an embrace that should've grounded Zio even if it couldn't soothe the terminal restlessness he'd been reborn with, but as Zio hid his face in his alpha's chest, he felt nothing but a scraping desire to run.

He pushed back from Varian. "Sorry."

Varian gazed at him, unblinking. "What for?"

"Dunno."

"Then don't be sorry, Zio. That's not something I've ever asked of you, is it? To show contrition for simply being yourself?"

Zio shook his head, hating that Varian's earnest care grated on him so much. "I don't know what I'm sorry for, okay? I'm just really fucking tired."

"If I let you go, will you go home and rest? Or will I wake in the night to you howling at the moon?"

"Does it matter?"

"Of course it matters. For shifters, our wolf instinct is what makes us who we are, but we are still men. Sometimes we must leave the call of the beast and take care of ourselves as humans."

"That doesn't make any sense."

"It doesn't have to. Just promise me you'll go home, or to Danielo, or Bomber. I know you have found comfort with your brothers before."

Zio fought the urge to roll his eyes. If Varian thought getting buzzed and hooking up with his friends would quench the fire roaring through him, there was a missing link in the mystical chain that bonded a wolf to his alpha. A short circuit. A fault. *It's you, dickhead. Isn't it always?*

"I'll take him home."

The new voice in the room startled Zio, but Devan's sudden presence seemed as if it had always been there. He glanced over Varian's shoulder. Devan was leaning in the doorway, his gaze— as it had been ever since they'd returned from the Leicester mission—trained anywhere but at Zio.

"I assumed you'd be going that way at some point." Varian's tone was dry. "But I'm sure Zio can manage the walk alone if you have other plans."

"I don't."

The flatness lacing Devan's words made Zio's teeth itch. How could someone so vibrant be the grey man? *This shit is so fucked up.* But Zio knew a defeat when he sensed one. Varian wasn't going to let him leave without a genuine promise to do as he'd been told, and Zio couldn't give him one without Devan to distract him from the urge to run riot in the forest all night. "Whatever. Let's go."

They walked home in silence, Devan in front, Zio trailing after him like a sullen teenager.

Devan opened the door and stood back to let Zio pass.

Zio scowled. "You don't have to act like my fucking chaperone. I'm not a child."

Devan didn't blink. "Then don't act like one."

Ouch. Zio stepped into the house and moved automatically towards his room, his bed, unslept in for so long, a siren's call, but every pace away from Devan added lead to his already heavy legs. *Fuck's sake.* Zio knocked his fist on his head *again* and turned to find Devan behind him. "What—"

Devan shook his head and closed his fingers around Zio's aching wrist. The pain disappeared, gone in a whisper. "Now you can rest . . . brother."

He released Zio and disappeared into the kitchen.

Zio followed him, naturally. "I'm not your brother."

"Suit yourself." Devan opened the fridge and pulled out a pizza, some green shit Zio hadn't known was in there, and two bottles of beer. "But whatever you think I am, my place in your pack is to heal your pain."

"I don't have any pain. I didn't have any before you put your weirdo hands on me."

"You didn't have a problem with my weirdo hands when we were foraging."

With all that had happened since, their forest encounter seemed like a lifetime ago. "That wasn't your hands, and I didn't ask for that either."

"Do you think I'm forcing myself on you, Zio?"

"That's not what I said."

"Then what are you saying? That I should take care of everyone else and not you? Or that I should've left Bomber to be scooped up by the humans to save him from the violation of me healing him?"

"What? No."

Devan sighed and switched on the oven. It buzzed and whirred, a clear sign as if Zio needed one that Emma had been the last to use it. "Look, I get that this is difficult for you, even without . . . this." He gestured between them, then began the task of relocating every mushroom on the pizza to one side. Zio's side, he presumed. "But however much I want to, I can't make any of it go away."

Dread churned coldly in Zio's stomach. "Make what go away?"

"Any of it," Devan snapped. "Gods, how dense are you?"

68

Zio didn't have an answer that wasn't a sickening rumble from his empty stomach.

Devan shook his head and showed Zio his back. "Go and rest. I'll bring you some food when it's ready."

His tone was final. Zio wore belligerence like a second skin, but something—*everything*—about Devan's stance warned him to back off.

He retreated to his room, leaving the door open enough that Devan would know to come in if he wanted to, but not enough that Zio would see him if he walked past.

Zio stripped his clothes and crawled into bed. The sheets smelt faintly of Emma—as she'd likely washed them last—but for once, it didn't hurt to smell her. In a world which had become all about scents and urges he didn't understand, her distant familiarity was an embrace he needed more than Varian's.

There was a TV in Zio's room. He switched it on for company and lay down. Sleep hovered at the edge of his consciousness, taunting him with sweet oblivion, but as he listened to Devan move around the kitchen, closing his eyes felt like sacrilege.

So he didn't. He lay awake with scratchy eyes and a restless mind until Devan appeared with a plate of food and a bottle of beer.

Devan handed Zio the food without comment and turned to leave.

Zio's healed arm shot out to stop him. "Wait."

"What for?"

"I don't want to eat alone. Come sit with me."

"In your bed?"

"*On* my bed. Please?"

Devan sighed and walked away without answering. Zio held his breath. His shifter hearing was sharp, but Devan seemed to have feet that made no sound, so he couldn't tell if Devan would return until he reappeared a few moments later, clutching a plate and second beer bottle. "This is a bad idea."

Zio scooted over to make room. "Why?"

"Because I'm trying to stay away from you."

"How does marching me home from Varian's help with that?"

"I didn't say I was doing a good job of it."

Zio took a bite of his pizza and watched Devan do the same. "When did you last eat?"

"What do you care?"

It was on the tip of Zio's tongue to claim that he didn't, but it simply wasn't true. Devan had been in his life for a matter of days, but the imprint he'd left on Zio was bat-shit insane. He did care about Devan, even if he didn't have the first clue why.

He's pack, remember?

But . . . no. It was more than that. It had to be.

Pizza disappeared. Beer too. And a comfortable, and yet somehow awkward, silence settled over them. Sleep once again threatened Zio's consciousness, but as he slid down the bed, his nakedness in such close proximity to Devan made his skin jump.

Devan closed his eyes and banged his head on the bed frame. "Stop it."

"What?"

"Whatever you're thinking. I can smell it, and even if I couldn't, I healed you, remember? I can feel what you're feeling."

"You don't feel it yourself?"

"That's beside the point."

"It's really not."

Devan let out a quiet growl that came from deep within. Deep and low, it resonated through Zio's every nerve, adding fuel to the fire he was finding harder and harder to ignore.

"I didn't like it when you were fighting," Devan said. "Not just that you were in danger, but how you felt when you killed. You expect to enjoy it, but you don't."

"That's what you're telling me to stop?"

"No, I want you to stop throwing out waves that make me want to jump you so we can talk about something real."

Real. Another kick to the gut. Was Devan seriously implying

that the attraction between them *wasn't* real? That it was a heady mix of booze, post-fight adrenaline, and shifter horniness? And if he was, why did Zio care?

I don't care.

But again, it wasn't true. "I don't want to talk about fighting. It's done for today, but there'll be more tomorrow. Leave it alone."

Devan set his plate on the bedside table, slid down the bed and onto his side so he was facing Zio. His hypnotic scent was stronger than ever. Zio swallowed thickly but held his ground, not blinking as Devan's soft fingers grazed his cheek, his jaw, his bare shoulder. "I want to leave you alone. I wish I'd never met you."

"That hurts."

"I know. That's why I wish it so."

Zio didn't understand and suspected he wouldn't even if Devan explained it. He was a soldier, not a thinker or a student of the mind. He knew what he needed to know to survive, and surviving had become less important recently. Hidden away with Devan, nothing except his gentle touch seemed to matter, not even his ominous words. A contented rumble escaped Zio before he could catch it, and he gasped. *Did that come from me?* In all his supernatural existence, he'd never heard such a sound.

Devan chuckled. "How old are you, Zio?"

"You don't already know? You seem to know everything else."

"I read the cover of your file. It had vague circumstances of your change but not when you were born. I assumed your human backstory would be inside."

"You didn't look?"

"No."

"Why?"

"Because you didn't want me to. I didn't look at your unit at all, as it happens. I didn't think it was fair when you were so openly hostile to me."

"Fair to who?"

"You, obviously. Would you want someone you perceived as an enemy to know intimate details of your life?"

"There's nothing intimate about my life. Danielo's might make you blush, though."

Devan laughed again. "I don't doubt it. I can sense the . . . uh, connection he's had with all of you, even Varian."

It was Zio's turn to chuckle. "Yeah, that's Danielo. I'm pretty sure he's in love with Michael, but he's pretty free with, um, well, you know, the rest of it. He says love and sex aren't always connected."

"Interesting."

"Is it?"

Devan shrugged. "He's right, obviously. But if he's in love with Michael, I think he'll know that having sex with him is very different to experiences he's shared with the rest of you."

"He's never had sex with Michael. Everyone else, but never Michael, and don't fucking say that's interesting too. You're not here to dissect us or to pretend that your Shadow Clan lot don't get up to some freaky shit."

"Tell you what." Devan's ghosting fingers stilled, and he cupped Zio's face with his warm palm. "I won't speculate on Danielo's sex life if you tell me how old you are."

"In wolf terms or human?"

"Both."

"It's the same answer."

Devan's fair eyebrows ticked up. "Explain?"

"Varian found me at the scene of an accident my entire family had died in. I was badly hurt at the bottom of a ravine, no human medics or supernatural healers close enough to help, so he bit me to keep me alive." Zio's hand fluttered to the mark on his neck. He traced it with his thumb and shivered. "That was twenty-one years ago."

"Wow." Devan covered Zio's hand with his own. "I knew you were young."

"How?"

"The way you speak, the gaps in your knowledge old age

would have filled. I didn't know you'd been reborn of such tragedy, though. I'm sorry."

Zio shrugged. "It's okay. I was only a few days old—I don't know what I lost. And Varian found good people to take care of me until I was old enough to fight."

"You shouldn't have to fight."

"But I do . . . and I need it, you know? It keeps my head quiet."

"Even if it's the killing that made your head noisy in the first place?"

"Who says it was?"

"Not me. Just speculating. Sorry. It's in my blood."

Devan went back to stroking Zio's face as though the conversation was done.

Zio leaned into his touch and pressed on. "Dash changed you, didn't he?"

"Yes. I told you . . . I asked him to."

"When you were eighteen?"

"Yes."

"How long ago was that?"

"What does it matter? Age isn't important to shifters."

"Then why did you ask me?"

A wry smile warmed Devan's boyish face. "Because I'm terminally curious."

"So am I."

"No, you're not."

"I am about you."

"Okay . . ." Devan licked his lips, not seeming to notice or care that the tip of his tongue darting in and out quickened Zio's pulse. "If you must know, it was thirty years ago, so technically, I'm forty-eight."

"Technically. You look eighteen."

"I feel it too when I shift. When I stop thinking."

"I get that."

"I know."

"You know everything, eh?"

73

"Not at all." Devan stretched his neck. "I have no idea how I'm going to leave your room without kissing you."

Zio jerked his head up. "You want to kiss me?"

"Among other things."

"What things?"

Devan rolled his eyes. "You're worldly enough to know that without me explaining it to you."

"I'm not. I'm young, remember?"

"Not so young you didn't know how to jump on me in that club."

"*You* jumped on *me*."

"Did I?"

Zio bit his lip. The world—his world, at least—had flipped a dozen times since then. He remembered how Devan smelt, how his hands had felt, so strong and safe, but fuck if he could remember who had touched who first. "Whatever. My point is that you should probably be clear about what you're saying. I have a habit of assuming things and losing my shit before letting people explain."

"Shocker."

"Fuck off."

Devan snorted. "That might be for the best. It hasn't worked out so well the last few times I've let this get out of hand."

"You've *let* this?"

"You said it yourself, Zio. You're young, remember?"

Zio couldn't tell if Devan was joking, but the idea that Devan had any kind of control over the madness that had occurred between them heated his blood to boiling point.

In a fluid movement, he kicked the bed covers away and pounced, straddling Devan, hands around his neck. "You can't control this. You can't control *me*."

Devan swallowed but otherwise appeared unfazed to find a naked Zio suddenly on top of him. "It's not about controlling you. It's about doing what's best for your—for *our*—pack. I don't know about you, but I don't have time for complications right now."

"Complications?"

"Yes." Devan canted his hips just enough for his hard length to press against Zio. "Complications. You think Varian needs to be worrying about one of his elite soldiers getting down with the only healer in the world prepared to help his pack in a time of war?"

Every nerve in Zio's body screamed at him to grind down on Devan's cock. To rip his clothes away and burn the bed to ashes as their simmering inferno exploded around them.

But . . . Devan had a point. If Varian disapproved of them hooking up, he might feel the need to send Devan away, and despite every thought Zio had thrown up to the contrary, the pack needed Devan . . . even more than Zio did.

With a rough growl, he rolled off Devan. "Fuck this, I'm going out."

Devan caught his arm. "Don't. You need to rest."

"You don't know what I need."

"I do." Devan's grip tightened, and he pulled Zio back on top of him. "And I've told you already that I want it too, but we can't, Zio. We just . . . can't."

Pressed so tightly together, it was impossible to comprehend that Devan could have been right. Zio gave in to the primal urge to grind against Devan and moaned as pleasure ripped through him with a brand new fire. *So good, so good, so good.* He circled his hips again and again, found Devan's hands, and squeezed, bending bones that would've broken if Devan had been human.

But Devan wasn't human. He was a shifter with strength that matched Zio's. Zio's weight was his only advantage, and he took it, fighting Devan for dominance until he won. Until Devan gave in and let Zio manhandle him and tear at his clothes.

Devan's T-shirt disappeared, his jeans and underwear gone in a swipe of Zio's clawed hands. Bare to Zio, he glared up at him. "What do you want, huh? You want to fuck me and let the whole world know? Because they will. They'll know it the moment we leave this house."

Zio didn't care. The desire to join himself to Devan in any

way Devan would let him was making him dizzy. His chest heaved, his head spun, and coherent thought was long gone. "I want—"

Devan growled and moved too fast for Zio to catch him, rolling them, throwing Zio onto his back and pressing his forearm against Zio's throat. "I know what you want. You can't have it."

"Why not?"

"I told you already. Because of the pack. The war. And a million other reasons."

"Then why are you playing me?"

"I'm not—"

"You are. How else do you explain the last few days? Or have you been healing my fucked-up soul with pizza and blowjobs?"

Devan's edible lips twitched. "You bought your own pizza last time."

"Didn't suck my own dick, though, did I?"

Devan groaned and dropped his head, platinum hair falling forwards, obscuring his face.

Zio ached to comfort him, punch him, fuck him. Punch him some more, then fuck him all over again. "This shit isn't fair. Why do you get to turn me inside out and walk away every time?"

"I can't walk away."

"What?"

Devan raised his head. "I said, I can't walk away. If I could, we'd have fucked already and that would be the end of it."

"What about all that crap about the pack and the war?"

"It would still stand, but if we'd had a one-time hook-up, I'm pretty sure life would've moved on by now." Devan removed his arm from Zio's throat and tugged him upright, faces inches apart, chests grazing. "Before this gets out of control, you need to know . . . I don't think anything that happens between us is ever going to be a one-time thing."

Devan pinned Zio's hands above his head. Somehow in the last ten minutes, he'd lost sight of all reason. Or maybe he'd never had it, and that was why it was now him straddling Zio. Him chasing the heated bolts of pleasure that blinded him so completely to anything else.

Anything except Zio.

Devan gazed down, drinking in Zio's fast-moving chest, flushed skin, and hooded dark eyes. Gods, he was beautiful. Devan pushed messy sweat-dampened hair out of his own face and leaned back. He ached to fuck Zio, to put an end to the yearning that was driving them both so insane, but he'd meant it when he'd told Zio that nothing they did would be a one-time thing, and his pack's warnings, though a distant memory while he kept Zio prisoner beneath him, still held true. *I can't fuck him. Not yet.*

But he had to do something. Had to set them both free, even if it was just for tonight.

"Devan."

Devan opened his eyes, unaware that he'd closed them until Zio's whisper broke through. "What is it?"

"Can I touch you?"

Devan blinked. "Why are you asking me that?"

"Because I need you to feel like I do when you touch me."

Devan found his hazed memory of the club and then the razor-sharp recollection of the forest. Zio had filled his throat perfectly, as though he'd been made to slide along Devan's tongue. He remembered Zio's crazed, ecstatic moans, and desire pulsed through him. "Touch me. Please."

Zio sat up and closed his hand around Devan's hard length. Fluid beaded at the tip and created the ultimate alchemy of wetness and friction.

Devan gasped. "Your hand is so warm."

"Does it feel good?"

"Yeah, Zio. It feels good."

Zio squeezed, pulled, twisted, bottom lip caught between his teeth. "I need you to be as crazy for me as I am for you. To lose your fucking mind before you come."

"Why?"

"I need to know it's not just me."

"I already told—"

"I need to *see*."

Devan shook his head. "You've seen it already, every day since we met."

"Then show me again."

Devan would show Zio anything he desired as long as he kept jacking him like that. He rarely gave into a shifter's natural urge to chase pleasure wherever it was available, even when he was alone, but Zio's touch was nothing he'd ever felt before. Electric. Addictive. And so consuming Devan forgot where he was. Who he was. Forgot everything except the growing pressure in his belly. "Let me touch you too."

"No."

"Please?"

"*No.*"

"If I begged, would it convince you I'd lost my mind the way you want me to?"

"Maybe, but I don't want you to move. Just lie there, Devan. Let me take this from you."

A groan tore from Devan's chest. He thrust up into Zio's hand and screwed his eyes shut. "I need you to come too."

"Trust me, I'm gonna. And it's gonna be quick. Are you ready?"

I'll never be ready for you.

Zio loosened his grip on Devan's length enough to wrap his fingers around his own, so they slid together as one, slicked with the silky fluid that had seeped from Devan.

Devan opened his eyes, instantly transfixed. His blood sang, and release ambushed him, spurting out of him a split second before sensation caught up and knocked the breath from his lungs.

It hit him like a freight train. He roared. White-hot pleasure carried him to the precipice of his human form. Raw power shimmered through every facet of him, and only fear of hurting Zio kept him from shifting as new light flared in the connection they shared.

Zio came with a ragged yell, the very tips of his claws scraping Devan's cock. Sweat and blood merged with their combined release. The scent was dizzying, and Devan fought to stay conscious as Zio fell forwards.

He caught Zio and broke his fall with his body. Zio reached out with trembling hands to rub his seed into Devan's skin, but Devan stopped him. "Don't. We won't come back from that."

Barely awake, Zio gazed up at him. "From what?"

"You really don't know?"

Zio started to shake his head, but the obnoxious buzz of Devan's neglected phone cut him off. For a long moment, they didn't move, then reality kicked Devan in the nuts, and he dove for the phone.

Varian greeted him. "Sorry to disturb you. They need you at the clinic. Human emergency. Can you help?"

Devan rolled off the bed. "Of course. I'm on my way."

CHAPTER TWELVE

"I didn't hear you in the woods last night," Varian said. "Did you find rest?"

Zio kept his gaze on the satellite navigation app he was using to map out the weakest points in their defence lines. Some were obvious—sparsely populated and scenes of previous conflict—others less so. He'd heard rumours of wolves duping their way into regiments of the human army. "Yeah. I slept."

Not on purpose. After Devan had run out on him, he'd fought to stay awake, but drained of his haunting desire for Devan—for a short while, at least—he'd knocked out. Slept naked and clinging to one side of the bed so there'd be room for Devan when he came back.

He hadn't come back.

Varian rounded the table and scented Zio's neck, a gesture that often soothed Zio.

Now, though, Zio battled a primal urge to shove him away. To protect any remnants of Devan's scent from anyone's attention but his. *Mine.*

Zio shuddered. *The fuck is wrong with me?*

Varian stepped away. "I'm struggling with you, Zio. You've always been somewhat of an enigma, even as a child, but I see things in you I don't understand, now more than ever. I wish you would talk to me."

Tell him.

It seemed like madness. Varian had never pried into the private lives of his pack, even the combat units he worked so closely with. Even Zio, who he'd changed himself and mentored his entire childhood. He'd never asked why much of Gale's crew, and Zio's alike, had all passed through Danielo's bed when it was obvious to the whole fucking world that Danielo was forever devoted to Michael. He'd never asked Shannon about his human companion in the township. Or Kate why she'd cried when Ishmail had found his mate. It wasn't that he didn't care . . . it was about respect.

They were a pack with many beating hearts.

Besides, confessing to Varian would mean Devan's Shadow Clan alpha would have to be told too, and Zio didn't know enough about that relationship to betray Devan's trust. Not even to Varian. *My alpha.*

Zio's heart skipped, and he forced himself to focus on the tablet screen. "If I was commanding the southern forces, I'd plan small incursions at the weakest spots in the divisional lines while infiltrating easy access points in the all-human areas."

After a loaded beat of silence, Varian followed Zio's gaze. "Where?"

"Here." Zio pointed to an area of the unmarked border that was notoriously hard to defend. "And here—at the NHS hospital a few miles north of the line. It's overused, understaffed, and lacks funding from the human government. It's ripe for corruption."

"So you'd do that? Use the misfortune of others to gain a strategic advantage?"

"If I was a heartless bastard, yes. But I'm not sure our enemies are that clever. I might be overthinking."

"Underthinking is far more dangerous. Say they did covertly take the hospital. What would the advantage be?"

"At the very least, a place to pool soldiers until the time came to deploy them. That way they wouldn't be seen at the border."

Varian nodded, though his eyes gave nothing away. "And what would you do if you were the military commander of this pack?"

"You're more than a military commander. You're the alpha."

"Humour me."

Zio shrugged. "We could infiltrate the hospital first, but the southern commanders would simply find another target. I think we should show strength at the border, repel any attacks with heavy firepower. Let them think that's our focus while we monitor the hospital."

Varian hummed and left the table to fiddle with the coffee machine. He came back with a mug for himself and a handful of biscuits for Zio. "In case you haven't got round to eating yet."

"I ate last night. Devan made pizza."

"That's nice."

"Is it?"

"Yes, Zio. I was worried you wouldn't get on with someone living in Emma's space, and I had no wish for you—or him—to endure more upheaval than necessary."

"You know, you could've put him in the spare room at Bomber and Danielo's place. Or asked Michael if he'd share his flat at the barracks."

"I could've."

"So why didn't you?"

"You may crave solitude, child, but it's not good for you." Varian cupped Zio's face. His palm held all the warmth of Devan's, but none of the heat. "And Devan is a natural healer. I'd imagine his close presence is benefitting you already, even if you don't yet know it."

I know it. Zio cleared his throat. "How many soldiers am I taking to the border?"

Varian let his palm drop. "Your unit and the ground company—fifty-six of you, in total, while Gale's unit will target the hospital."

"Fifty-six? That's bad maths, boss. Me plus my unit, plus fifty squadies is fifty-five."

"Plus our resident healer."

"Devan?"

Varian nodded. "Yes. For some reason, my gut won't allow me to separate you."

Zio left Varian's house at sundown. He jogged through the trees, eager to link up with Gale so he could search out Devan and go home.

Home. It was a strange concept that after weeks of avoiding it, there was presently nowhere he'd rather be.

Right, cos it's all about the bungalow. The shit hot-water tank and the broken springs in your mattress.

Zio let his mind drift as he emerged from the wooded area and circled the compound to where Gale lived. As ever, there seemed to be a separate place in his brain reserved for Devan and a fuzziness to his memories of the moments leading up to encounters he could recall with crystal clarity. He remembered every second he'd been naked in bed with Devan, but not entirely how it came to be. How his sensibilities had led him to believe it was a good idea. Away from Devan, he could think clearly, but the trouble was, he didn't want to. Because thinking clearly would bring regret, and he wasn't in the mood for that shit. Nah. Been there, done that, and what had it changed?

Fuck all. Devan was still living in his house, and for whatever messed up reason, Zio still wanted him. *But he's not a wolf. Not a wolf. Not a wolf. Not a wolf.* Three words that haunted Zio when he let them. But did it truly matter? *Shit, we're just hooking up. It's not like I'm marrying the guy.*

Huh. Perhaps that was it. Varian was always advising them to embrace their human nature. Maybe, just maybe, this was about men, not a wolf and whatever mutant creature Devan was—

Zio crashed into a warm, solid body. "The fuck?"

Devan steadied him, his grin as supernatural as anything Zio had ever seen from him. "You should pay attention to your surroundings better, even on the compound. Complacency is a bad habit."

"Yeah? Well, so is creeping up on people like a stalker. Again. How do you *do* that? Do you have a shield?"

"Nope. I took advantage of your distraction again, hence my advice to be more self-aware."

Zio glared.

Devan grinned some more.

"You're not funny," Zio snapped.

"I'm not laughing."

"Liar."

"No. I'm not a liar, Zio. Ask me anything, and I'll always tell you the truth."

Zio rolled his eyes. "Damn. Is this what you snuck up on me for? Deep and meaningful conversation?"

"I came to say hello. I haven't seen you since last night."

Oh. Mollified, Zio relaxed his stance. "Well, hello then. Where've you been all this time? Varian said you'd been called out for a human emergency, but he didn't elaborate."

"Childbirth." Devan motioned for Zio to keep walking. "I'm sure you don't want the details, but the baby was stuck. The human doctors could save the mother, but not the baby, so I assisted them."

"The baby lived?"

"Yes, and I was able to heal the damage done by the compression on the placenta."

Zio winced. "That sounds painful."

"It was, for everyone involved, but the outcome was good."

"Was the baby human?"

"It's not yet known. The father was a wolf—I think he works on the arable farm—but the mother is human, so I suppose we won't know until the child is older."

Zio couldn't name the emotions that rolled through him as he contemplated that. "I can't imagine growing up without knowing. I was raised by humans, but for as long as I can remember, I counted the days until my first shift."

"How old were you?"

"Eleven."

It was Devan's turn to flinch. "That's . . . young. The development in hereditary shifters is much slower."

"And much faster in adults who are bitten. Did your change hurt?"

"Yes. Very much. But I was never alone, and it was something I'd chosen. I think that helps."

"I didn't choose to be bitten, and it didn't hurt."

Devan's expression grew distant, the way Zio had noticed it often did when he was reaching for the wisdom Zio lacked. "There isn't much literature on shifters who are bitten as infants. Years ago such things were forbidden, and the ruling councils would've destroyed you and Varian both."

"Yeah, he told me that. He probably told me what changed too, but I never paid much attention to his history lessons."

"What changed was the leadership of the supernatural world. Vampires and werewolves were defeated by shifters. New alliances formed; new laws made. By the time you were born, it was no longer permitted to destroy supernatural infants without just cause . . . no longer up to, say, Varian, to prove you weren't dangerous, and instead up to the authorities to prove you were."

Zio turned his gaze to the sky. Varian had warned him many times that the world was far greater than he'd ever see, but the idea that shifters he'd never meet had held his fate in their hands disturbed him.

Devan stopped and caught Zio's hand, tugging him back until they were face-to-face. "I can't vouch for the ruling wolves of the world, but you were never in danger from Shadow Clan."

"You don't know that."

"I do. I may not have known about you, but I've heard of

other shifters who were bitten as infants, and never once witnessed Dash advocating their death."

"What about Luca? Your war general, huh? I bet he's not so—"

"So what? You've already admitted that you have little knowledge of supernatural history, so why do you have such concrete opinions?"

"Am I annoying you, Devan?"

Devan's gaze flickered, turning his bright eyes a stormy blue. "Would that make you happy?"

"I—" Zio opened his mouth. Shut it again. He couldn't deny that riling Devan was amusing. That his reaction was off the scale hot. But did upsetting him make Zio happy?

That was a hard no.

"I'm sorry. I didn't mean to offend you."

Devan's scowl remained for a moment longer; then his face softened, and he shrugged. "I'm not offended. Perhaps spending the last twelve hours with wolves who didn't care for my presence has left me more irritable than usual."

Irritable wasn't a word Zio had associated with Devan in the short time he'd known him. "What wolves?"

"The father of the baby and his extended family. They didn't want a non-wolf healer near his human mate and his child. It took some persuading and the actual threat of death to change their minds."

"I didn't want you here either."

"I know."

"But death didn't have to persuade me otherwise if it's any consolation."

"It's not, to be honest. Your pack is on the verge of being wiped out by a threat as grave to supernatural peace as many living shifters have ever known. Do you think your prejudices about those who aren't exactly like you are more important?"

"No—"

"Then perhaps you, a highly revered soldier, should do more

to educate the masses. That is, if you have truly changed your mind and you haven't merely developed a fetish for me."

"Wow."

"What?"

Zio squeezed Devan's hands. "You really are pissed off."

"Am I?"

"Yes. I can't feel your emotions the way you can mine, but you're doing a pretty good job of projecting."

"Sorry."

"Nah. I like it better than never knowing how to read you."

"I wasn't aware you spent much time trying."

Zio chuckled. "You'd be amazed what I do when you're not paying attention."

Devan closed the minute distance between them, his lips tantalisingly close. "I think you're overestimating my ability to ignore you."

Kiss him. But Devan's phone rang, once again interrupting them. He fished it from his pocket and checked the screen. "It's a Bratislava number," he said. "I have to take it. Go on with your work. I'll find you at home before it's time to leave."

Home. "Leave?"

"For the border mission."

"How do you know about that? It was only planned an hour ago."

"Wolves talk. I listen."

Devan's impish grin returned, and he backed away from Zio, gone as suddenly and silently as he'd appeared, leaving Zio to contemplate the notion that home was a state of mind they shared.

I like that.

CHAPTER THIRTEEN

Devan perched on the branch of the weeping willow tree, surveying the efficient activity on the ground. With Zio in charge, the defence force deployed by Varian to protect the border had wasted little time setting up camp. The operation was different to the last—less guerrilla and far bigger. Fifty northern wolves had accompanied Zio's unit to the border, soldiers, apparently, though they lacked the edge of Zio's fearsome crew.

The base was imposing and well equipped. Sleeping quarters and a makeshift medical tent were set up.

"What about the human authorities?" Devan asked. "They won't object to a military camp like this?"

Danielo shook his head from his position at the foot of the tree, using his gift to seek out a fresh-water source in case the enemy cut the current supply. "They don't know where the border is. As far as they know, this is a training camp. We're allowed those."

"To what end?"

"To keep our protection forces viable. Not even humans can deny our right to defend ourselves."

Devan absorbed the information. Coexisting with English humans seemed far more complicated than it was in Slovakia, where Dash's healer's commune was nestled deep within the densely populated capital city. In Bratislava, humans were openly fascinated by shifters. Not so afraid of them that they imposed draconian rules to control them. *This is war, though, remember? And war breeds fear.*

Fear that had been worryingly absent in Zio as they'd prepared to head south. They hadn't had much time before the mission had called them away, but they'd managed to eat—more pizza—and Devan had slept on the couch while Zio had packed.

He'd woken to Zio's hand on his shoulder, his whisper that of a dream: *"It's time to go."* Staring down at the operation below, it seemed to belong to a different lifetime. Zio was in his element here, shouting orders, directing wolves, demanding respect without ever expecting that it wouldn't be there. Devan thought back to the blissful half hour they'd spent in Zio's bed before Devan's duty had interrupted them. Zio had been in his element then too. Was that what he'd needed all along? To take what he desired rather than Devan simply giving it to him?

As though he'd heard Devan's thoughts, Zio glanced up. Devan was hidden by the sweeping leaves of the willow tree, and the frown creasing Zio's forehead bothered him. *Does he need me?*

The possibility that he did, and Devan was nowhere in sight, was enough to drive Devan out of his treetop sanctuary.

He dropped to the ground, startling Danielo.

"Fuckin' A. Stop doing that shit."

Devan grinned back. "Sorry."

"No, you're not."

Devan turned. Zio was behind him, an unfathomable glint in his dark gaze. "How can you tell?"

"Just can. Where do you want to sleep?"

"Huh?"

"Sleep, Devan. That thing we do when we're tired, unless you were planning on staying awake for however long we're stuck in this crap hole."

"I don't need much sleep."

"That's not the same as no sleep. Answer the question."

Danielo whistled. "Damn, you're like an old married couple. Maybe you should share a tent while the rest of us bunk in together."

Zio glowered at him. "Don't be thinking what you're thinking already. We've only been here ten minutes, and we haven't got time for that."

Devan sampled Zio's emotions. Irritation was his baseline, impatience, frustration, but there was heat there too, a different kind to the inferno Devan felt when they were together, but still. "Am I missing something?"

"No," Zio snapped in synchro with Danielo's deepening smirk. "Just this clown can never be dissuaded from getting his dick wet. Doesn't seem to matter where we are or what's at stake."

He turned on his heel and stormed away. Devan shifted his curiosity to Danielo.

The young wolf shrugged. "Zio needs to chill out. Before Emma died, he had no issue cutting loose when we had the chance. Needed it as much as the rest of us. We've been fighting a long time."

Comprehension clicked in Devan's brain. "You're lonely and jacked up by war, so you find comfort in each other."

It wasn't a question, but Danielo nodded. "Something like that. I'm not saying we have non-stop orgies when we should be working, but there isn't exactly much to do around here."

"And being together is safe, yes?"

"Yes."

It made sense. Devan had heard of such things in shifter packs before and always envied the sexual freedom—the ability to take pleasure without consequence. He imagined what it would be like with Zio, if Devan was as Danielo seemed to be to him—a pack mate who'd always be there, no matter what. A friend he could explore and enjoy without complication or fear. Devan pictured them in Zio's bed, no stress or hard limits. Zio open and relaxed, uplifted by his desire for Devan, not rigid with ingrained distrust. *He pushed Zio onto his back and spread his legs, trailing fingertips through the sweat beaded on Zio's heated skin as he brought his length to where Zio wanted him most. Zio—*

Danielo chuckled, drawing Devan from his fantasies. "You should definitely try it while we're here, if you find yourself in need of a distraction."

"A distraction from what?"

"From whatever's putting that look on your face."

Another day, another treetop hideout. But this time for strategic importance rather than Devan's natural instinct to sit back and watch.

He tracked the team of northern soldiers as Zio led them through the undergrowth towards the enemy group approaching from the east.

The attack had been expected and was predictable in its nature. Devan had learned that about the southern packs—that what they gained by their greater numbers, they lacked in imagination. It was one of many reasons Varian's pack had resisted them for so long. Another was undeniably the superior abilities of the elite combat squad.

Devan climbed higher in the mighty oak. The two groups were out of sight of each other, but close—thirty feet, if that. A gentle rumble shook the ground. At first, Devan thought he'd imagined it; then the lead wolves of the enemy disappeared, swallowed by the earth as a sinkhole opened beneath them.

Gods. But there was no spare heartbeats for shock and awe. In the time it had taken Zio to destroy the southern scouts, the northern forces had converged, breaking through the hedge barriers separating them, using the advantage of their downwind position. A flash of light. A shout. Growls filled the air as every wolf that was able shifted and charged into the fray.

The fighting was fierce. Blood scented the wind, filling Devan's senses as a dozen shifters fought for survival. Zio's team were outnumbered, but they had skill on their side. And Devan. He skirted the battle from his aerial position, leaping from tree to tree as he fought the urge to shift. Another enemy shifter fell, throat ripped out by a northern wolf Devan didn't recognise in its animal form. *Where's their healer?* Devan scented the air and reached out with the contact only another healer would notice but found nothing.

A northern wolf died, succumbing to catastrophic injuries before Devan could reach them. *Who is it? Who is it? Who is it?* It wasn't Zio. But was it Bomber? Or Michael? *Fuck this. I need to see them in their wolf form before they go out again.*

Devan dropped to the ground. The fighting was fading. A northern wolf rolled in front of him, a deep gash to its neck. Devan healed it and moved on, trusting his abilities to keep the wolf safe from further attack.

A southern wolf fell at his feet. Instinct warred with pack, but a tortured howl pierced the air before either urge won.

Devan spun around. Four feet away, a brown wolf writhed on the ground, northern by scent. A southern wolf moved in to finish it off, but Zio's black wolf, enhanced with his beta strength, appeared from nowhere. He pounced. The enemy wolf yelped, but the sound cut off, the wolf killed by a flick of Zio's powerful jaws.

Silence hit the clearing, save the pained moans of the injured. The battle was over.

The sudden calm was oppressive. Devan moved through the aftermath, healing wolves with the northern scent, thankful every enemy wolf he came across had died of their wounds. Human footsteps replaced the tread of huge paws. Michael appeared, Danielo, and finally Bomber. All of them drawn to Devan, even as men, their wolves recognising Devan as their healer.

Other northern wolves drifted closer too, but before Devan could absorb that more of the pack—*his* pack—had accepted him as one of their own, a waft of blood hit him. Of torn flesh and mangled bone. He spun again. Two wolves were on the ground. Southern wolves. The enemy had left their injured behind.

Devan stepped forward.

Bomber caught his arm. "No."

"They'll die."

"So? You think their healer is running around looking for our brothers and sisters to heal?"

"Who they are doesn't change who I am. Who *we* are. Besides, if I heal them, you can take them prisoner, no?"

"We don't take prisoners."

Devan shrugged out of Bomber's grip and continued forwards. He crouched by the closest enemy wolf, a young female. "You didn't have non-wolves in your pack either until recently. Things change."

"Don't touch that fucking wolf."

Zio's voice sent shivers down Devan's spine. Somehow, Devan had missed him returning to the scene of the battle in his human form, but even with his back to him, he knew he was naked, sinewy muscles bunched with tension, fists clenched, dark gaze fiercer than ever.

Devan sat back on his heels. It had been easier to disobey Bomber. Technically, Zio was his superior, his beta, though Devan didn't belong to his unit. "I can't leave them to die."

"Why not? They'd rip your throat out if they were capable."

"I don't doubt it, but the fight is over. Let me heal them."

"No."

"*Zio.*"

"Fucking leave it, Devan. It's not your call."

Devan didn't need to hear Zio's departing footsteps to know he was walking away.

CHAPTER FOURTEEN

"He's still there, you know. Devan. He's still sitting with them."

Zio glowered. He didn't need specifics from Michael to know what he was talking about. He knew Devan was still guarding the dying enemy wolves because his every sense was tuned to Devan whether he wanted it to be or not. And right now, he could've done without the mental image of the raw pain he'd seen in Devan when he'd refused him permission to be the shifter he'd been reborn to be. "He can sit there all night. Won't do him any good."

Michael said nothing, which was often his loudest voice.

Zio sighed and pulled his hands from the river. "Whatever it is, just say it. I've better shit to be doing than dealing with you silently judging my every move."

Michael stretched his legs out in front of him, turning his face to the night sky. "I'm not judging anything, but I don't think you're being fair."

"Fair to who? The hordes of southern wolves that were sent to kill us, or Devan?"

"Both. We were trying to kill them as much as they were us, and you've ordered Devan to go against everything he is, despite him offering a sensible alternative."

"Taking prisoners?"

Michael shrugged. "We've never done it, but that doesn't mean we can't. We don't know who those wolves are—they could be grunts, or conscripts, or maybe even betas. Given our current situation, we'd be fools to let that kind of intelligence die."

"Our current situation?"

"We're against the ropes, man," Michael said. "And we only came out on top today because Devan was with us. Even if you don't agree with him, at least hear him out and check in with Varian before you make an enemy of the only healer we've got."

"We don't take prisoners."

"Uh-huh."

Michael lay back on the riverbank and closed his eyes, apparently oblivious to Zio's deepening glare. He was the most perceptive of Zio's unit. The only subordinate wolf who would ever challenge him so freely . . . and so damn reasonably that Zio wanted to throttle him.

He huffed out another sigh and got to his feet. In the distance, northern campfires burnt, overtly defending the weakest points in the border, the message to the enemy clear—*we're here, come and get us.* The fires were guarded, the sleeping areas too, watch teams changing every few hours. Zio's gaze didn't linger on them, instead drawn to the dimly lit area where northern wolves were burying both their own dead and those from the other side, as human public health laws dictated. To the side of the death circle, a lone figure sat where Zio had left him, keeping vigil over the dying wolves of the enemy pack.

Devan.

The tug in Zio's chest was impossible to ignore. He threw Michael a last scowl and jogged to the scene he'd been hoping to leave behind until morning.

Devan heard him coming, naturally, but didn't turn around. "The male died an hour ago. Your clean-up crew is coming back for him."

"They're not my clean-up crew. They're burying their family."

"And someone else's. Is this how you'd want your brothers to be treated?"

"The southern packs have done far worse to my brothers," Zio snapped. "And my sisters."

"Doesn't make it right."

"Never said it did."

Devan turned to face Zio, shadows obscuring most of his face. "What if the enemy had found Emma injured and let her live?"

"They didn't find her. I did, and she died in my arms."

"Because you couldn't heal her."

"No one could've healed her, Devan. She was . . . fuck, there was nothing left to fix."

"Shadow Clan nurtures the most powerful healers in the world," Devan said. "Whatever side I'd been on, I might've been able to save her."

Rage, fresh and bright, flared in Zio's gut, merging with the pain of old wounds. "I don't believe you."

"You don't have to. Just try and see past your anger and grief. There are strategic reasons to keep this wolf alive, but you have to be more than a soldier, Zio. You have to be a man."

"I don't have to be anything you tell me to be. My responsibility is to my pack, and that means eradicating any fucker that's trying to kill us."

Devan laughed without humour. "She's not killing anyone right now."

"And she won't ever again. Fuck you and your strategic bullshit. If you want to be a healer in a war, you have to pick a side."

"Or what?"

"Or you're no good to us."

For the second time in as many hours, Zio walked away from Devan. He felt sick, but he blamed it on the heavy use of his gift in the fight. Exerting his supernatural abilities often left him with a headache, something Devan could've helped him with if he hadn't been hellbent on saving the enemy. *Why does he have to be so fucking difficult?*

With no answer forthcoming from Zio's subconscious, he repeated the question to Varian when he tracked down the satellite phone a little while later.

Varian sighed. "He's not being difficult; he's showing us an alternate path, just as we have shown him one in drawing him onto the battlefield. I'll admit, my own desire to destroy as much of the southern packs as we can has left me merciless. Perhaps it's time we tried something different."

"You're seriously considering saving a southern rat?"

"A wolf, Zio. Whatever they have become to us, they are still our own kind."

Zio growled loud enough for a nearby soldier to shoot him an alarmed glance. Reining himself in, Zio ducked into a tent, letting solitude embrace him. Calm him. "Whatever. I still think it's madness to waste our resources keeping them alive."

"If Devan can heal the surviving wolf with his powers alone, we haven't lost anything."

"And then what, though? What if the enemy comes looking for her?"

"I'd imagine they won't if they were happy to leave her behind in the first place. In any case, I will send an intelligence unit to your position to retrieve her. That way, no nearby enemy will sense that she's still alive."

Disquiet coursed through Zio's veins. "But what if she doesn't know anything? What do we do with her then? Kill her anyway?"

"If she's away from your base, Zio, it won't be your concern. Pass my orders onto Devan, and consider the matter closed."

The discussion was over. The soldier in Zio regretted mentioning the injured southern wolf at all, but as Zio sent a messenger to Devan with Varian's orders, the man Devan apparently wanted him to be felt nothing but relief. *I can't live with him being unhappy.*

97

Devan drifted back to base, weary. Emotions that weren't his own bombarded him from every direction, and he longed for his quiet couch in Zio's bungalow.

He longed for Zio too, but if today had taught him anything, it was that whatever mythical connection they shared was nowhere near enough to bridge the gaps where they were worlds apart. If not for Varian's eleventh-hour intervention, the female wolf would've died.

As it was, Devan had passed her over to northern intelligence. Who knew what would become of her now?

Fresh woodsmoke greeted Devan as he reached the tent city Zio's forces had erected for shelter. Devan's was at the back, the only way to get to it through the main area, crowded with off-duty soldiers letting off steam, and of course, he was sharing with Zio.

Devan picked his way through the clusters of men and women indulging in Danielo's prescription for the ultimate downtime. It was nothing Devan hadn't seen before, but as the scents of arousal and sex filled his senses, blocking out the blood and distress he'd brought back from the field, he felt no urge to join in.

He kept his gaze to himself until he found Michael in a quiet corner. Grateful for a familiar face that wasn't attached to a naked body, Devan dropped down beside him. "Not your scene?"

Michael spared him a soft grunt. "Not especially. I'm not as . . . well, horny, I suppose, as the rest of them. Perhaps that part of me is broken."

Devan hadn't healed Michael, and so it was impossible to tell if he was joking. Given that he'd never seen the serious young soldier laugh, he went with the instinct that he wasn't. "Being different isn't broken. Have you ever been with someone?"

"Once. But she was killed soon after, so I was never sure if the feeling was permanent."

"Emma?"

Michael shook his head. "Emma, to my knowledge, only felt that way about females. It was someone else . . . a friend."

"I'm sorry."

"It's okay. It was a long time ago."

"How long?"

"Five years."

A blink of the eye in a supernatural lifetime, but Varian's pack—Devan's pack now—were still young. Devan cast his gaze around the clearing. Campfires were lit, tended to by men and women grilling meat and roasting potatoes. Those that weren't cooking were generally fucking. Danielo and Bomber were both . . . occupied, though not, Devan noted, with each other.

Zio was nowhere to be seen, but Devan knew that without looking. Knew that wherever Zio was, he wasn't remotely close. He pondered where he might be, then cursed himself for caring. *I wish I'd never met him.*

Michael got up and fetched a plate of meat and potatoes. For campfire food, it was pretty good, but Devan couldn't bring himself to eat much. He'd healed so many today he'd carry their pain for a while. Food would've helped, but sleep would do more, and Devan craved the sweet oblivion.

He excused himself and left Michael, retreating through the amorous chaos, so intent on reaching his bed for the night that he walked right into Bomber. "Damn. Sorry."

"No worries." Bomber regarded him through hooded eyes. "Where are you headed in such a hurry anyway? Someone waiting for you?"

His grin was suggestive. Devan rolled his eyes. "I doubt it, especially after today. I don't think many people are gonna be queuing to hook up with the man who healed the enemy, do you?"

"I'll hook up with you."

Devan laughed, couldn't help it, despite his connection to Bomber telling him the offer was entirely serious. "Thanks, but it's okay. I didn't fight today, so my, uh, urges aren't quite as irresistible as yours."

Bomber laughed too and stepped closer, crowding into Devan's personal space, grabbing his arm. "If you say so, doc. The offer's open-ended, though, so come find me if you change your mind."

A lick of potent rage hit Devan. He blinked as his subconscious adjusted. *That wasn't me.* But with so many emotions roiling in the air, he couldn't pinpoint the source. As he glanced around, he extracted himself from Bomber's grip and gave him a gentle push back to the party, but no one was looking in their direction or giving any indication that they had ever been.

Unsettled, Devan continued his trek to the tent he was to call home for as long as this operation lasted. He fully expected to find it empty, but as he got closer, the tingling in his spine that had been present since he'd caught Zio's scent tripled in intensity.

Devan's heart thudded with every step, and he began to wonder if the anger simmering in his gut was his own after all. Part of him wanted to throw Zio down and kick some sense into him. The rest of him just wanted to throw him down.

Conflicted, Devan ducked into the tent. Zio was on the far side, sitting cross-legged on a spread-out sleeping bag, rubbing his temples. His discomfort broke through Devan's confusion. He stepped forward.

Zio growled. "Don't."

Fine by me.

It wasn't, but Devan didn't have the energy to force his powers on anyone, least of all someone who'd likely take his head off in return.

He retreated to the sleeping bag someone had kindly left on the other side of the tent. Head spinning with fatigue, he unrolled it and opened it out. The night air was cold, but the warmth of the fires, combined with the heat of dozens of oversexed wolves, was enough to keep it at bay.

Devan stretched out and closed his eyes. Sleep hovered at the edge of his brain, but Zio's pain and the weight of his fierce glare shone brighter. Sighing, he rolled over, turning his back on them both. After a moment, he sensed movement, and then a different heat as a body stretched out behind him.

Zio pressed his face between Devan's shoulder blades and threw his sleeping bag over both of them. He growled again. *"Don't."*

CHAPTER FIFTEEN

Zio woke at dawn. At some point in the night, Devan had rolled over, and Zio was now curled into his side, his head cradled on Devan's chest, his headache from the night before a dazed memory.

Great. Now he's healing me in his sleep. But Zio couldn't find it within himself to be resentful. He needed Devan like he needed air.

He just didn't know why.

And he couldn't deny that it felt good to be in Devan's arms. Safe. Right. If he could get back to sleep and rest a little while longer—

Michael stuck his head in the tent. "Drones have picked something up."

Zio blinked. "Okay. I'm coming."

Michael ducked out with no sign that he'd noticed Zio was wrapped around Devan.

But still. *Shit.* His unit up in his face about Devan was aggravation he didn't need. *At least we're not naked.*

Zio held the small comfort close until he spotted the wood he was sporting in his combat trousers—wood that was currently digging a hole in Devan's thigh. *Awesome.*

Somehow, Zio disentangled himself from the hot mess he'd

woken up in without waking Devan. His heart clenched. Loyalty and duty had roused his wolf, but leaving their cocoon of arms and legs felt like the end of the world and unsettled his wolf even more.

I don't want to go. But he had to.

Zio slipped out of the tent. Daylight hit him, along with a face full of rain, and he cringed. In wolf form, the weather didn't bother him. In human form? Yeah. It could suck a bag of southern wolf dicks.

Grumbling, he followed Michael's scent to the embankment where the drone pilots were embedded. Danielo was there too, viewing the captured footage on a laptop.

Zio peered over his shoulder, still half asleep. "You stink of sex."

"You stink of a Shadow Clan healer, brother. Care to explain?"

Zio had no verbal answer to that. He elbowed Danielo in the ribs and forced himself to focus on the grainy drone footage. "What have we got?"

"They're trying to flank us," Michael said. "See here? The unit coming our way split in two an hour ago, one vehicle headed east, one west."

"You sure those are the only vehicles?"

"No," a drone pilot spoke up. "But we are sure these two are gunning for us. We've got them loading up with weapons—bats and knives. Pretty sure we saw a silencer, though we didn't see any guns."

Zio felt sick. Varian had long feared that the southern packs would bring human weapons to a shifter fight, despite every law in the land forbidding them. Explosives could be explained away as accidents. But guns? The human authorities wouldn't stand for that.

"Maybe we should say fuck it and get guns," Danielo mused, voicing what was almost certainly on the collective pack mind.

Zio growled, lacing it with every ounce of beta authority he

103

possessed. "That's not who we are, what we've lost so many friends fighting for. No fucking guns, not now, not ever."

He got no argument, for that or the hastily formulated plan to intercept their would-be attackers.

Zio selected two teams. "I'll lead one, Bomber the other."

"He stinks too," Danielo offered as acquiesce.

"Shut the fuck up."

Danielo grinned before sobering and returning to the task at hand. "What about Devan? He can't be in two places at once."

"That's if he'll even come with us," Michael said, gaze on the laptop screen. "After yesterday."

Another growl built in Zio's chest. He swallowed it down. "Devan is under orders to be here as much as the rest of us. He'll go out with Bomber's team to the west. Go get your shit. We need to rock out in ten minutes."

The makeshift council adjourned. Zio exchanged a meaningful glance with Michael, grabbed the satellite phone, and dashed back to camp, unsure of what he wanted to find when he returned to the tent he was sharing with Devan. A grinding headache and a craving for peace, even if only for a few minutes, had driven him to invade Devan's bed the previous night— along with an irresistible desire to keep Devan warm—and he'd never intended to stay till morning, but he couldn't bring himself to regret it. *I don't regret anything about him.*

The realisation startled Zio. He'd spent so many long nights wishing he'd never gone to that fucking club, that he'd stayed home like a good beta—like Gale—and guided his unit through the grief they owned as much as Zio did. But it was true. Zio had little knowledge of the bonds and relationships shifters formed away from their units, sometimes even away from their packs, but what he shared with Devan was . . . something. It had to be, or he was losing his damn mind.

He slipped inside the tent. Devan was awake, sitting among the mess of sleeping bags they'd slept in, lacing his boots. "What are you fretting about?"

Zio crouched beside him. "I'm not fretting."

104

"Liar."

"Uh-huh. What are you going to do about it?"

Devan glanced up, his upturned face so close to Zio's that they could've kissed without moving a muscle.

Zio licked his lips, his wolf stirring and demanding something he didn't have time for.

Devan laughed softly. "This is getting complicated."

"I know."

"So what are *you* going to do about it?"

"I have no idea. I've never let wanting to fuck someone take over my life like this."

"That's what you think this is? A crush that's got out of hand?" Devan spoke carefully, like he always did among wolves, as though they were unexploded bombs that could go off at any moment.

Zio frowned. "I wouldn't call it a crush because I'm not twelve, but I guess so, yeah. The fuck would you call it?"

Devan blinked a few times, then shrugged. "Nothing. Whatever. Your words work."

He was the one lying now, Zio felt it in every fibre of his being, but he didn't have time for a deep and meaningful conversation. *Fuck it.* He gripped Devan's chin and kissed him, crushing their lips together hard enough to draw blood from both of them. Iron coated his tongue, and he slipped his tongue between Devan's lips, devouring him, dominating him until he abruptly found himself on his back, Devan pressing him into the nest of sleeping bags that smelt so deeply of both of them.

Devan kissed Zio hard, and then softer . . . sweeter, drawing a moan from Zio that sounded as though it had come from someone else. Soft hands combed through Zio's hair, fingertips stroked his cheekbone, and then . . .

It was over. Devan pulled away, shaking his head. "You really don't understand, do you?"

"Understand what?"

Devan let out a frustrated growl and gestured between them.

105

"What this is. Gods, didn't your parents, your alpha, teach you anything?"

Zio flinched. "I was raised by humans while my alpha fought a war that still isn't won. You think he had time to fucking school me? I'm lucky I can read."

"There's more to life than war, Zio."

"Clearly, but not right now. Fuck, I don't have time for this, and neither do you. We've got raiding parties to intercept."

"We?"

"Yeah. You're assigned to Bomber's team, if you agree."

Devan held Zio's gaze for a long moment, and then a tangible shift passed between them. The madness faded, and reality kicked back in. He rolled off Zio with a heavy sigh. "Of course I agree. Just because I fought you yesterday doesn't mean I don't understand how orders work. I'll go wherever you need me."

Mourning Devan's touch already, Zio sprang to his feet. "Good. Then head west with Bomber. I'm taking a team east. Hopefully we won't need you in two places at once."

He fled the tent without waiting for Devan's answer.

Devan trailed Bomber's team through the undergrowth, chasing down the southern force who were approaching the camp from the west. Dread filled his every step. Zio's plan to go around them and attack from behind was solid, but something in the air didn't feel right.

Hormones. He kissed you. And you kissed him back. Nothing was ever going to be normal after that.

Truth, but as ever, Devan was locked in a losing battle to put Zio out of his mind and focus on the task at hand. *How can he know so little about basic shifter biology?* The answer was simple: Zio and his closest friends were orphans and misfits who knew nothing but war. Mostly unmated, to them, attraction was a function that killed time and gave them respite from violence and pain. From grief and fear. Varian knew more, he had to, but

106

he was young too, by alpha standards at least, and no pack leader in the wolf world could've predicted the shitshow Devan and Zio were currently experiencing.

Your clan alphas didn't predict it either.

The taunt came from somewhere deep within Devan, from a place where common sense reigned, and he knew that even if Zio ever recognised what was happening between them, it could go absolutely nowhere. Hopelessness washed over him. He needed to speak with Varian, Dash too. Perhaps there was another healer who could take his place, and he could return to Bratislava. The current between him and Zio would fade in time, die out through forced neglect, and with Devan gone, Zio would be free—

An explosion rocked the earth, tearing up the ground in front of Devan. The wolf he'd been trailing disappeared in a gruesome cloud of shattered flesh and pulverised bone.

Devan sailed through the air and hit the ground with a dull thud, his ears ringing, both arms broken. *Damn fragile bones. Though stronger than the average human, they didn't hold a candle to his shifter form.* He bunched his stomach muscles and sat up, the fractures already healing, but that didn't stop the pain, some his, some that of his pack mates ahead.

A huge gash on Devan's leg seeped blood into the earth. With stiff, barely healed hands, he fixed it and crawled to the relative safety of a nearby ditch.

In the muddy puddle at the bottom, he found Danielo, hurt but conscious enough to flash a steely grin.

Devan healed him, and another brotherhood flared between him and the pack. "You've lost a lot of blood," he said. "You might be dizzy when you stand. Give it a moment."

"I don't think we have a moment," Danielo ground out. "And you're one to talk about losing blood. Doing okay, Devan?"

Devan glanced at his own healed wounds. His arms throbbed and would for a few days, but the rest of it barely scratched the surface. *My pack needs me.* "I'm fine. You ready?"

107

Danielo nodded. "Let's roll."

They scrambled out of the ditch. Wolf howls greeted them. Danielo grabbed Devan's arm. "I need to shift. Are you gonna be okay?"

"Of course. Go. I'll shift if I need to defend myself."

Danielo was gone before Devan had finished the sentence, bursting into his silver-grey wolf form and darting forwards, wobbly at first, but then straight as an arrow as he picked up speed.

Devan sprinted after him. Ahead, a fierce fight raged, punctuating the frosty air with battle cries and screams of pain. He was getting better at distinguishing between pack and enemy, his natural instinct to help everyone blunted by each new bond he forged with the northern wolves. In time, perhaps, he'd begrudge the fundamental change pack life had forced on him, but in the heat of the battle, protecting the pack was everything.

More explosions boomed. Trees splintered. There was no way the human authorities weren't going to respond. Devan pushed his human form to its limits, leaping into the trees and swinging through the branches to get a better view of what awaited him when he caught up to the wolves.

A scene of carnage greeted him, blood on the ground, bodies scattered. For the first time since he'd been reborn, Devan resented his enhanced ability to see in the dark. *So many dead.* From this distance, it was impossible to tell who had been lost, but his gut told him Bomber and Danielo were still alive.

Zio too. Devan had given up trying to quell their connection. Zio was angry and fighting, but for now, he was safe.

Devan sprang out of the trees and raced the last hundred metres. The beast within prowled and snarled, eager to end any creature who sought to harm his pack, but his instinct to heal won out. He didn't know the names of the northern wolves he passed his hands over, just that there were more of them than the southern wolves he ignored—for now. His connection with Bomber burnt bright. Devan found him at the foot of a tree, bloodied and broken in his human form.

Dread filled Devan as he crouched beside him. He healed the surface wounds he could see, but lifeblood poured from the gnarled stump that remained where Bomber's left leg had been.

"It's bad, isn't it?" Bomber gritted out.

"It's not good." Devan dug the berries he'd picked that morning out of the pouch slung over his back. He pressed them into Bomber's mouth. "Swallow. I'm going to drip sap onto the open wound, okay? It's going to hurt like the gods, but it'll buy me some time while I look for your leg."

Bomber laughed, flat and defeated. "There is no leg. It got blown to bits. Just leave me. Help the others."

Devan gripped his hands. "There must be something left of it. I can't make you whole again, but I can save you, if that's what you want?"

"Of course it's what he wants." Danielo dropped beside Devan. "Fix him."

Devan kept his gaze on Bomber. "It's up to you."

"You can't bring my leg back?"

"No. The damage is too great. If you survive, you'll be without it, both as a human and as a wolf."

Comprehension dawned in Danielo then. He sucked in a shaky breath, all the while glancing over his shoulder as the fighting continued. "Shit. I've got to shift, or it won't fucking matter." He turned back to Bomber and dragged a rough kiss over his split lips. "Do what you need to do. We'll be here, always."

He vanished. Devan didn't watch him go, his commitment to Bomber absolute. Battle sounds faded. He squeezed Bomber's hands tighter. *Whatever you need.*

Bomber swallowed thickly. "I'm no use to the pack if I can't run."

"That's not true. You have years of military experience. You can train, teach, assist Varian in command."

"But what if I can't shift?"

"That won't happen."

"How do you know?"

"Because I've seen it. Shifters can live happily without limbs just as humans can. And there's more to life, and to war, than being a soldier on the ground."

"You want to save me."

"Of course I do."

"Then why—" Bomber swallowed again. "Why did you give me the option?"

"Because you need to choose so you don't regret being alive later."

"That's some double bluff, doc."

Devan hummed and began the painstaking process of dripping sap onto Bomber's wounds. "It takes more than flesh to make us whole, so I guess we'll see, eh?"

Bomber didn't answer. Pain overwhelmed him, and he passed out. Devan was glad of it, though the concentration it was going to take to heal him was a huge risk. Without Bomber's eyes watching Devan's back, anyone could come up on them.

Focus. Devan sealed Bomber's wounds and searched the ground for any scraps of flesh and bone he could use to create a permanent fix. It was a gruesome task but necessary.

He gathered what he needed and returned to where Bomber was slumped, face grey, lips turning blue. *We're out of time.* Devan laid hands on the very worst injuries and closed his eyes. Magic filled his veins. Warmth spread through him, different to the heat he felt every moment Zio was near, but no less potent. No less the essence of his entire existence.

The world as he knew it faded. Devan couldn't say how long he would sit with Bomber like this. Time ceased to matter. Life, death . . . only Bomber's mattered. Energy flowed from his fingertips, magic warring with anatomy. The natural and the supernatural. Bomber's wolf accepted Devan's helping hand, but his human form rejected it over and over, until heartbeat by heartbeat, Devan won.

He opened his eyes. Though Bomber was still unconscious, colour had returned to his face and his leg. Though it would never be whole, it was healed, the stump smooth and marred only by scars that would fade with time. Devan slumped forwards, exhausted, but before he could give in to the fatigue washing over him, a panicked bark startled him back to life.

Devan spun around. Mere feet away, wolves fought for their lives in the dirt. Devan shielded Bomber with his body as the northern wolf closest to them held his ground. More wolves entered the sunken clearing created by the earlier explosion. The brindle male Devan knew to be Michael reached them. He sniffed Bomber and nudged Devan's shoulder, the message in his flinty gaze clear: *I've got him.*

The northern wolves in the clearing were winning. Devan locked gazes with Michael, and the wolf jerked his head east. An hour ago, Devan would've had to guess to interpret his meaning, but in that short space of time, their blossoming pack connection had forged a deeper bond with Devan's powers. Now he understood without question. *Go. Others need you.*

Devan shot back the way he'd come with Bomber's team, leaving a part of himself on the ground with the young wolf who would never be the same. But his grief and worry for the wolves behind him had nothing on the growing fear of what he'd find when he reached the end of the scent trail he'd picked up with no conscious thought. Zio's scent had consumed him for weeks, but with every step he took, a new desperation took hold within him.

He needs me. Even if Zio didn't know it yet—because, gods, Devan could sense his pugnacious temper a mile out from the furious fight he could hear in the distance.

The route Zio's team had taken was rockier than the path west and more exposed. With no trees to swing through, Devan leapt boulders and scaled chalky cliffs. As he got closer to the fighting, Zio's emotions changed. A rush of uncertainty and fear tainted his vengeful anger.

Devan scrambled up another cliff face. On the ground, dead wolves were everywhere, but he didn't stop to check who they were or who they belonged to, instinct driving him on through a small copse of trees and into a moonlit glade that might've been beautiful if not for the violence tearing it apart.

So much blood.

The scent of savagery had been Devan's constant companion for days. Nausea churned with exhaustion even supernatural strength couldn't mask. His legs wavered, and he started to fall, but before his knees touched the ground, a low whine broke through the fog, pushing him down. Devan rallied and staggered to his feet, hand flying to his chest as the ache there burnt his soul. *He's hurt.*

Heart in his mouth, Devan ran harder than he'd ever run before, feet barely touching the ground, but with every step came certainty that he wasn't going to get there in time. An overgrown path led to a stile, and then a long-abandoned sand processing plant. In the potholed yard, three wolves advanced on Zio. Outnumbered, Zio whined again, foreleg hanging limp and useless, blood dripping from his mouth.

More pain lanced Devan's chest. Zio was badly injured and too weak to move the earth beneath him. If the enemy wolves reached him before Devan, he wouldn't survive.

No. The vicious snarl in Devan's mind came from a part of him he didn't recognise. It rumbled through him, bringing with it bright light that blinded him to all else but getting to Zio. A chain reaction burst to life, instincts he'd fought for so long breaking free with a growl that echoed in the vast yard.

Devan hurdled a fallen tree and leapt into the fray, shifting with a singular thought in his mind. A vow. A declaration that he could never take back.

Mine.

CHAPTER SIXTEEN

Zio woke up backed against a wall, crumpled in his human form. He tasted blood on his tongue, but his shattered jaw was fixed. His ribs and legs too. He tried to sit up, but a paw large enough to span his chest pushed him down.

Breath caught in his throat. He looked up and met a bright blue gaze that was so familiar he wanted to cry, but at the same time, that of a stranger. *Devan.*

But was it? Zio had never seen his shifted form before, and the huge white tiger pinning him down was fucking terrifying.

Zio's hands reached out of their own accord to touch the big cat. Soft white fur awaited them, and beneath, corded muscles that made even Varian seem like a household pet.

The tiger growled. Zio snatched his hands back, but the beast wasn't looking at him, gaze trained instead over his shoulder.

Zio peered around him and gasped at the sight of a dozen bodies, all of them enemy wolves. He reached again for the tiger and buried his face in the fur that of course smelt of Devan. *He saved me.*

A violent shudder passed through Zio as he recalled his last moments of consciousness. How three wolves had become four, and then five . . . more. He'd pictured his own death. Resigned himself to it. Then something had changed. A burst of energy had rippled around the derelict yard, and the wolves were gone. He didn't remember the tiger, only the peace that had washed over him when its scent had reached him. Somehow, he'd felt . . . safe.

Zio sucked in greedy breaths of Devan's enhanced scent, gorging himself until he was drunk enough on it to think clearly. He looked around Devan again to see more wolves had joined them, a handful of soldiers, Danielo taking point.

He relaxed, but Devan was still growling, poised to attack. "Hey." Zio rubbed Devan's shoulder. "It's Danielo. You know him. He's pack."

Danielo crept closer. Devan snarled and sprang forward, sending wolves scattering like mice.

They backed off, leaving the yard altogether and gathering at the gate. The sour scent of fear reached Zio. *Fuck. They're scared of him.*

And he couldn't blame them. Dividing Zio from his pack, Devan paced, his rage so palpable that flames seemed to flare from his mouth with every warning growl. His message was clear: *stay away.*

Zio swallowed thickly, his mind a jumbled mess. His connection to Devan seemed stronger than ever—so solid he was almost sure he could see it shimmering in the dark—but he didn't know the shifter guarding him. Or how to reach him.

Healed leg throbbing, Zio stood and crept forward. His chest was so tight he could barely breathe. More than anything, he yearned to go to Devan, put his hands on him, and urge him to shift back to the form Zio recognised. Anything to help him make sense of the chaos he'd woken up to, but right now, it was about more than the two of them. It was about pack, and as long as Devan didn't recognise Danielo as a brother, he was a danger to everyone.

Zio moved level with Devan, arms outstretched. "Come here."

Devan stopped prowling and stared at him.

New energy flowed between them. Zio stepped closer and stretched up to stroke Devan's chest. "Stand down. It's over."

Devan didn't move, a simmering growl his only response.

Zio kept their gazes locked. "Danielo, shift back."

A low whine signalled Danielo's protest. Zio dug deep for the beta authority he rarely used with his closest brothers. "Now. He needs to see you're no threat."

A beat of silence. A shimmer in the air. Then Danielo, tired and bemused, was human. "A threat to who?"

"Anyone."

"Dude, I don't think he gives a fuck about the rest of the world right now."

"What?"

"How do *you* feel, Zio?"

Zio tore his attention from Devan and spared Danielo a glance. "The fuck are you talking about?"

Danielo raised his eyebrows. "I'm talking about the fact that a shifter with more control than all of us put together is about to burn the world down to protect you. Not anyone else, Zio. *You.* Don't tell me you can't feel it."

"Feel wha—" But the words died on Zio's lips before he could finish the sentence, eclipsed by the absolute certainty that whatever had happened tonight had changed him forever. "Fuck." His hand flew to his chest. "I do feel it. What is it? What's happening to me?"

"You've triggered a potential mating bond," Danielo said flatly. "With a Shadow Clan shifter who's ready to kill us all if we come any closer. Oh, and the humans are on their way, so you might want to think about fixing this shit so they don't shoot us where we stand."

Sarcasm was Danielo's baseline, but urgency laced his tone, and as if on cue, sirens sounded in the distance. It wouldn't be long before the helicopters went up—aircraft modified by the authorities with orders to shoot any shifters who could be considered a threat to the general population.

From a human perspective, a cluster of nervous wolves and a raging tiger would be a hard risk to ignore.

Brain spinning, Zio reached again for his beta authority, focussing it this time on Devan. "Stand down. No one is going to hurt me except the humans heading our way, and I need to get my pack to safety. If you can't shift back, you'll have to run until you're far enough away that they won't find you."

He gave Devan a gentle push.

Devan didn't move.

Zio tried again. "Please, Devan. For me, okay? If you stay and you're like this, the humans will shoot us all. I can't let that happen . . . to you or my pack. I need you to go."

For the longest moment, Zio feared Devan wouldn't budge, that he wouldn't do the only thing left to protect himself, Zio, and the pack that had brought them together, but as the approaching sirens grew louder, he finally seemed to hear them. He bent his neck and nudged Zio towards the rest of the pack. Then . . . he was gone, and the crushing pain of his departure drove Zio to his knees.

Zio sat on the cold ground by the fire no one had bothered to keep going. The humans had been and gone, unconvinced by Zio's explanation of a training exercise gone wrong but unable to prove otherwise. Danielo had taken a team back out to bury the dead, while Michael took care of Bomber.

Shannon had been the only one left to sit with Zio, and he did, shoulders touching, his presence a comfort, but nowhere near enough to soothe the pain ripping through Zio's soul.

"What if he doesn't come back?" The very thought brought fresh agony to Zio's heart. He rubbed his chest and repeated the question out loud with a scratchy whisper that hurt his ears.

Shannon wrapped an arm around him. "He'll come back— he's bound to the pack, and now he's bound to you too, even if you don't fulfil the bond."

"I don't know what any of that means."

"Neither do I, at least not when it comes to shifters from different clans. We have to wait for Varian; he'll know what to do."

Zio wasn't so sure. In all the years he'd served his alpha, Varian had rarely talked about bonds, even his own with Tomos, and Zio had never sought out friendships in the wider pack, preferring to stick close to his squad brothers and sisters. *It was never up to other people to tell you. Varian taught you many times that knowledge was the greatest power, but you never bothered to learn.*

It was true. The only thing Zio knew about mated pairs was that they never served in the same units, in his own pack and beyond. "I always thought if I triggered a bond, it would be with Emma, and that it would be easy. She'd leave the combat units, and she'd be safe."

"I thought you never slept with Emma."

"I didn't. But I was never sure that wouldn't change."

Shannon sighed. "Maybe it would be easier to bond with your best friend, but the supernatural world doesn't work like that. Bonds are . . . unique things. Magic. Unpredictable. You can't control them, no matter how bad you want to."

"Do you wish this had happened with you and your human friend?"

"No. I would never wish this life on someone I love."

Love. Zio craved to know more, but an approaching vehicle interrupted them. He scrambled to his feet. The guards had shouted no warning, so it had to be Varian.

Zio's stomach turned over, nervous for reasons he didn't understand.

Shannon nudged him. "Chill. It'll be fine. It's not like you've done anything wrong. You're as blindsided by this as the rest of us."

Zio shook his head. "I'm not. I should've known."

"How? It's not like you've been— Oh fuck, seriously?" Realisation dawned on Shannon's face, but there was no time to fend off his inevitable questions.

Varian had arrived.

Varian stood by the refreshed fire, flames dancing in his eyes. He'd listened to Zio's explanation from start to finish, sought out others to hear theirs, and checked on Bomber before he'd returned to Zio's side. "I knew there was . . . something," he said eventually. "I didn't believe you would keep something from me, more that you didn't know what you were hiding. Now it makes sense."

"I didn't know."

"You don't have to convince me, Zio. I believe Devan might've, though, or at least suspected such a thing was possible. He has seen far more of the world than you, and maybe more than I when it comes to such things."

"He never said."

"Perhaps he thought he could control it."

"Control it?"

Varian sighed. "Yes. It's a big ask, but Devan is an extraordinary shifter. Perhaps he believed such a thing was possible if the bond didn't trigger when you were intimate."

"I couldn't stop," Zio whispered. "Every time we were together, I knew it was wrong, but . . . I-I just couldn't stop."

"What made you think it was wrong? The unfamiliar doesn't have to be so forever."

Zio jerked his head up. "Of course it's wrong. He's not a wolf."

"So? Devan's own creator is bonded to a shifter from a vampire coven. Nothing in this extraordinary world of ours is wrong unless it is born of hate and greed."

"But—"

"No." Varian shook his head. "The potential bond between you and Devan is a dangerous thing, and there will be consequences if you choose to fulfil it, especially now he has been seen by the southern packs, fought for us, killed for us, but that doesn't make it wrong. Just . . . difficult."

Zio could hardly catch the words as Varian spoke them. So many things he'd never considered. Devan had killed every enemy wolf that had come within spitting distance of Zio, but their ambushing force had been vast. Many had escaped to run home with tall tales of a raging tiger that turned out to be true. "What do we do now?"

Varian laid a warm hand on Zio's shoulder. "To be honest, I don't know. I've asked to speak with Dash. Perhaps he will know more than I do about such things, but the fact remains that the southern packs will likely see Devan's intervention tonight as a sign Shadow Clan has joined our war. For now, that must be our greatest concern."

"What about Devan? Will he be punished?"

"For what? This wasn't a circumstance he chose. There is a chance, maybe, that Dash will feel that Devan should've been wiser or perhaps informed him that he'd nurtured a . . . relationship with you, but Dash knows better than most of us that these things can't be predicted. I'd imagine his priority will be staying out of this war."

Zio rubbed his temples. "Do you think Devan will come back?"

"I have every faith that he will find it impossible not to, but you have to accept that Dash may not let him stay if it puts his own people at risk."

"What will happen if he leaves?"

"To your bond?"

Zio nodded, tongue stuck to the roof of his mouth.

"It will fade, with time," Varian said. "But it will be tough for both of you. Painful until the yearning to be together is gone. And then you will grieve, because you'll know what you've lost. It will be hard to be with another."

"I—"

Varian silenced Zio with a shake of his head. "Don't even contemplate it right now. There is much to discuss with many people before any decisions need to be made, but know this, Zio. In a time of peace, such decisions would be yours alone, and I will do everything in my power to be sure you retain that right."

Zio believed him. Varian's humility was legendary. Their enemies believed it made him weak, but Zio knew it was his greatest strength. "I miss him."

"I know. And you will every moment it takes to unravel this mess. Which is why I must go. Bomber is in need of some loving care from Tomos, and there are many conversations I must have before this night ends."

"I'm so sorry."

"For what? I will not repeat myself, Zio. There is no time. Your orders are to hold this camp with as little bloodshed as you can until you hear otherwise. If Devan returns to you, make contact with me when you can, but do not risk the safety of your pack. Is that clear?"

Varian's alpha timbre vibrated deep within Zio, reaching parts of him even Devan couldn't. He nodded and accepted his alpha's scent mark. "I understand."

CHAPTER SEVENTEEN

Devan had been running for days and days. Weeks, maybe. Time had ceased to matter. White noise filled his head, the sounds of the never-ending forest drowned out by the screaming pain in his chest, agony that intensified with every mile he ran from his pack. From his newfound extended family. From Zio. But as much as it hurt, he couldn't stop. Frenetic energy filled his veins and had become the only thing standing between him and the primal call to claim his mate.

He's not your mate, though, is he? He's the commander of the wolf pack unit you've been loaned to, and the last thing on earth his pack or the clan needs is the complication of a cross-species bond.

The fact that Devan had long ago ceased to think of the northern wolves as anyone's pack save his own seemed a distant point.

I want him.

I need him.

I can't have him.

Thirst drove Devan to a spring. He had no clue where he was —just that he was far enough from Zio that the compulsion to kill for him had faded, but the desire to be with him in any capacity burnt as strong as ever.

Devan's paws itched. *I have to keep moving.*

Thirst quenched, he leapt the spring and ran on, not stopping even when the forest petered out. He darted across farmland and holiday parks, thankfully deserted for the winter. Across open fields in broad daylight.

At dusk, he came to the outskirts of a town large enough to house an armed police unit. *I could run through the church square. Scare enough people that—*

"Don't even think about it."

Devan froze, every fibre of him held in place by the unmistakable alpha timbre vibrating through his bones. *Luca.* He shouldn't have been surprised, but somehow in his distant, rational mind, perhaps he'd expected Dash.

"Shift, Devan. Now."

Devan was in his human form before his brain computed the order. After untold time running wild, it took him a moment to adjust.

Luca gave him that moment, eyeing him from a few feet away, arms folded across his chest, gaze stern. When he was apparently sure Devan was cognisant, he stepped forward. "We need to talk."

"About Zio?"

It hurt to even say his name.

Luca nodded. "Among other things. Have you eaten? I have food with me."

"I'm fine."

"Of course you are. But I'm not Dash. I will not force self-care on you."

"You're not a healer," Devan muttered absently.

"No, Devan. I'm not. I'm a soldier, which is why I'm here."

"You know, don't you?"

"If you're referring to your triggered bond with the wolf, then yes. But that's not my first concern."

"Then what is?"

Luca raised an eyebrow. "Everything else. Dash was called to a meeting in Berlin. Representatives from the southern wolf packs were present, and they were angry that a Shadow Clan shifter had joined forces with the northern packs and fought against them."

"Do they know it was me?"

"You weren't mentioned by name, but it is widely known that there is only one clan shifter on British soil right now. Dash couldn't deny it."

Devan winced. Luca's presence had gifted him the clarity of thought he'd been lacking ever since he'd caught Zio's scent in that damn club, but he couldn't decide if it was a good thing. Knowing he'd put his entire clan at risk made him feel sick. "I'm sorry."

Luca snorted. "We tasked you with joining a pack, to move among them as a brother. A potential bond was always possible, and it's unfeasible that you wouldn't act to defend it."

"That's what we're going with?"

"For now."

It was on the tip of Devan's tongue to apologise again, but a glance at Luca's stern face stopped him. "I didn't mean to shift. Varian specifically asked me not to."

"With good reason," Luca said. "He couldn't have predicted this outcome, but he was right to be afraid. I do not believe any shifter but Dash could've prevented the certain war we faced a few days ago."

A few days? Now the world had stilled, Devan found the fact that he didn't know how much time he'd lost to his countryside rampage more disturbing than his human form could cope with. His skin itched, and his heart pounded. Only Luca's imposing presence kept him present. "But he did prevent it? Dash, I mean?"

Luca nodded. "Dash has negotiated an agreement that you can continue your work with the northern pack on the condition that, barring self-defence, you do not fight again, nor do you complete your bond with their soldier."

"What?"

"You do not complete the bond, Devan." Luca spread his hands. "It's far from ideal, but the only other option is to withdraw you completely, which would leave Varian at war without—"

"I'm not leaving. I can't."

"I thought you might say that." Luca showed no flicker of annoyance at being interrupted. "And I won't press you to examine why, because it's just as well, but know this: Varian's enemies will not hesitate to escalate this war if they believe the clan has picked a side. If you act outside of self-defence again, no one, not even Dash, will be able to halt the consequences."

Devan dropped to the ground, head in his hands. Running free, it had been easy to narrow the impact of the situation to himself and Zio. Now, as reality set in, the gravity that came with it was terrifying. An all-out war would destroy the super-natural world, leaving human survival to the mercy of which-ever side prevailed. And there were no guarantees which side that would be. "Maybe I should extract and come home. Send someone else in my place."

Luca growled his disagreement. "It's not possible. We cannot separate you from the wolf while the bond remains unfulfilled. The risk to him is too great."

Devan jerked his head up. "What do you mean?"

"It's not important right now." Luca crouched and gripped Devan's chin, forcing him to look at him as he laced his next words with alpha power far greater than Varian's. "What is vital is that the northern pack holds the border and that they appear to do it on their own without outside help. Do you think your wolf can do that?"

"No one can run the border operation better than Zio."

"Then you have two tasks," Luca said. "Keep him where he needs to be, and keep him alive."

Zio couldn't remember a time when his lips didn't buzz with the energy of a kiss that seemed to have happened to someone else. It felt like a century had passed since that stolen moment, hidden away from the world in a tent that was still heavy with fragrant arousal and . . . something else. Something beyond Devan's unique scent.

It's the bond.

Zio screwed his eyes shut, willing the errant thought away. But it went nowhere, and neither did he, apparently rooted to his spot on the ground, waiting for something that would never come.

He's not coming back. After five long days, Zio didn't know much, but of that he was certain.

Danielo slipped into the tent. "There you are. Varian called the satellite phone looking for you, but no one could track you down."

"Didn't try very hard then. I'm hardly hidden in plain sight."

"All right, all right. Don't get shitty with me."

Zio spared Danielo a sour look, but it was fleeting. He didn't have the energy to be a dick to one of his closest brothers. "Did he say anything about Bomber?"

"Just that he's doing as well as can be expected. Tomos is taking care of him."

"He should've died."

"Uh-huh. But he didn't." *Because of Devan.*

The unspoken words hung between them like a cloud of poison gas. Danielo backed off and disappeared before either of them could say anymore.

Zio flopped onto his back, a low growl escaping him. He'd come to the tent convinced he'd be able to gather anything and everything Devan had touched and burn it on the nearest fire, but it hadn't happened. Instead he'd found himself overcome by longing, and sulking it out had seemed his only option.

He closed his eyes. *Five fucking days. Where is he?* No one knew, or if they did, they weren't telling Zio.

And by *they*, Zio meant Varian. Not that Zio had even asked. Pathetically, he'd been kind of hoping Varian would do his Jedi mind trick and throw Zio a bone.

You're not that lucky. Or maybe he was. Maybe not knowing

Devan's whereabouts was a gift, because without it, there was no doubt in Zio's mind that his wolf would want to follow.

On cue, his wolf stirred, urging Zio to shift and find his mate. To claim him and heal the gaping wound in his soul, but he fought it, clenching his fists until it subsided, the sharp ache fading to a dull roar. *I need to sleep.*

And after so many days without rest, resisting was a battle he lost.

It was early, barely dawn. Devan drifted through the camp, tracking Zio's scent, all the while telling himself to go straight to the military hub and announce his return. Though the camp appeared to be asleep, somehow he knew Zio would be up.

Zio's scent was freshest on the path that led to the tent Devan had once shared with him. Devan took a step closer, but a warm hand closed around his arm before he could take another.

"You're back."

Devan turned to face Danielo. "I am, and I have orders to stay."

"For good?"

"For as long as I'm needed."

The brief light in Danielo's eyes faded. "You're not going to complete the bond?"

"I can't." He spoke like a robot, rehearsing the speech he'd meant for Zio if Zio asked him such questions. "It would bring my entire clan into the war, which in turn would set every wolf pack in the world against you."

"So? If they want to fight us that bad, they'll find a way. Why not let it be this?"

"It's not just about wolves. The world is bigger than you."

"Your clan won't fight?"

"Why should they? Why would they risk everything because of a potential bond nobody wants?"

Danielo tilted his head sideways. "You're different."

"Am I?"

"Yeah. For real. The Devan who saved us from annihilation never looked at me like you are now."

"And how's that?"

"Like you already died."

Danielo let his hand slip from Devan's arm and walked away, his disappointment in Devan, for whatever reason, seeping from him in waves that only added to the despair lacing Devan's every breath. Didn't he understand? Devan had no idea if he truly wanted to bond with Zio, and he never would. It wasn't his choice. He had orders, and right now, in a war that wasn't his, nothing else mattered.

Rubbing his chest, Devan gave in to the instinct pulling him towards Zio. They'd have to face each other eventually, and while Luca's alpha command echoed in Devan's mind, fresh and uncompromising, stronger than any bond, now seemed as good a time as any.

As Devan drew closer to the tent where he sensed Zio sleeping, he was almost convinced. Then he ducked under the tarpaulin, and yearning hit him like a runaway train.

He fell to his knees, breath stolen, as Zio slept on, sprawled out on the crumpled sleeping bags, innocent, beautiful, and so peaceful Devan could've wept. He'd always longed to see Zio like this, face untouched by grief and pain, smoothed of war-weary fatigue.

Zio. Devan reached out with shaking hands, caught himself, and pulled them back. *Don't wake him.*

But it was too late. What little noise he'd made reached Zio, and the young wolf stirred. His eyes fluttered open; his senses came to life. He bolted upright, gaze fixed on Devan before the confusion of sleep had cleared, and when he spoke, it was a whisper.

"You came back."

CHAPTER EIGHTEEN

Devan sat by the tent entrance, muscles coiled and tight, as though Zio could blink and he'd be gone, leaving a void behind that no other could ever fill. Only his gaze was in motion, scanning Zio's body, clearly checking him for injuries.

I'm fine, Devan. You healed me before I woke up at that damn-fucking sand plant.

Zio moved slowly, untangling himself from the cosy pit he'd knocked out in. Every part of him was screaming to touch Devan, but deep-rooted instincts warned him off. *Don't scare him.*

It was hard to imagine that the last time they'd been alone like this, they'd been rolling on the ground, kissing, grinding . . . all the things they'd never do again if the set of Devan's jaw was anything to go by.

Zio's heart filled with dread.

He pushed it aside.

*This isn't just about that. And what do you **want** from him? To bond? To fuck? To fight?*

Arguments for all three battled in Zio's soul. He licked his lips. "Danielo told me what you did for Bomber. He thinks none of this would've happened if you hadn't put yourself at risk to save him when you were already hurt yourself . . . that you were too exhausted to resist your instincts."

Devan's gaze flickered. "I wasn't hurt when I healed Bomber."

"You had been, though. I can still smell your blood."

"Don't."

"Don't what? Smell? Hate to break it to you, but I have even less control over that than I do anything else."

A faint grin lit Devan's features before he seemed to catch himself. "From here on out, it doesn't matter what you can smell, you have to ignore it."

"What?"

"I have orders, Zio."

"From who?"

"My alpha, one of them at least. I've got three, remember?"

"Varian?"

"No. Luca."

Zio swallowed the lump in his throat. "What were the orders?"

"The same as before . . . to act as pack healer whenever I'm needed, but this time, with an add on not to fulfil any potential bonds."

"Your alpha has *ordered* you to ignore a potential bond?"

"He's ordered me to act in the best interests of everyone affected by it. Don't you understand?"

"You keep asking me that shit, and you know I don't," Zio snapped. "Explain it to me."

Devan sighed, and for a moment he was the same Devan that Zio had spent the last few weeks growing to consider a brother, a friend . . . and a lover.

Then his open expression shuttered. Jaw reset. "If we bond, your enemies will consider it confirmation that my clan has joined the war against them. If I leave, there's a possibility you will become so affected by the loss of the bond that you won't be able to hold this border and all kinds of other horrible shit Luca wouldn't even tell me."

"Loss of the bond—"

"Yes, Zio. The *bond*. Don't make the mistake of thinking this

129

is personal, because it's not. It's ancient biology that sometimes gets things wrong."

"So, we have to . . . what? Incubate this bullshit until the war is over and we can go our separate ways without causing a shifter apocalypse?"

"Pretty much."

"And it's not personal . . . it's biology?"

"Yes."

Zio growled. "I don't believe you."

"So?"

"So fuck you." Zio scrambled to his feet, skin already burning with the desire to shift. "You don't get to come back here and tell me to suck it up and get on with it. If it's *biology*, take it with you and fuck off."

He started for the tent entrance.

Devan caught his arm. "I already told you I can't do that. Besides, your pack needs both of us to win this war."

"It's your pack too."

"It won't be forever."

Zio had never felt pain like this. To lose Devan as a potential mate was one thing. To lose him as a brother too? Fuck. It would destroy him. "So what do we do?"

"Nothing, Zio. Absolutely nothing."

Zio understood the loaded meaning. He wrenched himself free of Devan's grasp. "Fine. Whatever. I don't give a shit."

Zio was good at walking away from Devan. He was, apparently, becoming less proficient at staying away. Devan sensed his return less than an hour after he'd stormed out of the tent and braced himself for another fight.

But as Zio approached, his emotions lacked the rage and aggression he'd left with. Devan tasted defeat and sadness that mingled with his own despair, and he closed his eyes. *Gods, Zio, I wish things were different.*

Different how, he had yet to reconcile, but not this. *Never* this.

Zio ghosted into the tent, his face the blank mask Devan was fighting so hard to maintain for himself. His hair was wet too and smelt of the river three miles away.

"Did you go for a swim?"

"Not on purpose."

Devan pursed his lips.

Zio scowled. "Piss off. What do you care?"

"As pack healer, if you can't control yourself enough to keep from falling in the river, I care a lot."

"But not enough to—" Zio clamped his mouth shut and snatched a breath. "Sorry. I didn't come back to have that fight again."

"I know."

"Of course you do."

"I don't know everything you feel, though. Especially not about . . . this."

"Good, cos that would really piss me off considering I have zero clue how I feel about anything right now."

Zio had war-weary eyes, but in that moment he looked so young and confused that Devan's resolve to never touch him again melted away. He rose up on his knees and held out his hands. "Come here."

"No."

"Come *here*."

Devan grabbed Zio's hands and tugged him further into the tent, and then down to his level.

Zio could've resisted. But he didn't. He allowed Devan to manhandle him until they were sitting side by side on the mess of the bed they'd only shared once.

Devan squeezed his hands. "I'm so sorry this has happened to you. I need you to know that I could've prevented this."

"Prevented it? How?"

"That night, in the club. I knew what happened to us there wasn't normal, but I convinced myself I'd never see you again, and then when I did . . . I don't know. Maybe I was caught up in

131

the bond before I realised it, or maybe I was just too arrogant to believe I couldn't control it."

"You knew." Zio spoke slowly, his words carrying no weight of accusation, but Devan shook his head.

"I didn't know anything for sure, and things kept changing . . . evolving. Sometimes I thought for real I'd have to do something to stop it; others I thought I was a fucking lunatic."

"I like it when you curse."

"What?"

"When you swear. It makes me laugh."

"Yeah, well. I like it when you laugh, so call it even?"

"I don't think anyone's winning here."

Devan's arm slipped, unbidden, around Zio's shoulders. "I was lying earlier when I said everything between us was biology. It's not. I like you, and I wish we'd had the chance to enjoy each other without this complication."

Zio hummed, leaning into Devan's embrace whether he knew it or not. "I wish you hadn't come back. Shit, I wish I'd never met you, but I'm glad you're staying. Thinking I'd never see you again was fucking me up."

"It's going to be really hard. We can't fool around anymore. The risk of losing control and biting each other is too great."

"Biting completes the bond, right? I mean, I know it does for wolves, but I wasn't sure if it was the same for you."

"We don't have to bite for a bond to solidify, sometimes the mating process is enough, but the strongest bonds are formed around both. I'd imagine your desire to bite me will be the same as if I were a wolf."

Arousal scented the air, instant, consuming, demanding.

Zio shuddered. "I never knew I wanted to bite you until you left. Then it was all I could think about. Mostly. I thought about other stuff too."

"Like what?"

"Like if you were thinking about biting me, or mating. What I'd say if you came back and told me you wanted to."

Don't ask him, don't ask him, don't ask him. "Did you ever figure it out?"

"No. I mean, I know I want all those things on a physical level, that the bond is making me want those things more than anything else, but I don't know how I feel about the rest of it. My head . . . it's never an easy place to be at the best of times. Right now, I feel like I'm underwater."

It was probably the most Zio had ever spoken to Devan at any one time, and every word made a sickening sense. In another world, another life, if they'd been born into different bodies, perhaps the decision to be together would've been easy. They'd have known each other well enough to love one another. To lie down on the forest floor and let instinct own them. But they couldn't do that, not now, and maybe not ever.

Zio broke the silence with a heavy sigh. "I've got to lead patrol tonight. I don't think you should come."

"What if you need me?"

"We have radio comms."

"That won't work in wolf form."

"I know, but it's all I have right now. I can't handle the idea of you being in danger, and if the last time we saw each other is anything to go by, it's as bad in reverse."

Devan couldn't deny it. "I'll take a radio and keep my distance, but I can't promise I won't kill anyone who tries to hurt you."

Zio sniggered. "There was me thinking it was a one-time thing."

"Zio?"

"Yeah?"

"Shut up."

CHAPTER NINETEEN

Devan squeezed his phone so hard the metal case bowed. "Do you think I'd be safe from it if I sat underwater?"

Dash's gentle chuckle was marred by the crackly connection. "Maybe. But you'd have to come up for air eventually, and then what?"

I'd go back down and stay there forever. Who needs air anyway?

Dash laughed again—he didn't need a physical connection to know what Devan was thinking. Then he sighed, humour gone as if it had never been there at all. "To be honest, I have no idea what would make this easier for you. My own bond was fulfilled before I truly knew what it was. I've never longed for Luca the way you will for the wolf because he has always been with me."

"Can you imagine how it would feel if he wasn't? Or if he was, but you couldn't be, like, actually with him?"

"No, Devan. Such a thing . . . I couldn't contemplate it. It's unfathomable to me."

"You're not really helping," Devan grumbled before he remembered he was talking to his most respected alpha, but Dash was like that, so . . . *normal* it was easy to forget he was among the most powerful shifters the world had ever seen. *He's so human.* A quality Devan had often admired, but today he resented it. *I need guidance, not friendship.* And the sense that

Dash wasn't telling him everything made him want to scream. "I don't know how long I can do this for. When he's close, I want him so much I don't care about anything else, and when he's gone, I can't rest until he comes back."

"That'll get easier."

"When?"

"I don't know."

"Why don't you know? You're hundreds of years old. You must've seen this before."

"It's true, I've seen bonds, Devan. And I can share with you, second hand, of course, the experiences of many others who've lived through this process, but they won't be yours, because we are all different."

"So you've never ordered anyone else to live in the pocket of someone they're forbidden to bond with?"

"No, and I'll regret to my last days that we've asked this of you. Devan, if you know nothing else, please believe that I'm doing all I can to end this before your bond with the wolf fades."

"And then what?"

"And then you will be free, both of you, to choose your path."

"This war has lasted decades. What makes you think you can end it before this bond fades?"

Dash sighed. "There are many things I can't tell you."

Devan closed his eyes, hopelessness washing over him. He'd called Dash for reassurance, for the soothing tone of his alpha's voice, the comfort that was lacking in his fledgling relationship with Varian, and that had never existed between him and Luca. Dash was his sire. His father, of sorts. And until this moment, his best friend.

But Dash's world was far greater than Devan; his responsibilities stretched wider than Devan could ever contemplate. *He can't help me.* And as he bid Dash goodbye, he realised no one could. The pain in his chest was permanent, until it wasn't, and when it had passed, Devan would mourn its loss for the rest of his existence.

He ended the call and resumed his stare-off with the river. The moonlight danced on the fast-flowing water, shimmering, and frost crunched on the ground. If not for the oppressive clutch of war in the air, the night might've been beautiful. But the unrelenting flow of the river matched the edginess grating him and didn't occupy him for long. Restless, he sprang to his feet and scaled a nearby tree. His night vision was stronger than that of the wolves, but as he scanned the horizon, he saw nothing of the small patrol group Zio had taken out a few hours earlier. He scented the air, testing for blood. Reached out for his connections with the wolves on the ground, but nothing came back. Wherever they were, it would take Devan too long to find them if anything went wrong.

Growling, he dropped to the ground. The radio Michael had presented him with the morning after his return fell from his back pocket. In four days, it had yet to make a sound. The temptation to kick it into the water was strong, but fear that he might miss something won out, and so he stayed by the water, straining every sense, every nerve. *Zio, where are you?*

A wolf approached from behind. Devan reached out but found nothing but the shifter's identity. Devan had healed most wolves in the border force by now in one way or another, but not the quietest of Zio's closest companions. Not Michael. "Everything okay?"

Michael sat on a rock a few feet from where Devan paced. "I think so. They'll be back soon, I think."

"How can you tell?"

Michael glanced at the sky. "It's nearly dawn. If there's been no fighting, Danielo will want his breakfast."

Devan snorted. "That's your barometer for the safety of your pack mates?"

"If I'm wrong, I'll give you the extra bacon he sneaks on my plate."

"That's cute."

"I try."

The conversation lapsed, but Devan was used to that with

Michael. Despite the close-knit pack, Michael was somewhat of a lone wolf. He didn't say much or ask for much in return.

"Are you going to complete your bond?"

Devan sighed. Scratch that. Maybe Michael was as annoying as everyone else seemed to be right now. "Why are you asking me that?"

"Because Zio's my brother."

"So ask him."

"He's never here."

"And there's your answer."

Michael ticked an eyebrow up. "Where? Come on, man. Zio doesn't tell us shit. I know it's your business, but we can't watch him get hurt. It's not fair."

Devan sucked in a shaky breath. "Believe me, hurting him is the last thing on my mind."

"So why not complete the bond and get it over with? I know it's weird that you're from different packs . . . clans, whatever you call it where you're from, but it doesn't really matter, does it?"

"Not to me, and maybe not to Zio, I have no idea where he is on that, but it's bigger than the two of us. I was loaned to you as a healer, not a fighter. Peace between my clan and the southern wolf packs depends on that."

"So don't fight."

"Impossible if I thought someone was threatening my mate— you know what happened when the bond triggered. And regardless, it's about perception. I'm Shadow Clan, Michael. If I pick a side, it would start a war far bigger than this."

"I thought Danielo was being dramatic when he said that."

"Danielo? Dramatic? No."

Michael huffed out a grunt. "So you really do have to wait it out and hope it fades without killing you?"

"Now *you're* being dramatic."

"Not really. Unrequited bonds can kill a wolf."

"What?"

"It's rare," Michael said. "And more common in hereditary

shifters than those changed by the bite, but it happens. It killed my father's cousin. When I was a kid, my mum used to say he'd died of a broken heart."

Devan absorbed Michael's words and matched them with Luca's. *"We cannot separate you from the wolf while the bond remains unfulfilled. The risk to him is too great."*

No.

That can't be true.

But one look at Michael's earnest face told Devan that it was. Fulfilling the bond risked the lives of every soul Zio cared about, but ignoring it could cost him his own life. "Does he know?"

"Zio?"

"Yes. Does he know he's at risk?"

Michael slowly shook his head. "I don't think so. He's never been interested in pack history, he doesn't pay attention to conversations that don't directly affect him, *and* I don't think Varian wants him to know."

Comprehension dawned in Devan's bond-clouded brain. "That's why you came to find me, isn't it? Because Varian ordered you not to tell him?"

Michael locked his gaze with Devan's. "Yes. And I get why Zio worrying he's going to drop dead at any moment isn't going to do him any favours, but *you* need to know how dangerous this is for him. Fuck the rest of the world, Devan. Don't let politics kill my brother."

Zio knew something had changed the moment he got back. After a long—and boring—night on patrol, he'd braced himself to face Devan's inevitable absence. The trail of his scent as he'd left the camp in response to Zio's return. The empty tent. And the gnawing hunger in his gut he could never sate.

But as he led his team out of the woods, a fire burnt bright in the centre of the camp, tended to by Michael, while Devan cooked sizzling bacon and stirred a vat of scrambled eggs.

"The fuck is going on here?" he murmured. "Michael's never lit a fire in his life."

Danielo bounded past him. "Who cares? I'm starving."

"Of course you are." Zio rolled his eyes, but that didn't stop the guilt he felt for keeping his team out long after sunrise. Patrol had been uneventful, like it had been ever since Devan had shifted and apparently scared every enemy unit away, but unsatisfied by the quiet, Zio had circled back again and again, checking and rechecking until the collective rumble of the wolves behind him had convinced him to come home.

Diligent or avoiding Devan? It was hard to tell once the pull between them reignited, Devan's close proximity, though he'd yet to glance Zio's way, bringing Zio to life.

Zio took an unconscious step forward. Stopped. Stepped back. Michael noticed his struggle and nudged Devan. Blue eyes found Zio's. Devan set his spatula down and shouldered through hungry wolves to get to Zio.

He stopped a foot away, hands twitching at his sides. "Morning."

"Morning." Zio kicked at a stone. "What's all this?"

"Thought you might be hungry."

"Why?"

"Because you've been out all night. Come. Eat."

"Thanks, but I'm going to crash."

"Uh-huh. After breakfast. *Come.*"

Devan's tone shot heat straight to Zio's groin. Warmth pooled in his belly, and his treacherous feet reclaimed the step he'd retreated. "I need to sleep."

But his protest was weak, rooted in nothing. Devan took his hand and tugged him to the fire, and Zio was powerless to resist.

He sat beside Danielo as Michael and Devan served breakfast to the returning patrol and then handed out leftovers to the rest of the camp. They'd cooked enough for an army far bigger than Zio had, and even when he was full, the food kept coming.

Danielo was like a pig in shit, but Zio's appetite—though he was hungrier than he cared to admit—was far smaller. At

Devan's third attempt to refill his plate, he pushed him away. "Stop. You're going to kill me."

Devan flinched.

Zio's overfull stomach turned over. "I didn't mean it literally. I've just had enough, okay?"

Devan shook himself. "Of course. Sorry. You want to go to bed?"

"Please—" *Gods, stop talking.* Zio cringed and tried again. "Yeah. I'm knackered."

He stood and backed up, expecting Devan to stay put. But Devan ditched the plate he'd been brandishing and darted to his side. "Come on then."

"You're coming with me?"

"Yup. Unless you'd rather I slept with Danielo and—"

"What? Fuck no."

Devan stopped walking. "I can, you know. I mean, not sleep with Danielo, but swap tents or try and not be around when you need to sleep. I can't go far . . . I can't be away from you like that, but if it's easier for you if I'm not here, I can make that happen."

"Don't."

"Don't what?"

"Go anywhere." Zio gave in to the urge to grab Devan's hands. "I know it'll probably make things worse, but I'm so fucking tired, I can't deal with you not being close. It hurts that we can't . . . *be* what we want, but I just need . . . fuck, I don't know what I need."

Devan's gaze pierced Zio's soul as he read Zio, tasted his every emotion, and for once Zio didn't mind that his heart was no longer private. That it had belonged to Devan long before either of them had known it. If their connection saved him having to explain the riot currently occupying his entire being, he could dig it.

He closed his eyes. *Please.*

Devan cupped Zio's face with a warm, grounding palm. "Of course. Let's go."

Hand in hand they drifted to their tent. Far from the chaos

Zio had left it in the previous evening, Devan had apparently been busy. Michael too, if the scent lingering in the air was anything to go by.

"He had a couple of pillows," Devan replied to Zio's obvious curiosity. "And he pinched some blankets from somewhere."

"What for?"

"To keep you warm. You're the only idiot who didn't bring a camp bed. No one else is sleeping on the ground."

"You are."

"Got a pillow now, though, haven't I?"

So many emotions tumbled through Zio, too confused to make sense of. He hadn't brought a bed because the only one left had smelt too much of Emma, and being cold as he slept was cathartic. At least, it had been until Devan had come along. "I don't understand."

Devan left his boots by the tent entrance and stepped into Zio's personal space. "You don't have to. Just let me take care of you a little, okay? It's all I can do right now."

Zio was struggling to remember a time when Devan's soft voice hadn't completely owned him. When he hadn't obeyed his gentle requests without question. "Whatever you want."

"No, Zio. Whatever *you* need."

Zio knocked his head against Devan's shoulder, trusting Devan to already know that what he needed was a few hours of solid sleep. A break from angsting over the mess lingering between them and fretting over the safety of his pack. His family.

Devan wrapped his arms around Zio, his embrace loose enough to be platonic if it wasn't for the supernatural chemistry swirling around them, trapping them in a vortex of instinct and desire. Zio greedily breathed in Devan's scent, saturating himself in it as a deep-rooted fear that he might not get the chance again drove him to cling to Devan, claws sliding out to hook into Devan's clothes.

"Easy," Devan murmured. "I'm not going anywhere."

"But what if you do?"

141

"I won't. Everyone making the decisions has ordered me to stay put. We can't bond or do anything that might cause us to lose control, but we can be together, Zio. Like this. Like *pack*."

Pack. The one thing, until Devan had come along, that Zio had believed he truly understood. "I can't handle you touching me, but I can't cope if you stop."

"I'll only stop if you ask me to."

"I won't. I can't."

"Then let it go." Devan pulled back. "I've tried to fight it, to stay away, and it only hurts more."

Zio couldn't imagine anything hurting him more than Devan's absence and the loss of his touch and his scent. He let Devan lead him to the bed-shaped nest he'd made of sleeping bags and pillows. "You're going to stay, aren't you? You won't leave while I'm asleep?"

Devan gestured for Zio to undress. "I'll only leave if someone gets hurt and they need me, but with the reinforcements Varian is sending today and no active patrols, that shouldn't happen."

"Famous last words."

"I know, but it's all I've got."

Zio stripped his clothes. Devan did the same, and they crawled into bed. Zio closed the scant distance between them the moment Devan's back hit the ground, twining their legs and laying his head on Devan's chest.

Devan's heart beat like a metronome, slow and steady, while Zio's pulse ticked like a broken clock. *How is he so fucking calm all the time?* Then he remembered the crazed beast who'd saved him from certain death, the shifter who'd been so out of control he'd have killed his own pack brothers if Zio hadn't stopped him. *He's as dangerous as I am. More.*

It should've scared him, but it didn't.

CHAPTER TWENTY

Zio talked in his sleep. Devan couldn't say how he'd never noticed before, but as the day passed to Zio's fidgeting and muttering, everything seemed brand new. Devan tracked the shadows across the tent as he lay on his back with Zio in his arms, fingers tangled in his silky hair. Zio's scent intoxicated him, and his bared neck called to Devan like a siren, but as the brief winter sun came and went, he resisted. *Pack.*

Withstanding the urge to investigate the hot length pressed against his thigh was harder. Human Devan knew that fooling around was among the most dangerous things they could do when it came to controlling their instincts to bond, but natural arousal, combined with the heady madness of simply being together, made rational thought impossible.

As Zio slept, Devan lay awake, imagining all the things they might've done if things had been different. Uncomplicated. How throwing each other around in bed would become less necessary and more fun. Perhaps they'd take their time. Find a patch of sunlight to roll around in. Devan had been with too many partners to count, but Zio—

"Gods, whatever you're thinking about, please stop."

Devan blinked and glanced down.

Zio stared back at him, gaze heated. Hungry.

"How do you know I'm thinking about anything in particular?"

Zio canted his hips and fluttered a hand over Devan's groin. "Are you taking the piss?"

Devan smiled in spite of himself. "Not on purpose. Sorry. My, uh, mind got away from me."

"Your mind is obviously a filthy place to be."

"It would seem so."

The tension in Zio's body melted away a little. He brought his hands back to Devan and ghosted them over his chest, his abdomen, and the very place Devan wanted him most. His touch was featherlight. Gentle. Curious.

Devan bit his lip. "If you want me to retrieve my mind from the gutter, you're gonna have to stop doing that."

"Uh-huh."

Zio's tone was noncommittal.

Devan groaned and flexed, chasing his magic hands. "Now it's your turn to stop."

"I don't want to."

"I know. That's why you have to."

"I don't have to do anything." Zio moved fast, straddling Devan in the blink of an eye. He dropped a hand either side of Devan's head and ground down, softly at first, but then, when he met no resistance, harder, with more purpose, drawing another moan from Devan. "We could fuck," Zio whispered. "Just once. No one would know."

"Everyone would know," Devan gritted out. "But that's not the issue."

"Then what is?"

"Don't play dumb." *Gods, why am I having this conversation again?* "You know if we mess around like this, the chances of us biting and completing the bond are a million times higher."

"I don't care."

With Zio playing him, neither did Devan. The bond swirled around them, tendrils snaking into his brain, clouding his

144

rational judgement, overriding everything, even his commitment to keep the pack safe.

He gripped Zio's wrists and flipped them over. They'd slept in underwear, but it was gone before Devan could contemplate what he was doing. Naked, all bets were off. His body ached to be inside Zio. He closed his hand around Zio's neck, the other shoving Zio's legs apart. His cock pressed against Zio, demanding entrance.

Zio snatched a shaky breath. "Kiss me."

Devan leaned down. Skin touched skin, and Zio's legs came around him, drawing Devan closer, their lips millimetres apart. *This is it. He's mine—*

"Um, guys?"

Reality crashed in, slamming into Devan like a tsunami. He reared back, a fierce growl escaping him. "*Fuck.* What do you *want?*"

Shannon looked on, expression an irritating mix of wary and amused. "The reinforcements have arrived. Varian came with them, and he wants to see you, Devan."

"What about me?" Zio asked.

"He didn't mention you, and he's not stopping. Just said to find Devan."

Confusion broke through the hormone-haze clouding Zio's eyes. He frowned but said nothing as he scrambled out from beneath Devan.

Devan's hand shot out to stop him, but he caught it in time and sprang to his feet. "Where's he at?"

"Comms tent. Peace out."

Shannon disappeared, taking with him the heat of the moment. Devan shook his head, trying to clear it. His body still throbbed with desire, but with alpha orders hanging over him, it was easier to control.

He retrieved his clothes from the floor and threw them on while Zio watched, the emotions seeping from him so conflicted Devan couldn't pin them down. Want. Relief. Sadness.

Devan stamped into his boots and crouched at Zio's side.

"I'm sorry. That was my fault. I let my imagination run away with me while you slept."

"'S okay. It's not like I did much to stop it."

"That's the point. You couldn't, because how I was feeling influenced you before you even woke up. I'll work on it, I promise."

"I don't want you to work on not wanting to jump me."

"Yeah, well. I have to, or I'll have to leave."

Like that'll ever happen. Even without the risks to Zio, it wasn't something Devan could contemplate, but the threat worked. Zio blinked. Shook himself. Banged his head on Devan's shoulder and nodded. "We'll both work on it. Should I come with you to see Varian?"

"No. Rest here."

"I just slept all day."

"Yeah, and you'll be out all night. Humour me."

Devan slipped out of the tent before Zio could argue. He was under no illusions that Zio would consider his instructions an order but had faith that he wouldn't want to leave their scent addled sanctuary unless he had to. Devan certainly didn't, and his displeasure at doing so led him to greet Varian with a surly grunt.

Varian scented the air. "Hard day?"

"Is that a joke?"

"I doubt it. Tomos has spent our entire relationship reminding me that I'm distinctly unfunny."

"Lucky you."

Varian's eyebrow twitched. Amusement or annoyance, Devan couldn't tell, and he didn't care. He folded his arms across his chest and leaned against a stack of crates. "What can I do for you, Alpha?"

"Michael let slip that he told you about the risk to Zio if you are forced apart before the bond completes."

"The bond we've been *forbidden* to complete?"

Varian sighed. "You will never know how much that haunts me."

Devan could debate that all day, but he lacked the patience. "The semantics aren't important. Michael confirmed what I had some vague knowledge of already, but I doubt I'd have found the willpower to leave anyway. And I've no intention of abandoning my pack."

"I knew that, which is why I didn't tell you of the risk to Zio. Perhaps I was wrong, but it never crossed my mind that you would leave him, even if your clan alphas ordered you to."

"They didn't."

"I know, and I'm forever grateful to Dash and Luca for their friendship. They have risked much to support us, and so have you. Devan, I need you to believe how much I appreciate all you've done in the short time you've been with us."

"I do know it, but this bond . . . it's leaving me a little irrational. I don't mean to be rude."

Varian smiled. "And I don't mean to irritate you, so I suppose we're even, but I *am* sorry I didn't tell you about Zio. I thought it was for the best, but Michael convinced me otherwise."

"I haven't told Zio."

"Hopefully you won't have to. It's a rare thing in my living memory, at least, but the way our luck is going, you never know."

"Trouble at home?"

"No. And not much here. Worrying, don't you think?"

"Perhaps your enemies have given up."

"If only." Varian straightened. "But after decades of this war, I think it would take more than a rogue tiger to scare them off. No offence."

"None taken." Devan observed Varian as he prepared to leave, all the while wondering if the point of the conversation would ever reveal itself. He found it hard to believe that a leader as stretched as Varian would summon him for a pep talk. "Is there anything else I can do for you?"

Varian took a last glance at the latest drone footage on the computer screens, his frown deepening before he schooled his features, and turned back to Devan. "Not that I can think of, but

147

stay vigilant. Look for things you've never seen. Right now, it's all we can do."

Devan saw Varian to his waiting vehicle, then let himself be drawn back to the tent, instinct reassuring him that Zio was exactly where he'd left him.

And he was, though he'd put clothes on.

"Did someone give Michael a lobotomy?" He waved a plate of food in Devan's general direction. "He's acting like he went to sleep one day and woke up the next thinking he's somebody's mother."

"Maybe Varian told him to chip in a little more."

"Why would he do that? Michael works as hard as the rest of us."

"How would I know? He's been your brother far longer than he has mine."

"You're hiding something."

"Yup." It was pointless to deny it. "But I can't tell you what, so don't waste your energy worrying about it. Speaking of which . . ." Devan fished his supply bag from beneath a pile of Zio's crap. "I want you to take some of these."

He pulled a pouch of herbal pills from his stash and held them out to Zio.

Zio hooked the pouch from Devan's fingers as though he'd been handed poison. "The fuck are they?"

"A blend from home. We use it to give shifters strength after injury."

"I'm not injured."

"But you have been, many times, and you're shifting every day."

"I'm a wolf, bro. I don't want to take these and grow whiskers or some shit."

Devan laughed. "You're ridiculous. Do you think I've only

148

ever healed my own kind? Granted, wolves aren't my speciality, but there's more to my world than big cats."

"Seems to me there's *only* big cats in my world right now. One of you, at least." Zio shovelled the last of his dinner/breakfast into his mouth. "And I'm not down with swallowing random pills, but something tells me I'll end up doing it anyway, so I might as well get it over with."

He tipped the chalky pills into his palm. "Why are they all different colours?"

"I made them on different days. Nature changes every minute. Some days the berries were red; by the end of the week they were black. Same with the leaves."

Zio held his hand up to the light. "I've never taken . . . medication before. That's a human thing."

"It's not medicine. It's holistic."

"I don't know what that means."

"It treats the whole person—shifter and human—rather than one specific thing."

"There's nothing wrong with me."

Devan ran out of rope. He sighed and flopped down on the bed. "I know that. Think of it more as a supplement. An energy boost. Or at the very least, a harmless intervention. If you have no faith, you'll feel no different, but if you do . . . it can't be a bad thing, eh?"

"Nothing about how you make me feel is bad."

Suddenly, Zio was on top of Devan. *Again.* Unwilling to lose control this time, Devan braced himself. "You don't make me feel bad either."

"Don't I? You don't smile as much around me as you do everyone else."

Devan's lips twitched. "I wasn't aware that I'd smiled much at all since I got here. No offence, but your way of life is kind of intense."

"True that, but you *are* different with the others. I've seen you with Michael, and Bomber when he was still here. You're relaxed with them . . . a brother. With me it's like you're waiting for a grenade to go off."

Devan turned it over in his mind and realised Zio was right. In many ways, being with Zio in any capacity was so right he couldn't imagine it feeling wrong, but the reality of fighting a bond was markedly different. It was hard to smile when his instincts were taking such a battering. "I don't mean to be miserable."

"That's not what I said."

"All the same, I am sorry. I like being with you. You *do* make me smile."

"Show me."

"What?"

"*Show* me," Zio repeated. "I have to go in a minute, and I don't want to leave again knowing you feel like shit."

"I don't feel like shit."

"Prove it."

In spite of himself, Devan smiled, and for a fleeting moment, his world narrowed to the grin he got from Zio in return. War, packs, clans, they faded to black. They were alone with the addictive warmth they shared, and its origins didn't matter.

Devan cupped Zio's face in his hands and tugged him down for a gentle kiss. His body thrummed with desire, but he ignored it—ignored everything save the sensation of lips that were made for his. Zio melted against him, his sharp edges a distant memory. The kiss went on and on and on. Fresh magic sparked, and Zio's contented wolf called to Devan's shifter soul.

Mine.

Ours.

Too soon, though, Zio pulled back. "I'm not sorry I jumped on you."

"I don't want you to be."

"Good, cos I'm not, and I can't promise it won't happen again before this operation is over."

"And what about after? Our orders are to deflect the bond until the *war* is over. That could be years."

Zio shrugged. "The bond will have faded by then, and we can be friends . . . maybe even friends who fuck. Seriously, man. I think we should stop worrying about it. Neither of us is going to disobey our alphas."

"You think the bond is going to fade?" Devan's stomach dropped through the ground, leaving a crater in its wake. "Even though we're both stuck here . . . together?"

"Of course. You have to fuck to complete it, right? And bite each other. We're not going to do that."

The glow Devan had absorbed from their kiss evaporated. There'd been moments when he'd been grateful for the fact that Zio had learned little about the shifter world in his short, tumultuous life, but in *this* moment, Devan wanted to scream. *How can he be that naive?*

But Devan already knew the answer—because he didn't know any better. "Zio, we—"

For the second time that day, they were interrupted. Danielo ducked into the tent. "Sorry to barge in." He looked anything but. "Drones are in, Z. Movement to the south. I think it's human, but we should check it out."

In an instant, Zio became the soldier Devan had been ordered to protect. He rolled off Devan and scrambled to his feet. "I'm coming."

"You might want to zip your jeans up first, mate. We don't all want to see your dick."

"Liar."

Danielo smirked.

Devan leapt to his feet. A growl rumbled out of his chest, deep and possessive. Zio gripped his elbow and motioned to Danielo to leave. "Easy. I'll do it up, see? And I'll even take your quack pills. Just don't kill my brothers, okay? I need them."

Devan needed them too, but with Danielo's scent still lingering in the tent, it was hard to think clearly. He pulled Zio close, rougher than he'd meant to. "Wherever you're going, hurry back."

CHAPTER TWENTY-ONE

The push and pull of a triggered bond was officially insane. And a complete ball ache. Zio couldn't see how anyone in his position ever got anything done, how the whole world didn't grind to a halt because shifters couldn't get their shit together.

Not that *together* was on Zio's radar. At least, it wasn't when responsibility put a safe distance between him and Devan. When the possessive, demanding current hummed weakly enough to gift them perspective.

Zio scanned the camp. His gaze automatically sought Devan out, but the skip in his pulse when he found him was bearable. Or maybe it was masked by Zio's concern for the soldier Devan was currently bent over, a scout from a returning patrol. Zio caught Danielo's attention and jerked his head in Devan's direction. "Find out what happened. Nothing came through on comms."

Danielo hurdled the hedge separating the communications base from the rest of the camp. The most agile of all Zio's team, he moved with a grace that was almost feline, though he had nothing on Devan—

Focus.

Zio forced himself to turn away from Danielo and Devan and study the intelligence spread out in front of him. Patrols over the last few days had confirmed the activity close to the border had been the human army setting up a base of their own, a clear attempt to discourage shifter violence, though all they'd truly achieved was to drive the enemy to a place where Zio couldn't see them.

He drew circles on the big maps with a pencil. "If the southern packs believe Shadow Clan have joined us, they'll want to attack as soon as possible. Catch us before clan forces arrive to boost our numbers."

"Shadow Clan have ways of moving their people without the rest of us knowing," Michael said. "The enemy might think they're already here. That's why they've pulled back, because they're scared."

Zio could think of a dozen enemies he'd rather face than the powerful clan Devan came from, but Michael's theory didn't sit right. For Shadow Clan's reinforcements to make a difference, they'd have to be substantial, and the enemy would see that. Without Gale on the front to shield Zio's soldiers, enemy drones saw as much as their own. "They're not scared. They're testing us. Waiting to see if we chase them down or stay put, shore up, and prepare to fight here."

"You think they'll attack the camp? Even with the humans there?"

"No. They'll either attempt to draw us out or they'll wait for the humans to move on, which they will if nothing happens soon. You know they're only here for the media coverage. They don't give a shit if we destroy each other."

Michael grunted, though Zio couldn't tell if he agreed or not, and his attention soon wandered again, drifting back to where Devan was still working on the wounded shifter. Gentle hands. Soft smile. Everything Zio's wolf wanted to claim as his own.

Danielo returned. "Idiot got hit by a truck. It flipped him into a tree and a branch went through his thigh. Missed the artery, but it's gonna take a while for Devan to put it right."

Zio scowled. "How does that even happen? We can sense approaching vehicles from miles away."

"Fucked if I know."

"Why don't you know? I sent you over there to find out."

"Dude's lost a bazillion pints of blood and crawled back here. Give him an hour, eh?"

Danielo wasn't known for being the voice of reason, but he possessed more patience than Zio right now. With a sigh, Zio waved him away. "Whatever. Find out later. I don't want defective scouts on my watch."

"Yes, boss. I'm off to get the dinner on. Can't have Michael and Devan showing us up."

Danielo ambled away. Zio brooded over maps and surveillance footage until nightfall, then returned to the tent, heart sinking when he found it empty, though he'd known from fifty feet away that Devan wasn't there.

Woodsmoke reached Zio's senses. Danielo's laughter as he called to anyone close enough to pay him attention.

Zio rolled his eyes, and his stomach growled. Somehow over the last few days, he'd grown used to the regular hot meals cooked up on the campfire, and his appetite had become befitting of a shifter. He was hungry all the time. He cast a glance at Devan's stuff, neatly piled in the corner, half-hidden by the chaos that was Zio's belongings. *He brought the kitchen sink in that tiny bag. I wonder if he's got any food.*

Searching through Devan's things was all wrong, but Zio's nose led him to a supermarket bag tucked under a coat. Inside he found nirvana—ginger biscuits, salt-and-vinegar crisps, and a packet of Rolos. *How did he know?*

Zio pondered on it as he ate his way through Devan's supplies but was no further to the answer when Devan returned a little while later, the scent of another wolf's blood clinging to him. A growl threatened in Zio's chest. He swallowed it down with the last of the biscuits and offered Devan the empty wrapper. "I'm not even sorry."

"I don't want you to be. I got them for you."

"How?"

"I went to a shop. We're not stationed on the moon."

"I meant *how* did you know everything I like?"

Devan's gaze flickered, wary. "Emma wrote it on the front of your file. She said it was the best way to cheer you up if you were terminally pissed off."

"I'm not terminally pissed off."

"Why do you think I hadn't given them to you yet?"

"Valid." Zio dusted his hands together. "I don't know why she kept notes like that. It's not like ginger nuts could ever help a healer reattach a limb or some shit."

"Not all injuries are physical. Sometimes kindness is enough."

"You sound super old when you say stuff like that."

"I prefer wise."

Devan smiled, but it didn't quite reach his eyes. He looked . . . tired, and Zio realised he'd neglected to ask after the injured scout. He opened his mouth to rectify his mistake, but Danielo called for dinnertime before he could speak, and the moment passed.

"Come on." He stood and held out his hand. "Let's go eat."

"You just ate."

"So? Those pills you gave me are turning me into a gannet. I'm still hungry."

"How do you feel otherwise?"

"About what? You?"

"No, Zio. I know how you feel about me . . . you couldn't hide it if you tried. I meant how are you feeling physically. Those pills are pretty powerful if the shifter body takes to them."

"What happens if the body doesn't?"

"Nothing."

It was on the tip of Zio's tongue to stake a claim on nothing, but as the words formed on his lips, he realised they weren't true. He'd spent his entire life in a bad mood, even before Emma's death. War had been his constant companion. Violence. Death. Grief and misery. But though the triggers were more prominent than ever and his emotions had been disrupted by Devan as he lost himself to introspection, a cloud had lifted.

155

Worries still gnawed at him, but for the first time that he could remember, there was a distance between him and them. Perspective. *How is that possible when we're in the middle of a fucking war?*

Zio had no clue, but he couldn't deny it—whatever was in those plant pills, he felt fantastic. "I think they're working."

Devan smiled for real then. "Good. Now let's go eat before we find new ways to get in trouble."

———

"Nothing to report?"

Michael shook his head. "We swept everywhere. Sent the drones up to check where we couldn't reach. No activity. Not even recon units. It's like they've disappeared."

Zio narrowed his eyes as Michael's choice of words sank in. Enemy forces didn't disappear unless they chose to, and why would they do that? Getting over the border was the southern pack's main objective—it had to be if they wanted to claim northern England as their own. Why would they retreat?

The hospital flickered into Zio's mind. He sent Michael to get some rest and searched out the satellite phone. It took a while to get hold of Gale. Waiting unsettled Zio's wolf, so he allowed his thoughts to drift to Devan. It was a strange state of flux to be fighting a war that seemed to have got lost in the post and to be fixated on a shifter that was unlike any Zio had ever known. The routine of patrols that went nowhere, camp meals that put him in a food coma, and games of verbal chicken with Devan were driving Zio slowly mad, but at the same time, in a world he'd ceased to understand weeks ago, he was . . . happy.

Devan, on the other hand, was not. He barely ate, and Zio rarely saw him sleep. *It's like we've swapped personalities.* Well, not exactly. Devan was still a better person than Zio, a fact Danielo reminded him of daily.

But still. *He's not happy.* And Zio couldn't live with that.

"Um . . . hello? Anyone there?"

Zio jumped, even Gale's soft voice enough to startle him. "Fuck. Sorry. I was distracted."

"Clearly. Everything okay? I heard about you and Devan."

"Of course you did," Zio grumbled. "Haven't people got anything better to talk about?"

Gale chuckled. "Not around here. Monitoring a human hospital is pretty boring, you know."

"That's what I wanted to talk to you about. The briefing I got yesterday said nothing unusual had been picked up, but I wanted to hear your take on it."

"The briefing was my take on it. I wrote it and sent it to you."

"Uh-huh." Zio let a speculative silence hang out. Gale was a black and white thinker, but when pushed, he had stronger instincts than even he knew.

Five, four, three, two, one . . .

"There was something, though," Gale said.

Bingo. Zio sat up straighter. "Go on?"

"Nah, it's probably nothing."

"So? If that's the case, we can eliminate it and move on."

"I guess."

"*So?*" Patience wasn't Zio's strong point.

Gale sighed. "We've been monitoring backroom staff—housekeeping, maintenance, the orderlies, all areas it's easy to sneak people in without proper records, but we've seen nothing in those departments. It's the medical staff. A year ago, the hospital couldn't keep employees longer than a few months, but recently, that's stopped."

"Did the working conditions change?"

"No. If anything, they've got worse. This is a failing hospital —cancelled surgeries, massive waitlists, huge queues in the emergency department. There's a lot of anger in the air, and front-line staff take the brunt of it."

"Shifters couldn't infiltrate a hospital like that. Even the humans would notice."

"I know. And we sweep the building day and night. No shifter has even come close."

"And no new humans either?"

"Not for a while."

Zio scrubbed a hand through his hair. It needed a cut, but only Emma had ever taken scissors to his hair. For now, he was content to go wild. "You're right. It might be nothing, but something about it feels off. Do you have any way of accessing the staff database?"

"Of course, but it will take time to do that undetected by anyone who's got there first."

"How much time?"

"A couple of days at least. We'd have to do it in stages."

"Then do it," Zio said. "And get to work checking out anyone who strikes you as suspicious—actually, check out everyone. We can't afford to miss anything."

Gale sighed again. "Okay. I suppose that means I'm not going home again. Vicky is going to kill me."

"No change there. How does that work anyway?"

"How does what work? Her wanting my balls for a hat because I haven't had dinner with her for a month?"

"No . . . your attachment to her. You're married, but you're not bonded."

Silence. Then Gale cleared his throat. "I'm not going to speculate as to why you suddenly give a shit about my private life, so I'll just say this: Me and Vic love each other, fancy the crap out of each other, and neither of us can imagine ever being with anyone else. It's been fifteen years. Yeah, we're not bonded in a shifter sense, but wolves aren't all we are . . . we're human too."

"But you *are* shifters. What if you trigger a bond with someone else?"

"Then I'd ignore it. Let it fade. It's not as though I haven't got a million other things to distract me."

An ache flared deep in Zio's chest. "I'm not sure it works like that."

"Maybe not for you, but you've never loved anyone the way I love Vic. The bond you've triggered with Devan is the first true affection you've ever had outside of the tiny circle of people you tolerate. And you're out in the field, fighting, hurting, healing. Living in each other's pockets. Everything's heightened, on top of the fact that you've been forbidden to complete it. If I know you at all, and I think I do, that's bound to make it more desirable."

Not it. It's not a thing. It's Devan.

Gale laughed. "Don't growl at me, Zio. You asked me a question; I answered it."

Zio pressed his hand over his mouth, as if he could shove his aggression down. Bury it. *As if.* He let his hand drop. "Do you think it would be different if we were away from the war . . . away from the pack, from everything? Do you think it would hurt less?"

"I don't know. Nothing about loving someone is easy, but you don't know Devan well enough to love him. What's between you is pack affection and a biological reaction determined by your shifter genes. I guess you have to figure out what that means to you."

Gale said other words, but Zio heard nothing more as he tried to rationalise his primal desires for Devan against the ever-increasing swell of his heart. His wolf wanted to bite Devan, to fuck him, claim him, and solidify all that swirled between them, but Zio wasn't just wolf, he was human.

And the man in Zio wanted so much more.

CHAPTER TWENTY-TWO

"Come out with me."

Devan squinted in the dark at Zio. "What?"

"Come *out*." Zio reached into the medical tent and grabbed Devan's hand. "You've healed everyone. No one needs you."

"No one?"

"Well, okay, I do, but that's not the same thing."

"Yeah. It's biology. I remember." Devan couldn't keep the sour note out of his voice, though he knew on some level, Zio's simplistic take on their situation made the most sense, *and* that he'd said it himself at some point . . . more than once. "What are you even doing here? Aren't you supposed to be out on patrol?"

"Been and gone," Zio said. "Next one's already headed out, which means . . . I'm free, and so are you, so let's *go*."

Devan had no idea what Zio was asking of him but let Zio tug him out of the tent and through the camp. It was early, predawn, and apart from the stag guards and the returned patrol, no one was up, save Michael who had already stoked the fire.

He watched Devan and Zio drift past him with a gaze that was, as ever, impossible to read, but Devan didn't try that hard. Couldn't when Zio's palm was so hot in his.

They neared the back of the camp. Devan frowned. "Where are we going?"

"I told you . . . out."

"Out where?"

"You'll see."

Devan was officially mystified, but given the direction his life had taken since he'd come to England, it wasn't an unusual state of affairs.

They slipped out of the camp. Zio retrieved a bag from a bush and slung it over his back. "Supplies," he responded to Devan's questioning stare. "I can't stop eating."

Devin grinned faintly. "That's good."

"Is it? I feel like it's the only thing keeping my mind off everything else."

"Everything else" could've meant anything from the war to their triggered bond and all that came between. Devan wasn't sure he had the stomach to investigate.

So he didn't. He clutched Zio's hand like a drowning man and let him lead him away from the camp and deep into the countryside.

They hiked miles on their human legs, up hills and across fields, wading across icy streams and tramping through mud. The weather was cold, but with their shifter blood, not unpleasantly so, and the scenery was glorious. Devan took advantage of mother nature and restocked his supplies, all the while trying not to lose his mind every time Zio trooped back to his side with a handful of leaves and a soft kiss.

"If you're trying to stop me getting attached to you, tactile foraging isn't the way," he remarked dryly when they'd stopped to eat.

Zio inhaled a hunk of stale bread that was wrapped around leftover sausages. "I'm not trying to *do* anything. I just figured getting away from the camp would do you good."

"Since when have you cared about doing me good?"

A muscle in Zio's cheek twitched and a faint flush stained his skin. He swallowed thickly and cleared his throat. "Do you think I'm some kind of monster?"

"Do *you*?"

Zio's gaze narrowed. "What's that supposed to mean?"

"Nothing." Devan folded his arms across his chest. "Just ignore me, okay? I'm not . . . feeling myself today."

Zio slid from the rock he'd been perched on and moved so fast he was a blur until he was suddenly right in front of Devan, crowding his personal space with his bewitching scent. "I upset you, didn't I?"

"When?"

"When I said our bond would fade and we could be friends. You've been in a bad mood since then."

Devan was used to sampling the emotions of those around him, not having his own served up to him on a plate. "I'm not in a bad mood. I'm frustrated."

"With me?"

"No. Yes. I don't know."

"I didn't mean it."

"Mean *what*?"

Zio flinched. "When I said it would fade. It's not going to, is it?"

Devan let his hands follow their natural path to Zio's hips, pulling him impossibly closer, then sliding his palms under Zio's clothes. Skin contact calmed him and settled Zio too. "I didn't like it when you seemed relieved by the possibility that this could all go away. That you might want to go back to your life before you met me. The human in me understands and maybe even feels the same. I don't know. But I'm not human, and neither are you. Our bond exists, and I want it. I want *you*."

"That's what it means," Zio whispered, his gaze distant, as though he spoke only to himself.

Devan gave him a moment, then brushed his lips along his jaw, barely resisting the urge to scent Zio as his teeth lengthened and venom filled his mouth. *Bite him.*

"Fuck." He pulled back, retracting his claws. "Sorry."

"What for?"

Devan growled and banged his head on Zio's shoulder, hard enough to hurt them both had they not possessed strong shifter bones. "Everything? I have no idea at this point. It feels like every breath I take makes it hurt more."

Helplessness tainted Zio's emotions. The healer in Devan longed to soothe him, but no words came. What could he say? Whichever way they turned, their situation was hopeless unless they disobeyed their alphas and set a grenade beneath a war that had already killed thousands of shifters on both sides.

"Devan." Zio eased two fingers under Devan's chin, pushing gently until Devan met his gaze. "I've said and thought a hundred times that I wish I'd never met you, but it's not true. We might not ever get to see what this could've been, but it's still everything to me. Before . . . fuck, before you, Emma was the only person I've ever felt understood me, but with you, it's even more than that. I feel like, I dunno, you *are* me, the good parts, at least. I can't give that up. I won't."

A fluttering sensation stirred in Devan's gut. "What are you saying?"

Zio sucked in a breath and fixed Devan with a steely gaze. "That we have to hold on, however long it takes. Protect what we have until we can make it permanent. I have my orders and so do you, but I won't take anymore. Devan, you *will* be mine."

Devan straightened and, with herculean effort, pushed Zio away. "Go over there and say that."

"What?"

"Go," Devan growled out. "I need to hear you say it when we're not entangled. When you're not as hypnotised by me as I am by you."

Zio backed up, moving steadily until he was as far away as Devan's heart could take, a genuine grin warming his usual flinty features. "Which part do you need me to repeat? That you're mine, or that I'm prepared to wait for you as long as it takes?"

"Those parts will do, and I don't need you to repeat it. I need *you* to be sure it's what you want."

"I am sure, Devan. Don't treat me like a child."

As if Devan ever could. "You're a warrior, Zio. I've never seen you as anything else."

"*Nothing* else?"

"Don't be pedantic." It was Devan's turn to close the distance between them in a flash. He shoved Zio against a tree and wedged a knee between his thighs. "But if this is what you dragged me out here for, there was really no need. We could've had this conversation in the tent."

"No, we couldn't," Zio said. "We've been together and apart, at war and naked in bed, but we've never truly been alone since the bond triggered. You were right to push me away and make me say it again, but you were too late. I've already lived twenty-one years without you. All I needed to be sure was to be *here*, Devan, with you."

Devan wondered who had swapped Zio's surly self for a young shifter so eloquent he was almost poetic. *This is a dream; it has to be.*

But it wasn't. The primal, *desperate* urge to bite Zio, to claim him, reignited stronger than ever. He pushed up against Zio, his desires clear.

Zio moaned and pushed back, hips canting to meet Devan, hard and demanding.

Devan bared his teeth, and only the alpha commands seared on his soul stopped him from following through. He groaned and rubbed his cheek against Zio's. "If we're going to hold on, we need to hold *off*."

"We could do it in secret," Zio whispered, gaze now hazy with instincts he couldn't control. "No one would know."

Devan chuckled. "They would. Your squad is young, but any shifter, wolf or otherwise, that's been around bonds, would know we'd completed it in a heartbeat. They'd smell it on us, sense the shift in our behaviour, our reactions to certain things. Besides, it's too dangerous while you're fighting. I've already killed for you . . . If we were properly bonded? I'd burn the world down."

"Gods." Zio shuddered. "I believe you because I've seen it, and my wolf liked it . . . it felt right, you know? But it scared me too. You were so different that day."

Devan eased away from Zio's body, every instinct he possessed screaming at him to do the opposite. "I *was* different that day, and I haven't been the same since. Even without . . . us, being in my animal skin was something I needed to do, and not being able to do it now is driving me slowly mad. Have you ever been in a situation where you can't shift for weeks at a time? Months? Years?"

Comprehension dawned in Zio's dark gaze. "That's what's bothering you?"

"I think so. I didn't realise it until I said it, and gods, there's other things going on too, but . . . yeah. I miss running free."

"Then do it."

"I can't. It's part of the agreement my alphas have with the southern packs—that I don't fight, shift, or do anything to bring my clan into the war."

"Surely that means you can't shift *to* fight. Not that you can't shift at all."

Devan sifted through his jumbled memories of the conversation he'd had with Luca in a place that had seemed like the end of the world. "*...barring self-defence, you do not fight again, nor do you complete your bond with their soldier.*" He hadn't outright forbidden Devan to shift— *But Varian did, remember?* "I can't do it."

"You can." A low growl punctuated Zio's words. "We're nowhere near the fighting—we're nowhere near *anything*. We can shift and run for miles without anyone knowing. And I'll tell Varian the truth when we get back—that you had to shift for your own well-being. He's not a monster, either. If it doesn't put the pack at risk, he'll understand."

"But—"

"*No*, Devan. You take care of everyone else; let me take care

165

of this for you. Shift. Run. Be your truth, even if it's just for a moment."

Devan couldn't remember a time when Zio asking anything of him wasn't so compelling he felt weak at the knees. Combined with the impatient beast demanding release, he stood no chance. He closed his eyes and summoned the power that would set him free. Bones lengthened and snapped. Senses came to life.

He shifted.

Zio's wolf was fast, but Devan's tiger was faster. The white cat zipped through the trees, bounding from fallen trunks and rocks as Zio raced to keep up. Wind and rain. Paws on the frosty ground. The aroma of damp earth merged with unmistakable scents of two excited shifters. Zio drank it all in, howling with delight in the rare moments he got close enough to Devan to nip his flank.

It was almost like running with his brothers, save the heady aura that kept pace with them, never to be outrun.

A few miles in, Devan slowed and jerked his head forwards, message clear: *show me the way.*

Zio shoulder-barged him on his way past. *Gladly.*

More miles disappeared as Zio led Devan through forests and open countryside. They climbed north into territory that hadn't seen a southern wolf in centuries. Stride by stride, the shackles of war and responsibility slipped away. With Devan a heartbeat behind, for the first time in forever, Zio tasted freedom. He ran on and on and on, until a familiar landmark came into view.

He skidded to a stop and dropped his head to let the bag he carried around his neck fall to the ground. Then he shifted back to his human form and turned to face Devan.

Blue eyes gazed back at him, wide and gleaming in Devan's black-and-white face.

Zio combed his fingers through soft fur. "I'm gonna walk the rest of the way. Come with me?"

Devan tilted his head sideways, absorbing Zio's touch, then a shimmer took him away.

He returned, very human and very naked.

Zio smirked, noting that the cold air had no effect on Devan's body either. "Ready?"

Devan shrugged. "Of course."

Zio shouldered his bag and grabbed Devan's hand, tugging him over the rocky terrain until they came to a sheltered path on the hillside.

"I hear water," Devan said. "Is there a spring nearby?"

"You'll see."

Moments later, the pathway opened out again, revealing the gentle waterfall that tumbled down the hill. It was no Niagara Falls, but for northern England, it was glorious.

Devan stretched his arm under the spray, cupping crystal clear water in his hand. He brought it to his face and took a sip. "This water is magic."

"I know. Emma brought me here a long time ago."

"Did she use it in her work?"

"I don't know. She talked a lot about stuff like that, but I didn't always listen."

"Why not?"

Zio shrugged and joined Devan by the water. "I didn't know how much it mattered."

"But you do now?"

"Of course I do. Without it, everyone I care about would've died three times over."

Devan hummed and dripped water down Zio's back. "I never realised how exhausting it was to use my gifts twenty-four seven. Some days I feel almost human."

"Yeah?"

"Yeah."

Zio stepped closer to Devan, his shoulder catching the spray from the fall. The water was shockingly cold, and he gasped.

Devan smirked. "See? Magic."

Zio caught a palmful of water and tipped it down Devan's chest. A tiny shudder passed through Devan, and Zio felt it in every bone. "Magic enough to let us forget anything else exists while we're here?"

"Maybe."

Devan dropped his hands to Zio's hips and pulled him flush against him. Desire flared. Zio gasped again, but this time it was heat, not frigid cold, and his cock rose to meet Devan's.

They hadn't been truly intimate for weeks. A few near misses had barely scratched the surface, dampened down by circumstance and responsibility. But as Devan brushed his lips along Zio's jaw, ties that bound them to the rest of the world faded to black. Wants and needs roared to life. The alpha orders forbidding Zio from bonding to his mate dulled to a distant hum.

"Zio." Devan's whisper broke through. "We can't fuck—I can't control myself—but we can do this, we can just be . . . for a little while, please?"

As if Zio could refuse him. He tugged Devan under the spray in the hope that perhaps the cool water would gift them perspective, then he kissed Devan, kissed him and kissed him and kissed him, and for as long as they stood under the waterfall, war was forgotten.

They were alone.

CHAPTER TWENTY-THREE

Devan reached the brow of the hill and scented the air. Zio was ahead of him, but their return journey held none of the promise of before. As darkness fell, so did Devan's mood, and lead laced his every step. He wanted to chase after Zio, but the reality that doing so would bring them closer to the last place on earth Devan wanted to be kept him dragging his heels.

Eventually, Zio noticed his slow pace and doubled back. He nosed Devan and whined.

Devan shook his head and shifted into his human form. "Sorry. I don't want to go."

Zio whined again, then shifted back too, brown eyes hooded and sad. "I don't want to go either, and I wish something had changed while we were out here."

"Something between us?"

"Maybe. I kind of wish we'd fucked, bitten, and bonded so it was done and we couldn't take it back—"

"Zio—"

"Yeah, yeah. I know all the bollocks that comes with it. We've been over it a thousand times, and I'm sick to fucking death of it. I just—fuck, I don't know. I wanted to make you happy, for a little while, at least. I'm sorry if I've made it worse."

"You haven't made it worse. I've had the best day."

"Really?" Zio's expression brightened enough to lift Devan's flagging spirits.

Devan smiled. "Of course. You think rolling around in the sun with you isn't my idea of a good time? It was magical."

And it was. If the world ended tonight, the sensation of the winter sun on his back while Zio's lips were fused to his would be seared on Devan's soul forever.

Zio retrieved his bag from the ground and opened it. He pulled out clothes and handed them to Devan. "Fuck it. Let's walk."

"As humans?"

"Yeah. Why not?"

"Because we won't get back until dawn."

"So? There's a hundred shifters in that camp now. No one will miss us."

Devan didn't believe for one minute that Zio wasn't fretting about getting back to his brothers. He wanted Zio all to himself until the end of time, but life was never going to be that way, and Devan didn't want it to be. Biology had brought them together. Mutual respect and an ever-growing love would keep them together. "They're already missing us. We have to get back, but before we go, can I kiss you again—"

Zio's lips cut him off, fierce and demanding before he drew back and shook Devan slightly. "Never ask me for anything that's already yours."

"Mine?"

"*Yours.*"

Devan's smile widened. There was much to be despondent about, but he couldn't deny the kick he got out of witnessing the effect their potential bond had on Zio. To see him turn from fearsome, to gentle, to territorial, all in the blink of an eye. Perhaps one day, Zio would utter those words and they'd take root, mean something more than wishful longing. "We need to go."

Zio licked his lips. "I know."

It would've been so easy to let the heat between them rise again, but Devan fought it, searched hard for the alpha orders keeping them apart, and allowed the hold that shifter lore had over both of them to win out. He kissed Zio one more time. Twice. Three times. Then he shoved the clothes back in the bag and shifted.

He towered over human Zio and propelled him forwards, ignoring Zio's indignant grumble. *Let's go.*

They reached the outskirts of the camp far quicker than either of them wanted to. A mile out, they shifted back and dressed in the dark.

Zio pulled his combat trousers on and scented Devan's throat. "I can smell that you've shifted. Do you think anyone else will notice?"

"Probably not. I don't think anyone else is as attuned to how I smell as you are."

Zio smirked, but his expression sobered a split second later. "Varian will know."

"Maybe." Devan stamped into his shoes and plucked twigs from his hair. "But he didn't outright order me not to shift again, so I haven't defied him. Besides, I didn't shift to fight his war, and we stayed in safe territory, so it should be fine."

"Should be," Zio deadpanned. "Awesome. And it's not Varian's war. It belongs to every wolf that doesn't want to be ruled by despotic southern wankers, thank you very much."

"Every *shifter*. I don't know if you've noticed, but I'm not a wolf."

"I've noticed."

"Glad we've cleared that up." Dressed, Devan snagged Zio's bag and slung it over his back. He jerked his head in the direction of the camp, then blinked hard as a wave of dizziness hit him. It was fleeting, gone in a flash, but in the time it took to pass, Zio had moved.

"What just happened?"

"Nothing."

"Liar." Zio gripped Devan's face. "What *happened*?"

"*Nothing*. I'm tired, that's all. Let's roll."

Zio frowned.

Devan nudged him. "Seriously. I'm fine. Healing just does weird things to me sometimes. You must've seen it in Emma."

It was a low blow, but it worked. Zio's face settled into his trademark scowl, and they set off for home.

They hiked down the hill and into the forest. Devan revelled in Zio's scent all over him and couldn't help stopping every few minutes to bury his face in Zio's neck. Their time together was running out, but he clung to it anyway. Who knew when they'd find more precious moments like these?

The scent of woodsmoke reached them, and it was Zio's turn to trail to a stop. He spun around and backed Devan against a tree. He didn't speak. Didn't have to. Just breathed Devan in.

Devan ran gentle fingers up the nape of Zio's neck and wove them into his wild hair. Zio smelt the same as he always did—of the earth he could bend to his will, of hope and promise, of blood and war. Zio was life and death, like Devan, but so very different it was hard to see how they fit together.

But they did fit together, flesh upon flesh, bone to bone. Even their breaths came as one.

Devan nosed the spot on Zio's neck he'd dreamed of biting a thousand times over. His teeth ached and venom pooled in his mouth. He wondered if the instincts flooding him would ever fade, if long after he'd bitten Zio and made him his own, the soul-deep craving for him would remain.

Craving that he'd be able to satiate.

It was almost inconceivable, but Devan's phone, buried somewhere in Zio's bag, buzzed loud enough to break the thraldom between them.

He fished it out. A rural Slovakian number flashed on the screen. "Fuck. It'll be Dash. I've got to take it."

Zio raised his head and stepped away, taking with him his intoxicating scent. "Go ahead. I'm gonna run back, though. We've been gone too long as it is."

172

Devan nodded, already speculating what his alpha could want. His hands itched to grab Zio and haul him back, unwilling to be apart, even for a few moments, but Zio was gone before he could.

He took the call. "Dash?"

"It's me."

"Why aren't you in Bratislava?"

"Because I'm not chained to the city. Luca wanted to visit the clan pockets in the mountains, but we're on our way home now. He's putting petrol in the car."

Devan didn't much care for Luca's whereabouts, but it was a rare thing for his clan alphas to travel by road. "Why didn't you move on foot?"

"We're running out of time," Dash said.

"For what?"

"For whatever is coming."

"Are you being cryptic on purpose? Or is there something I should know?"

"Nothing concrete, but be careful over the next few days. Something is in the air."

"You can tell that from Slovakia?"

"Of course. I sired you, Devan. Your distress is my own."

It made more sense than Devan cared to admit, even though it made no sense at all. "I'm not distressed. My head is clear . . . thanks to Zio, but I'm tired. I underestimated the strain full-time healing and an unfulfilled bond would put on me."

"Everyone underestimates the power of a bond until it hits them. But I'm glad you and the young wolf are working on it together. It bodes well for your future that it hasn't torn you apart."

It is tearing me apart. Devan sighed. "I don't know how long I can resist it. It's more than a potential bond, Dash. I love him."

"I know."

"You do? How is that possible when I didn't until I just said it?"

"Assumption, knowledge, instinct. You wouldn't be the

173

shifter I turned all those years ago if you didn't embrace the most difficult things. It was the quality that made you such a remarkable human."

Devan rolled his eyes. "I was a gangly student who didn't know which way was up."

"Even as a human, you were an industrious young man who already knew he'd been put on this earth to help people. I hope one day you meet someone truly ordinary so you can see the difference."

The whole world was ordinary compared to Zio, but Devan was pretty sure Dash hadn't called to hear him wax lyrical about his longed-for mate. *Actually, why did he call?*

But twenty minutes later, Devan bid goodbye to his alpha, none the wiser and further away from camp—and from Zio—than when he'd answered the phone. He searched his brain for threads of logic in the hope of tying some together but found none. He'd been entirely truthful when he'd told Dash he was tired, and beyond the need to link up with Zio as soon as possible, stringing coherent thoughts together just wasn't happening.

Lost in thought, Devan retraced the half mile he'd wandered from camp. His senses were naturally attuned to Zio, but as he walked, the cracking current between them faded, as though Zio was somehow getting further and further away from him. After a solid twelve hours in each other's company, the loss of their connection hurt. Devan rubbed his chest and picked up his pace, breaking into a run as he neared the camp.

Multiple emotions hit him at once, none of them pleasant, and none of them Zio's. *Panic. Distress. Fear. Anger.*

Devan leapt the boundary and faced the scene of dozens of shifters running around, vehicles revving, shouting, howls as humans became wolves and raced into the night.

He grabbed the nearest body to him—a young woman who manned the comms tent. "What is it? What's happened?"

"Raid. At the compound. They've attacked our home."

Devan let the woman go and she disappeared into the throng, but her panic remained and lodged itself deep in

Devan's soul. The compound was the pack's strongest position, the only place on earth where they felt safe . . . where *Zio* felt safe. It housed their families, human and shifter. It was the heart of the northern pack and the only home Zio had ever known.

And with Varian's fiercest fighters deployed to protect the border, it was woefully undermanned, unless the combat squad could somehow get back in time to defend it.

Fuck, fuck, fuck!

Devan whirled around, searching for Zio, for Michael, for Danielo.

He found Shannon and grabbed him, claws sliding out to dig into Shannon's flesh. "Where's Zio? And the rest of you? We need to get back."

Wild wolf eyes stared back at him. "They already left."

CHAPTER TWENTY-FOUR

Zio ran like the wind, abandoning the vehicles where the human police had stopped them at the roadblocks they'd set up to keep the fighting contained. Warning shots rang out behind him, but he didn't look back, his entire being fixated on defending his home. His *pack*.

He reached the safety of the thick forest and shifted, raw power, enhanced by rage and fear, shimmering around him. At his back, Michael and Danielo shifted too, and their pack connection burnt brighter.

Zio reached out, urgency lacing his command like never before: *Faster. Before it's too late.*

Danielo: *What about the guns?*

Zio: *They won't shoot anyone in human form; can't be sure we're shifters. As wolves we're safe in the forest.*

It was the only reassurance he could offer his brothers, but they didn't question it, their faith in him absolute, and their desperation to get home as strong as his.

With every wolf who'd followed them from the border camp at their backs, they fanned out and raced through the trees, enemy scents thickening with every stride, assaulting Zio's senses. In the back of his mind, the trauma of being separated from Devan burnt ever-bright. But for the first time in days, something burnt brighter, and he latched onto the fury building inside him, used it to push on as the sound of fighting reached him, laced with blood and smoke.

The eastern boundary loomed ahead. Zio burst out of the trees, and the scene that greeted him almost drove him to his knees. *Fire. So much fire.* From the meeting hall, to the barracks, and even Varian's house, the entire compound had been razed to the ground.

Shock hit Zio like a truck, but the impact was lost in the swelling rage. Through the smoke and chaos, he caught sight of the bungalow he'd shared with Emma for his entire adult life until her death, and her face was suddenly all he could see. Anger had been Zio's constant companion from the moment she'd died in his arms, but it had lessened in recent weeks, overwhelmed by Zio's every thought and emotion revolving around Devan.

But Devan wasn't there, and without his scent to calm Zio's wolf, the craving for vengeance returned full force.

Zio skidded to a stop on the brow of Varian's garden. He tipped his head back and howled, his call to his pack brothers and sisters clear: *This ends here.*

Danielo split their forces and disappeared. Moments later, Zio's paws were wet, soaked by the water pipes Danielo had ruptured with his gift. *Yes.* Zio howled again, jerked his head forwards, and leapt into the fray.

Enemy wolves were everywhere, dozens of them. Hundreds. The more Zio killed, the more seemed to appear. Northern wolves fell, each death a lance through Zio's heart he'd never forget. Somewhere behind him, Michael's pained howl ripped through the air. Zio whirled around, but an enemy wolf leapt at him before he could locate his wounded brother.

Fur and blood filled Zio's mouth as he grappled with the larger wolf. Zio was fast, but his assailant was heavy and strong, and his teeth tore into Zio's flank.

Zio yelped, distracted by the fiery pain, and it was the

opening the enemy wolf needed. He threw Zio down, knocking the breath from his lungs, and bared his teeth.

Saliva dripped from blood-stained fangs onto Zio's face. The stench of hatred left him dizzy, laced with the acrid scent of his own fear. He struggled beneath the weight of the huge wolf paw holding him down. The gash in his side opened up, exposing bone, and an agonised whine escaped him.

Buoyed by the herbal pills Devan had prescribed, Zio's body fought to heal itself as he battled to escape. More blood. More pain. Zio raked his claws down the enemy wolf's chest, twisting and scraping, inflicting as much damage as possible. The wolf cried out. For an instant, Zio surged, and the ground shook beneath him, but the size difference between them was too great, and he found himself on his back again, throat exposed, ready for certain death.

Caught in a vortex of fear and acceptance, he stopped struggling, gaze snared on the fangs baring down on him. The enemy wolf dipped his head to end Zio. He braced himself for searing pain, for the lifeblood to be torn from him and spat on the ground, but the final, finishing bite never came. A brindle wolf crashed into them from the side. The huge paw constricting Zio's chest disappeared, and sounds of a fierce fight reached him as he gasped in air. But it was over in a flash, and then Michael stood over him, panting, bleeding, eyes wide with concern.

Michael: *You good?*

Dazed, Zio rolled over and sprang to his feet, nosing Michael's wounds as his own knitted together. *You need Devan.*

Michael: *He's not here.*

Of course he wasn't. Zio had made sure of that, commandeering every vehicle to race his forces back north before Devan had returned to camp from his phone call, an action he bitterly regretted as Michael limped towards him. In a split second, he'd had to decide their course. He'd put the need to protect his potential mate above the lives of his brothers. Of his *pack*. And now they were outnumbered without their healer, and dozens of them were already dead.

"*Zio.*" Hands shook Zio's shoulders—human hands.

Zio blinked, and Michael stood before him, battered and bruised. Zio nudged him with his nose. *Change back. It's not safe.* He punctuated the command Michael couldn't hear with a low whine.

Michael shook Zio again. "Whatever you're thinking, stop. We don't have time. If we can't win this fight, we need to retreat."

No.

"Yes." Michael knew Zio well enough to counter his wordless protest. "I don't smell Varian anywhere. He's either dead, or they took him away. Gale too. We're outnumbered, brother. We're not getting out of this unless we fall back."

Varian. In Zio's haste to enter the fray, he'd barely stopped to consider their alpha, but Michael was right. Zio scented the air. There was no fresh trace of Varian or Gale's unit anywhere. *Where are they?*

Michael shot a nervous glance over his shoulder. "I don't know where they are. But we need to regroup to find out. Fighting blind is just going to get us all killed."

He was right, like he always was, but in the five seconds Zio had wasted forcing Michael to ram the truth down his throat, the scene in Varian's garden had changed. Ten enemy wolves had become twenty . . . thirty, to Zio's nine, and new fires burnt.

They were surrounded.

Devan followed the scent of blood, battle, and Zio as though he was being dragged behind a bullet train. His tiger ate up the miles, a silver-white blur to any human who saw him, but it still felt like a lifetime had passed by the time the burning compound appeared on the horizon.

The air was thick with humans and their army vehicles. Their weapons. In the sky above, a helicopter hovered. Devan slowed his pace and slunk along the tree line until he found a safe place

179

to shift into human form, grateful he'd possessed the where-withal to sling his clothes in a bag around his neck before he'd torn away from the border camp.

He dressed in a flash and emerged from the forest, tracking Zio and his brothers to the smoking ruins of Varian's house. Bodies, enemy and pack, littered the ground. Devan healed every soul who carried the pack scent. Most faces he didn't catch. Over and over, he dug deep for his powers and emptied his pockets of the tinctures and herbs Zio had helped him gather.

Unknown time had passed when his supplies ran dry. He fell back on his heels as the wolf in front of him staggered to her feet and darted away on wobbly legs. An enemy fighter lunged for her. She evaded, barely.

Devan rocked back and stood, gaze caught on the enemy wolf as it scanned the smouldering mess that remained of Varian's garden. Blood squelched beneath his feet. So much blood. Devan's only comfort was that none of it was Zio's or any wolf he'd called brother over the last few weeks.

The enemy wolf was big, with muscular shoulders that signalled enhanced beta strength, perhaps even that of an alpha. Shock hit Devan as their eyes met. Most shifters possessed a human touch even in animal form, but not this one. Face caught in a snarl, gaze manic with the rush of violence and death, the wolf was pure evil, like nothing Devan had ever seen.

And he wasn't alone.

More enemy wolves entered the garden. They seemed to be looking for something, and when their collective attention fell on Devan, a warning growl built among them.

Devan widened his stance, the first ripples of a shift hovering at the edge of his consciousness. Under the terms Dash had negotiated, he had every right to be on the ground, healing the pack he'd been embedded with. Any reasonable pack leaders would know that, but as the enemy wolves advanced on Devan, he realised that the crazed glint in the first wolf's eyes hadn't been unique to him. *Damn. They're all like it.*

For the first time, a shimmer of fear ran through Devan. Until that moment, he'd been so hellbent on finding Zio—and helping as many as he could along the way—that his own safety had barely occurred to him. But the sheer number of deranged wolves creeping closer was fucking terrifying.

"I like it when you curse."

"What?"

"When you swear. It makes me laugh."

"Yeah, well. I like it when you laugh, so call it even?"

Warmth tried its luck against the disquiet coursing through Devan's gut, but even Zio's voice echoing in his head wasn't enough to distract him. *If they come for me, I'm dead. I have to shift.*

The rush of energy that came before a shift gathered power in Devan's senses. His vision sharpened, hearing zeroed in on sounds he hadn't noticed in his human form alone. The scents of his assailants intensified.

A quiet pop pierced the air. A thud hit Devan's side, as though he'd been punched.

He snorted. *They're throwing things at me? They really have lost their minds.* He steeled himself for the shift, eager for his bones to snap and elongate. He'd always enjoyed the pain, embraced it, revelled in it. As he'd got older, he'd taken the thrill for granted, but that had changed since he'd come to England and lived within the limitations of his complex new life. Now, every sensation that zipped through him was something he'd never felt before. Every jolt and shudder. The flashes of pain stretched out longer, deeper. And his shift didn't come.

What the—

But the thought didn't complete. Senses that had been fleetingly sharp dulled as though a dark cloud had been dropped on the world. Weakness replaced power. Bile surged in Devan's throat, and he fell forwards, bracing himself on the burnt ground until his arms crumpled and his head hit the concrete with a sickening crack.

Devan woke up in a cage in a damp, dark room. His own blood stained his skin and clothes, and the scent was overpowering. He retched, the sensation as alien to him as having four legs had been the first time he'd ever shifted. His stomach emptied, and his head swam. White dots danced in his eyes. *Gods, what happened to me?*

He fell onto his back. The ceiling above was as black as the night sky, and he possessed no idea what it meant. *Everything hurts.* He ran his hands over his body but found no open wounds. The blood he smelt was fresh, but where had it come from?

"Don't move," a voice murmured from somewhere close by. "You healed from the shot, but you were already too weak to recover from losing so much blood."

It took Devan a long moment to compute the words. He forced his heavy eyes to open wider and searched for the source. His gaze fell on a young woman crouched in the corner of the cage, blonde hair matted, skin streaked with grime. "It's you," he slurred.

She offered him a half-smile. "If by that you mean I'm the enemy wolf you rescued from the death sentence your mate passed on me, then, yeah, it's me."

"I don't have a mate."

"I think you do—"

The girl was cut off by approaching footsteps, heavy with enemy scent. Devan forced himself upright, bones and joints screaming with every movement. Three shifter men were at the cage bars before he could blink, each one a head taller than any northern pack Devan had ever seen. Stronger, maybe, than even Luca.

No—

"Where is he?"

Devan blinked. Somehow he'd missed the first shifter crouching in front of him, only iron bars between them. "Who?"

"Your alpha."

Which one? But Devan's muddled mind snared the question

before it escaped. He hadn't shifted. There was still a chance his captors hadn't figured out who he was. That somehow they hadn't noticed his scent was unlike any wolf they had come across before. *You're not that lucky.*

But perhaps he didn't need luck. The air was saturated with the blood of a hundred wolves. To Devan, only a faint trace of Zio stood out. He swallowed thickly. "I don't know where my alpha is."

"Liar."

"If you say so."

The huge southern shifter growled and punched the iron bars of the cage, bending them with the force of the blow.

Broken metal spiked millimetres from Devan's face. He winced. The shifter grinned. "Wherever they are, they're not coming back for you. We killed each one we caught, and there's no way they'll get back through our lines to collect their dead."

Laughter bubbled in Devan's chest, but once more, he swallowed the reaction down at the very last second. "They wouldn't come back for me anyway. I'm of no consequence to them."

"That right?"

"Yes. I'm nobody."

Another menacing growl rumbled between them. Devan sensed the gaze of the young woman on him but resisted the urge to glance at her. She knew exactly who he was, and these were her people. Why hadn't she given him up? They shared a connection—he'd healed her—but he hadn't seen her since. What was he to her?

And why the hell is she still in a cage?

The shifter questioning Devan lost interest and wandered off, taking his brothers with him. Exhausted by the exchange, Devan slumped on the cold ground. It took him a moment to remember the girl.

He forced himself to look at her, though the cracked floodlight somewhere behind her hurt his eyes. "Why are you still in this cage?"

She shrugged. "I don't recognise anyone, so I'm assuming they don't recognise me."

"You don't recognise the scent of your own pack?"

"My pack was decimated at the border. I don't know who these clowns are."

"I don't understand."

"It's not that complicated. The northern pack is just that—one pack. In the south we are many, brought together to fight one war."

"So you fight with strangers? To what aim? And why didn't they kill you if they thought you were northern?"

Something flickered in the girl's eyes. "Twenty years later and I still don't know what the aim of this war is, and as for why they haven't killed me, they've figured out I have enhanced hearing and they're trying to figure out if I'm worth more to them alive. But whatever, dude. *You're* the one fighting for a pack that's not your own."

"They *are* my pack."

"How? You're not a—"

The end of the sentence was drowned out by a wave of pain so intense Devan cried out, rigid as it coursed through him, searing every nerve. His skin burnt and his eyes watered as if he was corroding from the inside out. *Gods, this feels like radiation poisoning.* He'd seen such things in eastern Europe many years ago, and the memories were indelibly etched in his mind.

His brain buzzed as he tried—and failed—to apply logic to the increasingly outlandish theories that zipped through his mind. Bright images of death that were fascinating and terrifying at the same time. "I think I'm hallucinating."

"I think you're right." The girl's voice was closer than ever. "I'm so sorry, but I think you're really, really sick."

CHAPTER TWENTY-FIVE

Vengeance had carried Zio from the border to the compound. Had kept him alive as they'd fought against an enemy that outnumbered them four to one.

They'd barely escaped.

Fear kept him upright as they fled their home and regrouped in the forest. *So many. How did they amass those numbers undetected?*

Having been absent from the compound and township for weeks, Zio had no idea. Perhaps Gale might've known, but Zio would never get to ask him because Gale was dead. His unit ambushed and destroyed at the hospital. At least, that's what wolves he'd managed to gather for the retreat were telling him.

In the relative safety of the forest, Zio skidded to a stop and shifted into human form. Cuts and scrapes healed in an instant. A gash to his thigh took longer, even with his self-healing powers enhanced by Devan's magic-laced pills. *It's not the pills that are magic—it's him.*

But Zio shook off the thought. Pushed Devan out of his mind, keeping him safe at the border camp where he'd left him.

More wolves joined him beneath the thick canopy of trees. Soldiers, brothers, workers from the administration building.

Thankfully, all the children had been in school in the township and were now guarded by humans. But it was a small mercy. Hundreds had died, all of them someone's child once.

Danielo limped into the glade in human form. Drawn to Zio, he joined him beneath a large oak tree, gaze haunted. "Where's Michael?"

Pain flared in Zio's heart. "I don't know, but he's not dead. We'd feel it."

"How do you know?"

Zio laid his hand over Danielo's racing heart. "We'd *feel* it, brother."

For a moment, Danielo seemed almost convinced, but whatever he saw in Zio's eyes clearly didn't match the conviction in his voice. They both knew that their psychic connection wouldn't hold if they were too far from each other to keep it alive.

Zio's hand slipped from Danielo's bare chest. "How many do we have?"

"Fighters? Or in total?"

Zio glanced around. "Both. We're going to need every able soul we have if we're going to retake the compound."

Danielo's expression morphed from grief-stricken to one filled with fury. "Are you fucking serious?"

"Of course I'm serious. What do you suggest we do? Hide out here until the bad guys get bored and go away? Until the *humans* get bored of guarding the township and go home, leaving the rest of our people to the same fate as the others?"

Danielo shook his head. "It's not possible. There's hundreds of them in the compound, probably more by now if they were hiding reinforcements at the hospital too. We don't even have a healer among us."

"Not yet. We can bring Devan here."

"You want to bring your mate on a suicide mission? Gods, you've lost your mind."

"He's not my—"

"Yes, he fucking is!" Danielo exploded, his shout ringing out around the small clearing. "Whatever the technical state of this bond bullshit, if he comes with us, he'll fight to protect you and you to protect him, which leaves the rest of us exposed to your bad fucking judgement."

Zio flinched, flayed open by the very thought of Devan in danger and Danielo's clear disgust at his leadership. "We have to do *something*. If we don't, the township will fall too."

"I know that," Danielo snapped. Then the fight seemed to drain from him, and he slumped against a nearby tree. "But what *can* we do? Because it seems to me, whichever way we turn, we're gonna be wiped out."

Wiped out. Decimated. Destroyed. All the terms fit, and each one left a deeper trail of fear to Zio's heart. His own death he could live with, but not his brothers. His family. His *pack*. And what about Devan? With Zio gone, who would protect him? Love him? Make him smile that damn-fucking smile that lit up the whole world?

No. There had to be another way.

Another wave of wolves made it to the clearing. Zio scanned them with unseeing eyes. The need to separate the injured from those who could fight was as pressing as anything else, but his focus was shot. Danielo was right—he was no leader right now. Perhaps he never had been.

"The fuck?"

Danielo's murmur broke through Zio's daze. He followed Danielo's stare to the wolves trooping past them but found nothing untoward.

"What is it? What's wrong?"

Danielo pointed at the wolves who'd escaped with them and the ones just arriving. "No injuries."

Zio frowned and flicked his gaze between the two groups, one huddled together on the ground, covered in blood and filth, the other without a scratch on them. It didn't make any sense.

He grabbed the nearest wolf to him. "Shift."

With a fleeting shimmer, a young man carrying pack scent but an unfamiliar face appeared in front of Zio. In human form, the healing scars on his bare skin were clear to see.

A slow thud began in Zio's chest. "Who healed you?"

The kid shot a confused glance at Danielo.

"Answer him," Danielo said. "You're not in trouble."

"It was Devan," the young man said, as though it made perfect sense. "He healed everyone."

A growl burst out of Zio's chest. "That's not possible. We left him at the border, and we took all the vehicles."

"Yes, but . . ." The young man bit his lip.

"Go on," Danielo said.

"Shadow Clan are faster than wolves. If Devan shifted and followed us—followed *you*—here, he wouldn't need a vehicle to catch up."

A roar sounded in Zio's ears. It took him a moment to realise it had come from him. He stepped towards the young northern wolf. Danielo grabbed his arm, but Zio shook him off and seized the boy, drawing him close enough to run his nose up his throat. A scent so faint it was barely detectable sliced through what little composure he had left. He swallowed another pained roar. "What are you saying? That he's back there? In the compound?"

The young man nodded. "He was."

Was.

The past tense hit Zio like a speeding freight train. He dropped the boy and whirled around, raw power already surging through him.

Danielo grabbed him again. "Don't. If you go, we'll follow, and we'll be slaughtered."

The conflict that had raged since the very first time Zio had caught Devan's scent was a sharp pain that lanced his chest. He couldn't put his family in danger any more than he could leave Devan at the mercy of the savages at the compound.

He summoned what little remained of his beta authority and laid a hand at the base of Danielo's throat. "You will stay here and give shelter to any wolf who escapes the compound. Retreat as necessary, treat the wounded if you can, keep the pack safe—"

"Zio—"

"Keep them safe—"

"*Zio.*" Danielo fought Zio's superior strength until he fell to his knees with an anguished cry. "Don't, Zio. Please—"

"Let him go."

Varian's command cut through the clearing, his authority absolute.

Danielo crumbled, collapsing in a heap at Zio's feet. Zio wavered but managed to stay upright and turned to face his alpha.

Varian was dirty and bloodied, a healed gash on his temple. In his arms he carried Tomas, limp and lifeless.

His mate was dead.

"Zio," he said. "You must do what your wolf commands you to do. Follow your heart. In these dark moments, it is all we have left."

"I need to find Devan."

"Yes. You do. And you have my blessing."

"He'll be killed," Danielo said.

"Maybe. But he will not live if he fails to do all he can to save his mate." Varian laid Tomas on the ground. "Go, Zio. Fight hard and fight clever. I believe Shadow Clan forces are an hour away. If you can find Devan and keep yourselves alive until then, you may stand a chance."

Zio crept through the thick undergrowth at the east of the burning compound. His heart screamed at him to storm ahead, but Varian's last words kept him hidden. *Fight hard and fight clever.* Charging the compound would achieve the first, but not for long. The compound was heavily guarded. Even fuelled by wolf-deep instinct to get to Devan by any means possible and lacking the logical thinking of his human form, there were too many for Zio to fight alone, and he couldn't risk unleashing his gift while he didn't know Devan's location.

With growing desperation, he slunk along the perimeter, scenting the air every few seconds, searching for any recent trails that would lead him to Devan. The air was thick with unfamiliar shifters, with blood and death, but a hundred metres from Varian's house, he froze, nose twitching. It wasn't Devan's scent, but . . .

Zio followed it out of the bushes in the wrong direction and found Michael at the foot of a tree, bleeding heavily but conscious.

In a heartbeat, Zio was human. "Did you see him?"

"Who?"

"Devan."

"No. I didn't see anyone."

Zio took Michael's hand. "I thought you were dead."

Michael hummed. "Me too, but I took the herbs Devan gave out for blood loss. They're working. Just need a few minutes."

Judging by the still-open wound to Michael's abdomen and the wan tone of his skin, he needed more than a few minutes, but regardless, it was time Zio didn't have. "I'm alone," he said. "Varian, Danielo, and some others are gathered in the forest. I don't know if they'll be able to launch a counter-attack any time soon. Tomos is dead, Gale, Track, Kate, Ishmail, and Xan. All of them."

Michael shook his head. "No, not Gale. I felt him, I think . . . from a distance. He was alive."

"He was here?"

"Somewhere. I don't know. Not Vicky, though. I found her outside the intel building. Maybe he was looking for her."

Zio closed his eyes, committing the information to his brain to deal with later. His heart ached for his pack, for his *family*, but he could do nothing for Vicky now, and with no clue to Gale's whereabouts, he couldn't help him either.

"Z, there's something else."

Zio refocused on Michael, squeezing his hand tighter. "What? What is it?"

"Vicky. She wasn't killed in a wolf fight . . . she was shot . . . with a gun."

Michael's eyes fluttered. Zio shook him. "Are you sure?"

"I smelt it—gun smoke."

Zio sniffed the air and found nothing he hadn't smelt before. *But . . .* "We saw them. On the drone footage. They had guns and a silencer."

Michael nodded. "And they're not afraid to use them, even though the humans are all over us. It's like they've lost all reason."

Zio agreed, but he'd run out of time. "I have to go."

"I know."

"Are you going to be okay?"

"Soon, brother."

"As soon as you can walk, you need to get away from here. Get to the clearing by the oak glade. Find the others."

"I will."

"I don't want to leave you."

"*Go,* Zio. You *have* to find Devan, no matter the cost. Find him and come back to us. Make our pack whole again."

Zio stood and, after a lingering glance back, shifted and darted for the undergrowth again. The air still held no trace of Devan's scent, but as Zio circled the compound, whispers of it reached him. *Devan.* He called out with every instinct he had, but there was no reply. Desperation clawed at him, the primal need to find his mate overwhelming his wolf. He had no idea how Devan had come to be in the compound or what had happened to him since, but of one thing he was certain, Devan was in danger. Every thud of his heart and twist of his gut confirmed it. *Something's wrong.*

A silent howl burst from Zio's chest. *Hold on. I'm coming.*

Devan lay on the ground, his head pillowed by flesh that wasn't Zio's or Dash's or anyone else he'd ever sought comfort from before. His mind was thick with pain and grief, not all of it his own, but beyond his links with any nearby wolf, something else simmered. A fog he couldn't shake. *I'm dying.* He couldn't say why or when, but every facet of his being—human and beast —knew it.

A cool hand touched his face. "There's fighting not far from here. I think your mate has come back for you."

Devan could no longer speak, and he'd given up denying that Zio was his mate hours ago. The southern female—Mari— didn't care for his arguments.

"The technicalities don't matter anymore. You've claimed each other, whether you know it or not, and this won't end until you're together or you're both dead."

At this point, death seemed the most likely conclusion. Agony racked him, shuddering through his body in angry waves. Mari tried to soothe him, but her touch was alien, her compassion inexplicable to Devan's jumbled mind.

He drifted, straining his ears when it sporadically occurred to him to try and hear what Mari could hear. But it was no good. As he faded out a final time, he remembered that the abandoned bunkers Varian's pack had hurriedly repurposed to house Mari were sunk into the ground, designed from wars past to mask sound and scent. Even if Zio was still close enough to find him—if he'd survived the assault on the compound long enough to pick up Devan's scent among the chaos of the battle —the chances of him tracing Devan to the cells were next to zero.

I'm gonna die underground in the arms of a wolf from the wrong pack.

———

Devan's scent was everywhere. Strong and perfect, it seeped into Zio's senses, pulling him forward, step by step, as he fought to stay downwind of the enemy wolves guarding the compound. *Our compound.*

Fresh anger flared in his veins, tainted by the vengeance that had carried him from the border to the moment he'd realised Devan had followed him, but he swallowed it. Owned it. Only the rare patience Varian had battled to instil in him for moments like these kept him from breaking cover and slaughtering every enemy wolf he found until they cut him down with their damn-fucking guns.

Devan's scent was strongest around Varian's house, in the garden, where Tomas fed the birds every morning. Zio crept as close as he dared, grateful to Varian and Tomas that their penchant for privacy had led them to grow tall and thick conifers around their home. He was pushing his luck, though. A few more paces and his black fur would be visible to the shifters patrolling the garden. In human form, they were vulnerable to Zio's wolf, but once they'd caught wind of his presence, they wouldn't be human for long. *Take out the biggest dude before he shifts. Bury the rest.*

Zio summoned his powers and set his sights on the hulking shifter by the garden doors. Getting to him required evading the three other shifters between them, but Zio barely glanced at them, his focus so absolute even Devan's scent faded a touch.

The respite was fleeting, though. Panic flared in Zio's chest, but it wasn't his own. Fear, pain, defeat. And something else too —love, warmth . . . regret. *No. Don't give up.* A growl built in Zio's throat. Devan was close; he had to be for his emotions to be blasting Zio through the connection they'd forged since they'd met. And he was dying.

Zio knew it like he knew water was wet.

No! He tensed, ready to spring, but as he prepared to launch himself out of hiding and obliterate any wolf that got in his way, the air shimmered with an inhuman power that sent him flying.

He hit what remained of the garden wall and slid to the ground. The impact knocked the breath from his lungs, and he couldn't contain a yelp of pain.

For a moment, he lay immobile, dazed, eyes unblinking as he gazed at the unfolding scene in Varian's garden.

The wolves were gone, dead on the ground. In their place roamed dozens of great cats—tigers, leopards, pumas.

A huge lion threw back his head and roared. The wall at Zio's back shook. Bricks crumbled to dust.

Shadow Clan had arrived.

CHAPTER TWENTY-SIX

"Get up, Zio. We need you."

Zio blinked. Somehow he was human but couldn't recall shifting back.

A young man crouched at his feet, blond hair and glowing blue eyes like Devan's. He smelt of fighting. Of blood and war. He was a soldier, like Zio, but he was Shadow Clan. *Like Devan.*

The man held out a hand. "*Hurry.* You need to lead us to Devan. There isn't much time."

Devan. Bewilderment fell away. Zio took the man's hand and scrambled to his feet. He scented the air. Still thick with blood and a hundred strange shifters, Devan's scent was fainter than ever, but Zio didn't need it. The pull in his chest was enough.

He turned into the fading sunlight. "This way."

Despite Varian's house being where Devan's scent was strongest, instinct led Zio away from it and to the barracks. Friends and brothers lay dead inside, but he forced himself to keep moving until he came to the intelligence buildings.

Michael's scent was strong. Zio followed it inside. In the surveillance bunker, he found Vicky, long hair fanned out in a pool of blood. "She was shot. Look."

The Shadow Clan soldier peered around him. "And she's not

the only one. We're sorry for your loss, but we need to keep moving."

Zio nodded and stepped over Vic's body. If Gale really was dead, he'd bury her himself . . . after he'd found Devan.

Beyond the surveillance bunkers, deep underground, dank corridors led to the interrogation units Zio had rarely visited. Built to conceal scent and noise, they were cut off from the world, both human and shifter.

Zio shuddered, but with every step, the call to Devan grew stronger. "It's this way."

"What is?" the Shadow Clan soldier asked. "What's down there?"

"Cells."

"You don't take prisoners."

"We changed our minds. Devan wouldn't let us kill them."

A soft snort answered Zio. Distantly, he wondered how well his companion knew Devan, but the curious thought evaporated before it could take hold, beaten back by the increasing certainty that they were running out of time.

He darted along the corridor, the Shadow Clan soldier a heartbeat behind. At the end, a thick door, coated in scent-masking sealant, separated them from the cells the intelligence unit had hastily constructed a month ago.

There was no key—it was lost to the enemy—and the door had been designed to keep people out, humans and shifters alike. Zio reached out with his gift, summoned his powers from the depths of the earth, but as the ground shook, the door didn't shift.

Furious, Zio hammered on it with his fist. Kicked out and roared. The clan soldier stepped around him. "Let me try."

He laid his hands over the lock and his hands glowed. Molten brass dripped from the lock to the floor, taking the surface of the door with it. Heat filled the tight space. Energy crackled.

Gods. But there was no time to stand in awe. Zio blinked, and the door was open.

He pushed past the clan soldier and charged through the door. Devan's scent hit him like a punch to the gut, and he almost fell to his knees, but the smell of fresh blood—Devan's blood—kept him upright.

Zio shot down the new corridor, closing the distance between the door and the cages in a split second. "Devan!"

But there was no answer. Their bond had led Zio to the right place, but they were too late. Crumpled on the filthy ground and guarded by a wolf Zio didn't recognise, Devan was already dead.

Grief was a slow tsunami, creeping up on Zio in sharp, brutal waves. He roared but didn't hear it. Fell to his knees, but the impact of the cold ground was a lifetime away.

The Shadow Clan soldier pushed passed him, putting himself between Zio and the female wolf. He advanced on her, power shimmering around him in a way Zio had only ever seen in Devan, but he didn't shift. He stopped in front of the wolf and spread his hands. "Move."

A low whine pierced the air.

"*Move*," the soldier repeated. "I know you're protecting him, but you don't need to anymore. Devan's mate is here. His clan. His *family*. We'll take care of him now."

The present tense broke through Zio's haze. Confounded, he watched as the female wolf submitted and the clan soldier tore the front panel from the cage and tossed it aside. "Come, Zio. Devan needs you now."

"He's dead."

"Is he? Come closer and see for yourself."

The only thing worse than knowing Devan was dead was seeing it with his own eyes, but as the clan soldier reached for Devan, the bond surged to life.

Zio darted forward and shoved the soldier's hands away. "Don't touch him!"

The soldier smiled. "Why not?"

"He's my *mate*."

"Of course he is. Now save him, Zio. Only you can."

Zio crawled across the cold cage floor. He pulled Devan into his lap, noting the coldness of his skin, the grey tinge, his slack muscles. "He's dead."

"He's *not*. If he was dead, you'd feel it. Reach out, Zio. Your wolf knows who you've lost today—brothers, sisters, friends, but not your mate. Not *Devan*."

Helplessness warred with defeat, but authority laced the soldier's words, overriding all else.

Zio gasped, sensing the weight in every nerve. "You're an alpha."

The soldier nodded. "I am. And you will heed my orders and save your mate."

It wasn't an order Zio needed. His soul cried out for hope. He looked down at Devan again and laid his palm over his heart.

A faint pulse greeted him. Zio gasped again. "He's alive."

"Because of you."

"How? What's wrong with him? I can't see any injuries."

"They shot him with a human gun. His body healed the flesh injury, but he was too weak to recover from the blood loss."

The new voice startled Zio. He threw a glance over his shoulder.

A girl as filthy and bloodied as Devan crouched in the corner. "You were separated with an unfulfilled bond," she said. "If the bond is too strong to be ignored, it can kill a shifter, especially one with a catastrophic injury who's already exhausted from healing a hundred wolves."

Zio swung a panicked gaze to the Shadow Clan alpha. "Is that true? He can't heal because of me?"

"It's not you, Zio. It's the bond. It was stronger than anyone realised, even without completion. But none of that matters now. We can talk about it later. Right *now*, you need to heal your mate."

"I'm not a healer."

"For him, you are, always."

"I don't know what to do."

"Keep your hands on him. And sunlight. We need sunlight."

Zio slid his arms beneath Devan and lifted him from the ground. Skin touched skin. Warmth flared . . . for Zio, at least.

He followed the alpha back along the corridor, the strange girl at his back. An enemy wolf surged out of the darkness. The alpha cut him down with a wave of his hand. Wolf bones crunched. Blood spattered. It was over in an instant, and they kept moving.

The time it took to get above ground seemed a fraction of how long it had taken to descend, and they emerged into bright winter sun.

In the courtyard, the dead enemy wolves had been piled in a corner, guarded by clan shifters. Milling around were a dozen new faces, some slightly built, with blond hair and blue eyes like their alpha, others dark and hulking.

The alpha pointed to the path that led to the bungalow—and the bed Zio had so briefly shared with Devan. "Take him home. Stay with him every moment. I'll be with you as soon as I can."

Zio kept walking. In his arms, Devan weighed nothing, as if life had left him and he'd chased after it, leaving Zio to tie him down to the world. New panic seized Zio. *What if—*

Three wolves appeared from nowhere, blocking Zio's path. Three *brothers*. Danielo, Michael, and . . . Bomber, standing strong and proud on three legs.

Danielo shifted back, his hand a steady weight on Zio's shoulders. "Varian's taken a force to secure the border. Shadow Clan have moved out to protect the township and beyond."

"I don't care about any of that right now." It was sacrilege to say it, but to lie to his brother was worse.

A tiny smirk graced Danielo's face. "Neither do we. We're gonna guard your house, brother. At least until Devan wakes up."

"What if he doesn't wake up?"

Danielo snorted, the sound so normal in this strange new world that Zio almost laughed, and Danielo squeezed Zio's shoulder tighter. "He *will* wake up, Z. So much life he's given for others, how can he not?"

CHAPTER TWENTY-SEVEN

Warm hands brushed Devan's sensitive skin. Soft words he couldn't decipher graced his shallow consciousness. Instinct told him Zio was close, but the lingering pain in his bones denied it. Being with Zio was nirvana—there was no pain, only bliss.

"Devan."

No. The voice wasn't right. It was familiar and almost comforting, but it wasn't Zio.

A low chuckle came next, distant enough to ignore but irritating enough to drag him from the shadowed place he'd made home.

New hands touched him. Devan flinched, and the hands fell away.

"He's awake."

I'm not.

The warm hands returned with the hot breath against his cheek. "Devan?"

It was barely a whisper, but somehow louder than anything else. Devan took a breath. It rattled through his chest, and his muscles throbbed with new aches. *No. Not even that magic voice is worth this—*

"Devan, it's Zio. Wake up . . . please?"

A lightning bolt of want and need flashed through Devan.

His eyelids fluttered, and his body jerked as his every sense locked onto Zio. Brightness hurt his eyes, and his limbs protested at the slightest movement. Blackness threatened to pull him under, but he fought it, and for the first time in however long it had been, he won.

His eyes settled open. For a long, painful moment, he saw nothing then Zio's face solidified, perfect and beautiful. Dark skin, full lips, and wide brown eyes, full of yearning and worry.

I don't want him to worry.

Devan's hands moved of their own accord to smooth the lines of concern from Zio's face. The effect was instant. Zio smiled, and the sun came out. He leaned down, his lips so close Devan could've kissed him if his neck hadn't been so stiff. "You're awake."

"Not on purpose." Devan licked his dry lips. "How long was I asleep?"

"A week."

"What?"

Zio's expression clouded. "You don't remember?"

"Remember what?"

"Anything, I guess. Though I reckon I should be grateful you seem to remember me."

Devan swallowed thickly. "Of course I remember you. I feel you . . . here." His hand landed on his chest with a dull thud.

Zio was briefly amused again, then he sighed and rubbed his face.

"You look tired," Devan said.

Zio snorted. "I shouldn't. I've spent a lot of the last week asleep too."

"Why?"

"Because Dash said it would help you heal if I lay down with you. I didn't realise he meant your body would draw strength from mine, though. That shit is insane."

It felt so good to hear Zio curse. To see him scowl. To see the sparks fly from his dark gaze. Devan lost himself for a moment

202

before the entirety of what Zio had said hit him. "... *Dash said* ..." *What on earth?*

Zio frowned. "What's the matter?"

"Hmm?"

"You look like you're in pain."

Devan *was* in pain, but he could live with that as long as Zio was close. The gaps in his head bothered him more. "Dash."

"Do you want me to get him? He's outside."

"What? How?"

"Your clan came to our rescue. Stormed the compound and took it back. Luca led them. Dash helped me find you. I didn't know it was him, though."

"He's good at the ... incognito."

Zio cringed. "Yeah, I thought he was a kid. You could've told me the most powerful shifter on the planet looks like a twelve-year-old."

Devan almost laughed, but it hurt too much. "Tell me the rest."

"What do you mean?"

"All of it. Last I knew we were at the waterfall, or did I dream that?"

"Nah, that was real." Zio lay down on what Devan suddenly realised was his bed in the bungalow he'd shared with Emma. "And I'm kind of glad it's the last thing you remember. I was scared you'd die with only war on your mind."

"You look older."

"I am older ... by a week, at least."

"That's not what I meant."

"I know."

"Who died?"

"What?"

Devan flailed his heavy arm around until it landed on Zio. He made a feeble attempt to draw Zio closer. "If Dash and Luca felt the need to intervene, I'm guessing it was bad."

Zio's gaze flickered. "It was ... so fucking bad. Tomas, Vic, all of Gale's unit."

"No."

"Yeah. Gale's unit was ambushed at the hospital when they figured out what was going on there. Only Gale survived, but we didn't know until yesterday when Luca secured the hospital. Tomas was killed when he put himself between Varian and a gun. Vic was shot too . . . like you were."

Devan's head swam. "What?"

"They shot you, Devan. Dash said the bullet went straight through your liver and punctured your spleen. If you'd been human, you'd have died in minutes."

"I'm not human."

"No, you're not. But I wish you were. I wish we both were."

"Why?"

"Because I want to lie in this bed and eat pizza with you again. I want to spend every minute with you as if it's all that matters. As if this war never happened."

"But it did happen—" Devan cleared his throat and tried again. "It did happen, and it shaped us, Z. Like everything does."

"I like it when you call me Z. It reminds me that we're brothers too."

"*That* wouldn't happen if we were human."

Zio laughed. "Yeah, maybe not."

Devan started to smile too, but something unsaid gnawed at his gut. "There's something . . . someone. I can't remember. But I need to know they're okay."

"I think you mean Mari."

"Who?"

"Do you remember the wolf we took prisoner? The girl? I wanted to kill her, but you wouldn't let me."

"You didn't really want to kill her."

"I did."

"You didn't."

"Whatever. I didn't kill her. I handed her to the intelligence unit, and they kept her in the cells. That's where . . . that's where I found you."

"Who put me there?"

"I don't know exactly. Your clan pretty much wiped out the enemy packs as soon as they got here. I've never seen anything like it. It makes sense, though. I've seen you fight, after all."

"Stick to the story."

"Sorry. *Anyway*, there weren't many left to interrogate, that's my point. And the ones who were captured were still . . ." Zio waved his hand.

Devan frowned. "Still what?"

"Still lit . . . as in, off their tits. That's the other thing. At the hospital, remember?"

Devan ran out of rope. He'd lost a week, and others he cared about had lost far more, but he was too tired to take any more in. He shook his head and closed his eyes.

Zio's touch was instant, soothing, and wonderful. "It's okay," he whispered. "Sleep. I've got you. I'll tell you the rest later."

Time passed like a speeding bullet. Every moment Devan slept robbed him of hours and days he'd never get back. Hours and days he could've spent with Zio or doing something useful to help his pack.

"You really are one of them," Dash mused.

"It's what you wanted, isn't it?"

"Perhaps. With all that's happened, it's hard to fathom what I was thinking when I sent you here."

Dash's strength as an alpha went beyond his unrivalled powers. It was his ability to be so human that made him a leader. Devan stood, testing his legs, and joined him at the window. "You were thinking I could help your friend. And maybe I did, but this war still cost him his mate."

"Perhaps it would've cost him a lot more and a lot sooner had you not been here. Dozens of your wolf pack survived the battle here because of you."

Devan would have to take Dash's word for that. Despite

205

nearly two solid weeks in Zio's bed, he still had little memory of the horrors that had befallen the compound. Only second-hand accounts filled in the blanks. And death. Devan's heart ached for the brothers and sisters he'd lost, even those he'd never known. "Do you know how Gale is?"

"I visited him yesterday. His wounds are healing, thanks to the human doctor who saved him. I cannot speak for his soul."

"And Varian?"

"Much the same, though he has taking care of his pack to keep him busy. He came every day when you were unconscious. He is very much a father to Zio, no?"

"I guess."

Dash drew patterns on the glass. Devan had spent years trying to decipher his habit, but he couldn't find the will to try now. "Today is the first day I have felt like myself. It's . . . strange to have missed so much time. I don't *know* anything. Only what people tell me."

"But you believe them, don't you? These people are your family, and you know Luca and I would never lie to you."

"You didn't tell me that an unfulfilled bond could physically harm me, though, did you?"

Dash's gaze was steady. "I didn't know it could. As long as I have been alive, I've only seen such things in wolves."

"So you knew about the risk to Zio?"

"Yes, I did, which is why your orders were to stay with him —orders that, no doubt, along with your baser instincts to protect him, drove you to follow him here and save so many lives."

"I got shot, Dash."

"I know. Luca destroyed the shifters wielding the guns himself."

"What happened at the hospital? Zio's told me some . . . but I can't remember most of it."

"You think you will remember if I tell you?"

"Maybe. Yes. I think so." Devan sighed and turned away from the window. The ache in his chest at being apart from Zio

206

for even an hour was becoming unbearable. "I feel like I need to know everything before I can put it aside and move forward."

Dash kept his gaze on the frosted glass. "The tale from the hospital is not a pleasant one."

"And what happened here is?"

Silence. Then Dash cleared his throat. "My point is that what happened at the hospital is far from over. The ramifications will live with us for generations."

"Zio seems to think the other side had human assistance."

"They did. Zio was right to suspect the hospital as a staging ground for infiltration, though not all human participation was willing, from what I understand."

"Not all, but some?"

Dash shrugged. "It's not yet clear. What we *do* know is that doctors from a laboratory in London were recruited to work in the hospital and, over time, develop a stimulant that would enhance the strength and resilience of shifters. While they worked, shifters from the south used a shield to enter the north and live in the flats across the road undetected by Gale and his unit."

A shudder passed through Devan. He hadn't known Gale's people as well as he'd come to know Zio's, but they'd been kind to him when he'd joined their pack. Warm and welcoming. "What was the plan? To build an indestructible army?"

"I'd imagine so, but it seems they acted before they were entirely ready."

"How do you know that?"

"Luca didn't kill everyone. We kept some of the lower-ranked soldiers alive, and they seemed to be surprised the raid had happened so soon. A unit leader let slip that something had triggered it."

"What?"

It was rare that Devan ever saw his alpha uncomfortable, but as Dash shifted his weight from one foot to the other, horror washed over him. "They saw me and Zio together, didn't they? When we left the camp before the raid?"

Dash nodded. "Drone footage. To them, it confirmed that it was inevitable that Shadow Clan would join forces with the northern wolves sooner or later, and they knew that not even chemically enhanced shifters would be enough to resist us, at least not on the scale they had planned here."

"They might be one day, though. If they take this madness elsewhere. Continue to use human weapons against us."

"Maybe. We must prepare for the worst, and perhaps we should've done a long time ago. If we had, the conflict may have been over before your lifetime, and you'd have been free to bond with Zio from the start."

Devan allowed his mind to take an instant detour from pain and war. To imagine simpler times where alliances and loyalty to anyone but each other didn't matter. Would he have found Zio without clan orders throwing him into Zio's path?

Only the gods knew.

"What happens now?"

"To who, Devan?"

"Anyone. Everyone."

"That's entirely up to you."

"Is it?"

"Of course." Dash's tone deepened. "Luca is taking our forces south to drive the enemy back into the mainland. From there, we will fight until they are defeated. But Varian's pack —*your* pack—needs time to regroup and recover from what has happened here. Any northern wolf who wants to fight can join us, but we expect many to remain here. Perhaps you should too, if only to keep your mate safe. I can't see him leaving you ever again."

It was a lot to take in. Devan couldn't imagine being apart from Zio either, but it was also hard to picture Zio allowing the war to continue without him. "I don't know what Zio will do. He will want to avenge his brothers and sisters, though. Of that, I am certain."

"Have you talked to him?"

"No."

"I think that maybe you should."

"Why? Do you have an inside line to Zio's deepest thoughts?"

"Not even close. Your mate is somewhat of an enigma."

It was the second time Dash had referred to Zio as Devan's mate and the second time Devan had failed to correct him. His gaze drifted to the window again, seeking Zio out despite knowing he was on the other side of the compound with his unit, rebuilding lost homes. "Will it hurt Zio when I bite him?"

After a beat of silence, Dash came closer and nudged Devan's shoulder. "Our kind don't have to bite to seal a bond."

"I know that, but . . . I want to."

CHAPTER TWENTY-EIGHT

Zio knew the moment something changed, even though they weren't together. A veil of despair lifted. Fog cleared. The winter sun shone brighter, and somehow the darkness shrouding the entire pack seemed lighter.

Varian felt it too. He pulled Zio into a fatherly embrace and kissed his head. "It won't be long now."

He didn't elaborate, but he didn't have to. Zio's wolf knew. *My mate is coming for me.*

Zio leaned against Varian, selfishly enjoying the attention of his alpha before it occurred to him how such kindness had cost Varian. "Are you okay?"

"That's not something you need to worry about, Zio."

"Don't I get to decide that?"

"Not right now, no." Varian pulled back and grasped Zio's shoulders. "The only way we carry on is to continue to do what we've always done, to be who we've always been. My only regret from the last few months is that the choices I made kept you and Devan apart."

"But—"

"No. I cannot speak for Dash and Luca, but *my* wolf knows I made a mistake."

Any further argument died in Zio's throat. How could it not

when Zio's wolf had believed in the bond from the start? His human brain had fought it over and over, but not his wolf. Never his wolf, even if the man in him had failed to realise it.

Varian released him. Zio stumbled backwards. Strong hands caught him, and Zio turned to find Gale behind him. Their eyes met, and loneliness poured out of Gale before he caught himself with a wry smile. "Something is in the air," he whispered.

Zio resisted a shit-eating grin.

Gale laughed, and a trace of real humour danced in his sad gaze. "I take it you're going to need me to look after your unit for a while?"

"I wasn't going to ask you to do that."

"Well, I'm offering. It's not like I don't have the time."

Zio couldn't imagine how it felt to lose not only his partner but his entire unit too. Gale had been badly injured. Without Shadow Clan healers and human doctors, he wouldn't have survived. Zio wondered if he wished he hadn't, but Gale was a closed book. As reticent as Zio was volatile. *We can't let him suffer alone.*

"I won't be alone, Zio. Your boys will take care of me."

Zio blinked.

Gale's smile widened a touch. "You're doing that thing again where you think out loud. It's okay . . . really. I imagine I'll have my hands full trying to keep track of Danielo."

"Hey." Danielo glanced up from laying bricks. "I'm a reformed man."

"Bullshit," Shannon shot back. "You've already knocked off one of the human doctors they brought back from the hospital."

"And that's my cue." Varian rolled his eyes and walked away, as ever the good sport, even with the weight of the world on his shoulders.

Gale watched him go, then turned back to Zio. "Did you hear what happened at the hospital?"

"Some. It's so fucked up, though, I can't really make sense of it."

Gale nodded. "Me either. I mean, a stimulant that can withstand a shifter's metabolism? That's insane. I can't even get over that they attempted it, let alone that they succeeded. Can you imagine if they'd held off their attack until they'd developed it properly? If they'd administered it to every enemy wolf in England right now?"

"It's my fault they attacked when they did." Guilt twisted Zio's gut. "They caught me and Devan together with a drone."

"Then you did us a favour. I'm the one who failed to notice a troop build-up across the road."

"They had a shield, G. *No one* noticed."

"Yeah, well—actually, never mind."

Zio spun around as Devan stepped out of the trees. Somehow, despite Zio expecting him, he'd snuck up on them.

A slow tattoo thudded in Zio's chest. His breath caught, and he waited with painful anticipation as Devan greeted the whole unit with warm, lingering hugs—Bomber first, then Shannon, Danielo, and Michael, ending with Gale until he *finally* had eyes only for Zio.

Gale said something. Bodies disappeared. Grief and responsibility faded, and the universe narrowed to just them. *Just us.*

Zio drank Devan in, absorbing his scent, his slow smile, and the fact that he looked a world away from where he'd been a week ago. The grey skin and sunken gaze were gone, replaced with hair that shone like a halo and eyes so dazzling Zio wondered if they'd always been like that or if Devan had emerged from his brush with death brighter than he'd ever been. "You look . . ."

"Better?"

"Yeah, but that's not the right word."

"Then what is?"

"Dunno. Words aren't my thing."

"What is your thing, Zio?"

Before Devan, Zio might've said war, that he lived for the fight, for the defence of his pack, but his perspective had shifted that fateful night in the club, and he'd long ago accepted that it would never shift back. That perhaps meeting Devan had opened his eyes to the man Emma had seen in him all along. "Family is my thing. I lost sight of that for a while and thought I was alone in the world, but I never was. Haven't been since Varian saved me."

"We are lucky that even without each other we are loved."

"Without each other? Fuck off. That's not what I meant."

Humour flickered in Devan's hypnotic gaze. "I know what you meant. I wasn't suggesting that we should be apart—"

"Good. Because that's not going to happen."

"No?"

"No. And that's why you're here, isn't it? Why you've come to find me? Because *you* want what I want."

"How do I know what you want?"

In a flash, Zio had Devan pinned against a nearby tree. "You've always known. It's *me* that took too long to see it."

Devan's gaze darkened. "See what? Be clear, Zio. I need to hear you say the words."

"I love you."

Devan blinked. "What?"

"I said, I love you." Zio pressed impossibly closer. "Fuck the bond. Fuck biology, I *love* you."

He hadn't realised how true it was until he spoke the words aloud, tracked them through the cosmos, and registered the moment they collided with whatever Devan was thinking. But it *was* true. *Every fucking syllable.* Shifter fate had brought them together, war had kept them that way, but nothing on earth could keep Zio from Devan now. Nothing could keep him from claiming his mate. That he was lucky enough to be head over heels in love with him already? He'd thank the gods for it every day he lived.

Devan cupped Zio's face in his magical palm, seeking out his gaze. "I didn't know you loved me. I knew your wolf wanted the bond, felt it from the start, but I didn't think you'd ever— Gods. I love you too, you know that, don't you?"

A rush of joy flooded Zio's veins. "I do now. Devan, I-I

almost lost you to this bond bullshit. I had no idea it could put you in danger like that. If I had—"

"What? You'd have disobeyed your alpha's orders and completed the bond? *I* knew, Zio, and I couldn't do it."

"You knew not being together could weaken you?"

"No. I knew it could weaken *you*. Michael told me. It's why I didn't let you out of my sight when all I wanted to do was run and run and run until my heart didn't hurt anymore."

Puzzle pieces clicked into place. "I knew Michael was hiding something. And I knew you were unhappy too. I thought it was because you were homesick, not that you were trapped by a misguided responsibility to me."

"Misguided?" Devan moved like a snake and reversed their positions before Zio could blink, forearm pressed to Zio's throat . . . the way Zio liked it. "There was nothing *misguided* about it. I was unhappy because I couldn't handle the thought of a bond you didn't appear to want putting you in danger, *and* because I knew on every level that bonding with you was everything I'd ever wanted."

"You want the bond?"

"Of course I do. I want to claim you, bite you, and bond us forever. Loving you just makes it easy."

Nothing about the two of them together had ever been easy, but as Devan sealed his words with a brush of his lips over Zio's, the shackles of everything that had come before this moment fell away. The kiss deepened. Tree bark dug into Zio's back, and he lost himself in all that was Devan—his scent, his taste, his unyielding body holding Zio hostage against the tree.

Zio's teeth ached and his neck arched of its own volition, desperate for the bite. "Now, Devan. Please. We have to do it now."

Devan pulled back, eyes wild. "You never said you wanted it."

"I love you."

"That's not the same as wanting this bond. You can't take it back. It's forever until one of us dies."

214

"I know that. I want it. Please."

"You want me to bite you?"

"*Yes.*"

Another kiss, sweeter than before, and though Zio's blood still boiled red hot, a sudden calm blanketed him, the itch in his heart soothed. Devan kissed him one more time, then pulled back. "I knew you wanted it . . . just had to hear you say it."

Zio bounced on the balls of his feet. "And I've said it, so bite me already."

Devan laughed. "We should probably have a conversation about what happens after—"

"We've had a thousand conversations. What difference would another one make?"

Another slow smile spread across Devan's *insanely* beautiful face. "I'm trying to be sensible, but maybe it's time I stopped. I want this, Zio. I want *you*, like, *right now*, but—"

"But what?"

"Is this how it's going to be for the rest of our lives? You interrupting my every sentence?"

Zio opened his mouth. Shut it again. Then shook his head to clear it. "Sorry. I just . . . I don't know. I feel like we've wasted enough time, you know? I nearly lost you. I honestly thought you were dead when we found you in that cage, and the whole world stopped. It was worse than when Emma died."

"I'm sorry."

"Why? You were only there because of me. If you had died, it would've been my fault."

"No, it fucking wouldn't."

As ever, the coarse words slipping from Devan's velvet tongue sent a bolt of heat sluicing through Zio. He tried to ignore it. Failed, and flexed his hips enough to make himself groan.

Devan pressed his forehead tight against Zio's, gaze fierce. "I followed you into battle because you're my mate and I couldn't be apart from you, but even if I'd never met you—if all we have had never existed—I'd have followed my pack. It's the only reason I was ever here. It's who I am."

"You're my brother," Zio whispered.

Devan smiled. "I am."

Silence stretched between them, broken only by thudding heartbeats. The declaration wasn't new. Devan had sworn himself to the pack many times over, but somehow as they gazed at each other, every nerve yearning for that final connection, their bond grew ever-stronger.

Zio swallowed. "What was your but?"

"Hmm?"

"You were trying to say something when I interrupted you."

"It seems unimportant now."

"Say it, please?"

Devan glanced around. "I want to bite you and for you to bite me, but . . . not here. So much death and heartache, I don't know. It doesn't feel right."

It was on the tip of Zio's tongue to remind Devan that much love had been born and nurtured on the very ground they stood. Instead he smiled and held out his hand. "Come. I know the perfect place."

CHAPTER TWENTY-NINE

They raced through the forest. Zio led, and Devan let him, happily losing himself to the thrill of the chase. The ground beneath his paws was damp with morning dew, the wind cold in his face, and the warmth of the morning sun was second only to the heat of anticipation heating his veins.

From time to time, Zio glanced back, dark eyes gleaming. Devan wished he could smile in return. Then their connection sparked, and he remembered he didn't have to. Zio already knew how happy Devan was, how much he was loved, and soon enough, the crackle of instinctive empathy would solidify enough to become permanent.

Forever. Devan liked the sound of that, and he liked the sound of Zio's excited howl even more. Wherever they were headed, they were close, and Devan couldn't wait.

Zio finally came to a stop at a crystal-clear loch in the highlands of Scotland. An area known for its harsh weather, somehow the sun prevailed, bouncing off the water. Even the rocks at the shoreline glittered.

They shifted back.

"There's a cabin on the far side of the water," Zio said. "It's pack owned, but no one's been here in years."

"How do you know?"

"Because it belonged to Emma's father, and I have the key."

"Did she give it to you?"

"Yes."

"Why?"

Zio shrugged. "She never said, but I think she'd be pretty happy that this was the first time I came here."

Devan couldn't argue with that. With Dash's help, he'd spent a few days working through Emma's files, separating out those still of use and respectfully disposing of those that belonged to the dead. When Dash had gone, he'd lost himself in Zio's file, finally reading it from cover to cover, laughing and wiping away tears as she'd painted uncannily perfect pictures of his mate. *I wish I'd known her.* But if he had, perhaps they wouldn't be here.

Zio took Devan's hand and led him around the loch to a wooden cabin nestled in the trees. It was small and basic and not unlike the cabin in the snow where he'd visited the wolf pack elders so long ago. At least, it felt like a long time ago. In reality, it had been mere months.

"Stop thinking."

"Hmm?"

Zio shut the cabin door behind them and tapped the side of his head. "Stop *thinking*. None of it matters anymore."

"I know that." Devan's gaze zeroed in on the bed covered by a plastic dust sheet. He stepped around Zio and ripped it away. A bare mattress greeted him. Bathed in the sunlight pouring through the windows, it seemed fitting.

They were already naked from their cross-country run. Devan trailed a finger down Zio's chest. His skin should've been cool from the bracing winter air, but he burnt red hot.

Zio shuddered and bit his lip. "Are you going to draw this out? Because I think I might literally die."

Devan chuckled. "It's tempting . . . to draw it out, not see you spontaneously combust, but you're overestimating my self-control. Do you know how many times I nearly jumped you on the way here? Threw you down and claimed you in the snow?"

"So why didn't you?"

"Because I wanted it to be perfect."

"That *would've* been perfect."

"But so is this."

Zio didn't argue. Just tipped his head back as Devan continued his exploration of his body with a single, featherlight fingertip. With one hand pressed over Zio's speeding heart, Devan traced his smooth skin as though it was the first time he'd ever seen Zio like this—so vulnerable.

It wasn't, but it was different now. With so much behind them, they had all the time in the world. And nothing to fear.

Possessiveness swelled in Devan's gut, fuelled by desire and the love that hadn't been there at the start. He pulled Zio closer, so Zio's spine moulded to his chest, and kissed his neck, softly at first, but then with more purpose as the heat between them amped up.

Zio moaned, a slow tremble starting in his long, muscular limbs. "Please, Devan. I can't—please."

Devan couldn't deny the kick he got out of Zio's premature incoherency. The urge to claim him was so strong Devan felt it in every fibre of his being, and the beast within him preened at the knowledge that Zio wanted it too. Craved it. Would beg for it if Devan was cruel enough to make him.

But you're not cruel. And you love him.

Devan spun Zio around, relinquishing his position at Zio's glorious throat. He pushed Zio's hair back from his face, tucking it behind his ears. *My wild boy.*

Zio still trembled.

The healer in Devan ached to soothe him, but the man in him knew it wasn't what Zio wanted. What he *needed*. He edged Zio closer to the bed and gave him a gentle push. Zio took the hint and scrambled backwards, tugging Devan along with him. Their lips met, the air shifted, and Devan's mind emptied once and for all of anything that wasn't Zio's lips on his, the collision of their heated skin, and the hardness trapped between them.

They fought for dominance, rolling over and over. Zio was taller, heavier, but perhaps he wanted to win less. Lips fused together, Devan pressed him into the mattress, hooking one leg beneath his arm. Zio gasped, and a flicker of uncertainty coloured their connection.

Devan deepened their kiss and gripped Zio tighter. *I've got you. I won't hurt you.*

The uncertainty faded. Devan found Zio's cock and worked it gently, slowly drawing more plaintive groans from Zio. Venom dripped from his fangs as they lengthened and sharpened, eager for the bite, but he wasn't ready to end this yet. *I want him to love this as much as he loves me.*

Devan had pleasured Zio before, made him shout and shake, but this was different. He didn't need Zio to tell him he'd never allowed a man inside him before Devan. Still working Zio's cock, he slipped a finger inside Zio, a jolt of desire thundering through him as hot, wet heat enveloped him.

Zio growled, arching his back, welcoming the sensations that licked through him, chasing more. For long minutes, Devan held off, but the need to claim his mate eventually won out.

Caution gone, he manhandled Zio until he was exactly where he wanted him, on his back, legs wrapped around Devan's waist. He lifted Zio from the mattress and aligned them. A possessive growl built in his chest and he eased inside. Held still a moment, then gave in to the primal desire to make love to his mate.

Zio's snatched breaths turned to drawn-out moans, then shouts of pleasure as he chased all Devan could give him. "Fuck yeah, harder, Devan. So fucking good."

Devan hunched over him, driving into him as hard as he dared as the beast in his soul roared. *Now. Do it now.* Urgency overcame him. Desperation. Base instincts he couldn't and didn't want to control. Heat exploded in his gut, spreading fiery tendrils through every nerve. His heart swelled with the love he'd never thought possible, and he yanked Zio upright and onto his lap.

The change in angle drove his cock deeper inside Zio, and they both cried out. On his knees, Zio wrapped tight around him, Devan brought his teeth to Zio's neck. Fangs sank into soft, heady flesh, and as his body poured his seed into his mate, his mind carried only one thought. *Mine.*

Zio cried out as the pain of Devan's bite gave way to the bliss of the blossoming bond. He fell backwards, Devan still moving inside him, dizzy with pleasure, head spinning so fast he was sure it would never stop.

And it still wasn't over. Zio's wolf stirred again, rising inside him, demanding back everything he'd just given up for Devan.

He eased away from Devan's still hard cock, separating them for a painful split second. "On your knees."

Chest heaving, Devan obeyed without question, and Zio was inside him before he knew what he was doing, fucking him far harder than Devan had fucked him. Harder than he'd ever fucked anyone. The slap of skin against skin beat like the familiar metronome of Devan's heartbeat. In his dreams—and there'd been many—he'd taken Devan slowly in the forest, the dirt beneath them, the birds in the trees, but as the sun bounced off Devan's alabaster skin and made his hair shine like a damn halo, Zio knew he'd been right to follow his heart and bring him here. The thought that Emma was watching him fuck his mate was a thought too far even for him, but with the faint trace of her scent surrounding him, every puzzle piece clicked into place.

Harsh moans brought him back to the present. Zio gripped Devan's hips ever tighter but slowed his pace. The brutal dig of his cock became something sweeter, and the craving to bite he'd carried for so long throbbed inside him, filling his every sense until it spilled over and white light blinded him.

He yanked Devan upright, bringing his back to his chest and marvelling at their perfect fit. His lips found Devan's neck and he buried his face a moment, losing himself to Devan's scent, already laced with his own. *I want to smell like him. I want his scent to be mine, always.* "I'm going to bite you."

"Do it," Devan ground out. "Make me yours."

Zio sank his teeth in before Devan finished the sentence, biting down deep and hard, his mouth filling with Devan's blood as release burst out of him. He howled, and it merged with Devan's ecstatic cry. Devan's shudders became his own. His laboured breaths and flailing hands.

His seed poured into Devan and the stars aligned. They were joined in every way possible. Finally. Absolutely. Forever. The bond solidified. Warmth filled Zio's chest. Bliss. But it wasn't just his. The joy seeping from him radiated straight back, and when a stunned chuckle broke the silence, he wasn't sure if it was his or Devan's. Where Devan ended and he began.

Slowly, he slipped out of Devan and turned him around. He laid his mate on the bed as though he was made of glass and dipped down for a kiss. "We did it," he whispered.

Eyes shining, Devan laughed. "We did."

CHAPTER THIRTY

"I don't want a prosthesis."

Devan rolled his eyes and hauled Bomber out of the car. "We've been over this. If you don't want a prosthesis, then you have to live with the fact that you'll spend the rest of your human life on crutches."

"Fuck that."

"Exactly, now get in the damn doctor's office."

Bomber slipped his crutches over his arms and manoeuvred himself away from the car, swinging himself the way Devan imagined a ten-year-old boy would, but that was Bomber—his wolf a seasoned warrior, forever a delinquent teenager in his human form. And yet *both* his identities carried the scars of war. Bomber's wolf was hardly a fraction less formidable than he'd been before, but he'd found it harder to adapt in his human form, something Devan was hoping to fix today.

They made their way inside the hospital and took a seat in the newly built waiting room. Bomber's scowl remained. "Why does it have to be a human doctor?"

"Because he's the best. He saved Gale's life."

"That was him?"

"Yes. Don't you remember?"

"No, I wasn't at the hospital. Besides, *you* saved *my* life. Why can't you do this?"

"I'm not a doctor."

"As good as."

"Not really. I work with magic and flesh. These guys have science and technology . . . unless you want me to attempt to construct a new limb from berries, bark, and wishful thinking."

"Zio's a bad influence on you. You never used to be so sarcastic."

Just the mention of Zio's name tugged at Devan's heart, but six months since they'd made their bond permanent, it no longer hurt. Loving Zio was as consuming as ever, but in all the right ways.

Didn't stop Devan rubbing his chest, though. Or Bomber smirking.

"Shut it," Devan said. "Or I'll take your other damn leg off."

The doctor called them in before Bomber could reply.

Devan followed Bomber into the consulting room and took his place hovering protectively in the corner. Of all his wolf brothers, he felt most responsible for Bomber. His injuries had been severe, and healing him had taken something from Devan he'd never get back. Didn't *want* back if it meant giving up anything he had now.

The human doctor smiled at them both. Bomber glowered back, and Devan sighed. It was going to be a long consultation if he kept that up. The doctor had already made it clear he had no time for shifter intimidation tactics. And why would he when he'd endured enough of that to last him a lifetime? After being one of the hospital doctors who'd fallen victim to the rogue enemy blackmail tactics, they were lucky he'd been willing to help Bomber at all.

Still, the distrust on both sides was strong.

The doctor fitted the leg he'd had made for Bomber, showed them how it was removed and kept clean. "Obviously we haven't tested it for resilience if it's still attached when you shift, but I'd advise taking it off beforehand if you can."

224

"Won't work if we're in the field."

"True, but if your Shadow Clan friends keep the war out of this country, that won't be a problem, will it?"

Devan bristled. He'd long ago decided to build his life within the wolf pack he now called family, but the mention of his clan set his teeth on edge. The war was far from over. People were still dying.

Bomber's gaze flickered to Devan. "Chill, D. You know humans talk shit."

A low growl cut off as Devan refocused. *Huh.* Maybe he *was* more influenced by Zio's personality than he'd realised.

Twenty minutes later, the doctor—a good-looking blond in his thirties—walked them out of the office. Danielo and Zio waited by the car. Despite Devan's continued surprise at how Zio and his brothers seemed to appear from nowhere with no prior arrangement, his attention was instantly hooked on his mate, but he didn't miss the flirtatious glance Danielo sent the doctor's way.

"You smell nice," Danielo said.

The doctor glanced at him. "If you say so."

"I do. Every time I see you."

Flushing, the doctor sent Danielo a heated stare, then backed off as though he'd been burnt. After an hour of his clinical bedside manner, his animated reaction tickled Devan, and he hid his grin in Zio's delicious neck. "We should go."

Zio hummed his agreement. "Not in the car, though. I want to run with you."

They left Bomber with Danielo and escaped to the forest, taking the scenic route back to the rebuilt compound. Running free with his mate, Devan had never felt joy like it, but even that couldn't last forever.

Soon enough, they were home.

Barely through the door, they tumbled to the hardwood floor. Since they'd completed the bond, Zio had rarely let Devan fuck him, preferring to throw Devan around whenever the mood took them—which was a *lot*—and stake his claim on his body as he had on his heart. Devan wasn't complaining, but from time to time, he fought back.

He wrestled Zio to the rug at the end of the hallway. He got Zio on his back, legs splayed, head thrown back, clothes a shredded memory.

Devan slicked his cock with herbal oil and pushed inside him. Over the last six months, they'd mastered the art of the long, sensuous fuck—they'd had to, to save everything around them from certain destruction—clothes, furniture, ancient forest trees—but Devan didn't have the patience for that right now. It had been a long day.

Just breathing Zio's scent was enough to bring him to the point of climax, and it wasn't long before orgasm ambushed him.

Zio arched his back, his cock jutting out from his hips, hard and weeping. Devan caught it in his hand and squeezed, and Zio's answering yell tipped him over the edge. He came hard and fast, then sat back on his heels to watch Zio fall to pieces. His bite mark stood out in the darkening light, raised and white. Devan bent and ran his tongue along it, drawing a tortured shudder from Zio, a moan, and more seed to seep from his cock. "Gods, if you do that, I'll never stop coming."

Devan laughed. Sated for now, he let Zio be and pulled him close. Zio was a fierce lover, but after, regardless of how it had played out, he often sought the comfort of Devan's arms. And Devan wasn't complaining about that either.

They slumped lazily against the wall, Zio lounging with his head in Devan's lap. "I'm hungry."

"Uh-huh. What are you gonna eat?"

"Whatever you cook."

"Who says I'm cooking?"

"You always cook. Feeding me makes you horny."

Devan didn't need any help being hot for Zio, but he couldn't deny that taking care of his mate brought a certain thrill. He grunted, and Zio smirked in victory. Then his grin turned sleepy and he let out a happy sigh. "I can't believe how much I like being at home now. Like, it's the best thing ever. Being in bed, dozing on the couch, hanging out in the bathroom like a weirdo. I think you've turned me human."

"Nah, you've just remembered *how* to be human. You never had the chance before."

"I've been thinking about that."

Devan forced open his drooping eyes and sat up straighter. Since Shadow Clan had chased the southern packs out of England, the war had, as they'd feared, escalated beyond the realm of wolves. The thought of Zio fighting vampires made Devan's blood run colder than theirs, and he'd been trying not to dwell on it. To make the most of Zio while he had the chance. "Are you leaving me?"

"What? No!"

"Sure about that?"

"Yeah, but—"

"But what?" Devan braced himself. He'd spent enough time with Michael, Danielo, and Shannon to know that so long away from the fighting was a life they'd never learned to live. Rebuilding the compound had kept them occupied for a few months, but that was nearly done.

Zio poked him in the arm. "Dash told Varian that Luca would take a unit from the pack to fight with the clan if there were any of us that wanted to go."

"Do you want to go?"

"Of course I don't."

Relief flooded the sharp edges of Devan's nerves. "You don't?"

Zio shrugged. "I thought I did for a little while, but there's thousands of shifters fighting all over the world. It doesn't have to be me."

"I didn't think you'd ever see it like that."

"Even after we bonded? Think about it—if I went south to fight, I'd either have to leave you behind or accept that I'd be putting you in danger. I can't live with either of those scenarios, and it's more than that. I'm *tired*. At least I was six months ago. I

227

can't—fuck, I can't go back to that. I thought I'd be a soldier forever, and I'd still die for my pack, for my mate, and my brothers, but not if I don't have to. It matters to me now that I don't."

Devan took a slow breath, Zio's words carving a place in the soul he'd already claimed. "I wish no one had to die."

"Me too, but I heard what that doctor said when Danielo made me peek through the window, and he was right. As long as the fighting stays out of this country, we can be safe here, we can be *free*. I want that more than you'll ever know."

A rush of love hit Devan, so profound it took his breath away. He cupped Zio's face in his hands and stroked his stubble-rough cheeks with his thumbs. "What if the clan asks for help? Would you go then?"

"Yes, but they haven't so far, and I've heard it on good authority that Luca doesn't need our help."

Devan could believe that. "Dash already gave me leave to stay here forever."

"I know, and you know what *you* should know by now?"

"What?"

Zio rose up on his knees and kissed Devan slow and deep. Then he pulled back with a crooked grin that narrowed Devan's entire existence to the quiet life they'd built in Emma's bungalow. "That I'm counting on you for that forever."

FURTHER READING

Curious about Dash and Luca? You can read their beginning in Shadow Bound by signing up to my newsletter HERE.

NEWSLETTER

Get free stories!

For the most up to date news and free books, subscribe to my newsletter HERE.

This is a zero spam zone. Maximum number of emails you will receive is one per month.

PATREON

Not ready to let go of Zio and Devan? Or looking for sneak peeks at future books in the series? Alternative POVs, outtakes, and missing moments from **all** Garrett's books can be found on her Patreon site. Misfits, Slide, Strays…the works. Because you know what? Garrett wasn't ready to let her boys go either.

Pledges start from as little as $2, and all content is available at the lowest tier.

ABOUT THE AUTHOR

Bonus Material available for all books on Garrett's Patreon account. Includes short stories from Misfits, Slide, Strays, What Remains, Dream, and much more. Sign up here: https://www.patreon.com/garrettleigh

Facebook Fan Group, Garrett's Den... https://www.facebook.com/groups/garre...

BOOKBUB: https://www.bookbub.com/profile/garrett-leigh

Garrett Leigh is an award-winning British writer, cover artist, and book designer. Her debut novel, Slide, won Best Bisexual Debut at the 2014 Rainbow Book Awards, and her polyamorous novel, Misfits was a finalist in the 2016 LAMBDA awards, and was again a finalist in 2017 with Rented Heart.

In 2017, she won the EPIC award in contemporary romance with her military novel, Between Ghosts, and the contemporary romance category in the Bisexual Book Awards with her novel What Remains.

When not writing, Garrett can generally be found procrastinating on Twitter, cooking up a storm, or sitting on her behind doing as little as possible, all the while shouting at her menagerie of children and animals and attempting to tame her unruly and wonderful FOX.

Garrett is also an award winning cover artist, taking the silver medal at the Benjamin Franklin Book Awards in 2016. She designs for various publishing houses and independent authors at blackjazzdesign.com, and co-owns the specialist stock site moonstockphotography.com

Connect with Garrett
www.garrettleigh.com

ALSO BY GARRETT LEIGH

Lightning Source UK Ltd.
Milton Keynes UK
UKHW011833170622
404606UK00008B/151/J